KT-426-340

:CIAL MESSAGE ...

ULVERSCROFT FOUNDATION
stered UK charity number 264873)

stablished in 1972 to provide funds for
, diagnosis and treatment of eye diseases.
:amples of major projects funded by
the Ulverscroft Foundation are:-

Returr
or any
Ple
by
C

- Children's Eye Unit at Moorfields Eye
  spital, London
- Ulverscroft Children's Eye Unit at Great
  nond Street Hospital for Sick Children
- iding research into eye diseases and
  tment at the Department of Ophthalmology,
  iversity of Leicester
- Ulverscroft Vision Research Group,
  titute of Child Health
- n operating theatres at the Western
  nthalmic Hospital, London
- Chair of Ophthalmology at the Royal
  tralian College of Ophthalmologists

You c help further the work of the Foundation
by naking a donation or leaving a legacy.
very contribution is gratefully received. If you
would like to help support the Foundation or
require further information, please contact:

THE ULVERSCROFT FOUNDATION
**The Green, Bradgate Road, Anstey
Leicester LE7 7FU, England
Tel: (0116) 236 4325**

WITHDRAWN

website: www.foundation.ulverscroft.com

X000 000 049 3774
ABERDEEN CITY LIBRARIES

One of the most frequently translated authors in the world, Jules Verne was born in 1828 in Nantes, the first child of a successful lawyer who fondly imagined his son would follow in his footsteps. However, Jules's love of sailing and literature would lead him down a very different path. Moving to Paris, where he would befriend Alexandre Dumas, he started his literary career, spending most of his spare time in the Bibliothèque Nationale and accumulating piles of notes on a vast range of scientific topics and discoveries. His first novel, *Five Weeks in a Balloon*, was inspired by the real-life experiences of his friend Félix Tournachon. Later he penned his enduring classics of science fiction and adventure: *Journey to the Centre of the Earth*, *Twenty Thousand Leagues Under the Sea*, and *Around the World in Eighty Days*. Public figures who have declared that they have been inspired by Verne's stories are many and varied, including Edwin Hubble, Sir Ernest Shackleton, Jacques Cousteau, Yuri Gagarin, and the the crew of the Apollo 8.

FIVE WEEKS IN
A BALLOON

Five Weeks in a Balloon was Verne's first novel. It documents an apocryphal jaunt across the continent of Africa in a hydrogen balloon designed by the omniscient, imperturbable and ever-capable Dr Fergusson, the prototype of the Vernian cerebral adventurer. The story gives readers a glimpse of the exploration of Africa, which was not completely known to Europeans of the time, with explorers travelling all over the continent in search of its secrets. Finding the source of the Nile, rescuing missionaries and avoiding flocks of condors all feature in this unparalleled adventure.

Books by Jules Verne
Published by The House of Ulverscroft:

AROUND THE WORLD IN EIGHTY DAYS

JULES VERNE

FIVE WEEKS
IN A
BALLOON

Complete and Unabridged

ULVERSCROFT
Leicester

First published in Great Britain in 1869

This Large Print Edition
published 2014

The moral right of the author has been asserted

A catalogue record for this book is available
from the British Library.

ISBN 978–1–4448–2113–0

Published by
F. A. Thorpe (Publishing)
Anstey, Leicestershire

Set by Words & Graphics Ltd.
Anstey, Leicestershire
Printed and bound in Great Britain by
T. J. International Ltd., Padstow, Cornwall

This book is printed on acid-free paper

CONTENTS

1

*The end of a much-applauded speech
— Introduction of Dr Samuel Fergusson
— 'Excelsior!' — Full-length portrait of
the doctor — A convinced fatalist
— Dinner at the Travellers' Club
— A long toast list*

There was a large audience at the meeting of the Royal Geographical Society of London, 3 Waterloo Place, on the 14th of January, 1862. The President, Sir Francis M — , made an important announcement to his honourable colleagues in a speech frequently interrupted by applause. This rare piece of eloquence was at last brought to an end in a few sonorous sentences into which patriotism was poured with a lavish hand:

'England has always marched at the head of the nations' (for it is noticeable that the nations invariably march at each other's heads), 'through the intrepidity of her travellers in the sphere of geographical discovery. (*Hear, hear.*) Dr Samuel Fergusson, one of her famous sons, will not fail the land of his birth. (*Hear, hear, from all sides.*) This venture, if it succeeds (*It will succeed!*), will link together and complete the present scattered knowledge of African cartography, and — (*vehement applause*), and if it fails (*No! No!*) it will at least live as one of the most audacious conceptions of the human mind!' (*Frenzied cheers.*)

'Hurrah! hurrah!' shouted the assembly, electrified by these stirring words.

'Three cheers for brave Fergusson!' cried one of the more exuberant members of the audience, and there was an outburst of enthusiastic cheering. The name of Fergusson was on all lips, and we are justified in thinking that it gained considerably from its passage through English throats. The Session Hall was shaken with it.

Yet this was a gathering of bold explorers, aged and worn, whom their restless temperaments had dragged through the four quarters of the world. Physically or morally, they had practically all escaped from shipwreck, fire, the tomahawk of the Indian, the club of the savage, the torture-stake, and Polynesian stomachs! But nothing could restrain the leaping of their hearts during Sir Francis M — 's speech, and this was certainly the greatest oratorical success within the memory of the society.

In England, however, enthusiasm does not confine itself to mere words. It coins money faster than the engines of the Royal Mint. A sum of money voted on the spot for the encouragement of Dr Fergusson reached the figure of two thousand five hundred pounds. The importance of the sum was in proportion to the importance of the enterprise.

A member of the society questioned the President as to whether Dr Fergusson would not be officially presented.

'The doctor holds himself at the disposal of the meeting,' replied Sir Francis M — .

'Have him in!' they shouted. 'Have him in! We should like to see a man of such extraordinary audacity with our own eyes!'

'Perhaps this incredible scheme is only intended to hoax us,' said an apoplectic old commodore.

'What if Dr Fergusson didn't exist?' cried a malicious voice.

'He'd have to be invented,' replied a waggish member of this solemn society.

'Show Dr Fergusson in,' said Sir Francis simply.

And the doctor entered amid a thunder of applause, and without the least show of emotion. He was a man of about forty, of average height and build. His full-blooded temperament betrayed itself in the florid colouring of his face. His expression was cold, his features regular, with a prominent nose, the figure-head nose of the man predestined for discovery. His eyes, very gentle and intelligent rather than bold, gave great charm to his face. His arms were long, and he placed his feet on the ground in the confident manner of the great walker. The whole person of the doctor exhaled calm gravity, and it would never have occurred to anyone that he could be the instrument of the most innocent hoax.

And so the cheers and applause did not cease until the moment when the doctor, with a good-humoured gesture, called for silence. He made his way towards the chair prepared for his presentation, and then, upright, rigid, his eye radiating energy, he raised his right forefinger towards heaven, opened his mouth and uttered the single word: 'Excelsior!'

Never did an unexpected interpellation by Messrs Bright and Cobden, never a demand by Lord Palmerston for extraordinary funds for armouring the cliffs of England, meet with such a success. Sir Francis M — 's speech was thrown into the shade, and that easily. The doctor was at once sublime, great, self-controlled and restrained. He had struck the keynote of the situation: 'Excelsior!'

The old commodore, completely won over to this strange man, called for the insertion, verbatim, of Dr Fergusson's speech in the

Proceedings of the Royal Geographical Society of London.

What, then, was this doctor, and to what exploit was he about to devote himself?

Young Fergusson's father, a worthy captain of the British Navy, had from his son's earliest youth associated the latter with himself in the dangers and adventures of his profession. This estimable boy, who never appears to have known fear, quickly displayed a bright intelligence, an inquiring mind, a remarkable propensity for scientific work. In addition, he displayed unusual skill in getting out of difficulties. Nothing ever perplexed him, not even the handling of his first fork, with which children are not as a rule very successful.

Soon his imagination was kindled by the reading of bold enterprises and exploration by sea. He followed passionately the discoveries which signalised the early part of the nineteenth century. He dreamed of fame like that of Mungo Park, Bruce, the Caillies, Levaillant, and even to some extent, I believe, that of Selkirk, Robinson Crusoe, whom he placed on no less high a level. What absorbing hours he spent with him on his island of Juan Fernandez! The ideas of the solitary sailor frequently met with his approval, but at times he disputed his plans and schemes. He himself would have acted differently, perhaps better, certainly as well. But one thing is sure; he would never have left that joyous island, where he was as happy as a king without subjects, not even to become First Lord of the Admiralty.

I leave you to imagine how these tendencies developed during his adventurous youth, when he was tossed about between the four corners of the earth. His father, as an educated man, lost no opportunity of consolidating this alert mind by serious study of hydrography, physics and mechanics, with a dash of botany, medicine and astronomy.

After the death of the worthy captain, Samuel Fergusson, now twenty-two years of age, had already travelled round the world. He joined the Bengal Engineers and distinguished himself on several occasions. But a soldier's life did not suit him and, with little ambition to command, he was reluctant to obey. He resigned and, partly for purposes of hunting, partly botanising, he made his way towards the north of the Indian Peninsula, which he crossed from Calcutta to Surat: a mere jaunt.

From Surat we see him cross to Australia and take part, in 1845, in Captain Stuart's expedition to discover that Caspian Sea which was supposed to lie in the centre of New Holland.

Samuel Fergusson returned to England about 1850 and, more than ever possessed by the demon of discovery, passed his time until 1853 accompanying Captain MacClure on the expedition which traversed the American continent from the Behring Straits to Cape Farewell.

In spite of every form of fatigue, and in every kind of climate, Fergusson's constitution stood the test wonderfully. He lived cheerfully amid the most complete privations. He was the type of the ideal traveller whose stomach contracts or distends at will, whose legs grow longer or shorter to match the improvised couch, can go to sleep at any hour of the day and wake at any hour of the night.

Nothing is less surprising than to find our indefatigable traveller from 1855 to 1857 exploring the whole of western Tibet, in the company of the Schlagintweit brothers, and bringing back from this expedition curious ethnographical observations.

During these various journeys he was the most active and interesting correspondent of the *Daily Telegraph*, a penny paper whose circulation reaches 140,000 copies daily, which is hardly enough to satisfy several millions of readers. He was therefore well known, this doctor, in spite of the fact that he was not a member of any learned institution nor of any of the Royal Geographical Societies of London, Paris, Berlin, Vienna or St Petersburg, nor of the Travellers' Club, nor even of the Royal Polytechnic Institution, where his friend Cockburn, the statistician, was supreme.

This learned man, in fact, with the idea of making himself agreeable, one day asked him to solve the following problem: Given the number of miles traversed by the doctor in going round the world, how many more would his head have covered than his feet as a result of the difference between the radii? Or, given the number of miles covered by the feet and head of the doctor, respectively, calculate his height to one place of decimals.

But Fergusson always held aloof from learned societies, as talking was not his strong point. He thought his time better employed in seeking subjects for discussion and discovery than in making speeches.

It is said that an Englishman one day went to Geneva with the idea of inspecting the lake. He was put into one of those old-fashioned carriages in which the passengers sit sideways to the horse, as in an omnibus. Now it happened that our Englishman was seated with his back to the lake. The carriage quietly completed its circular trip without its having occurred to him to turn round, and he went

8

back to London delighted with the Lake of Geneva.

Dr Fergusson, however, was in the habit of turning round more than once during his travels, and to such good effect that he had seen much. In this, moreover, he was obeying his nature, and we have good reason to believe that he was a bit of a fatalist, though a very orthodox fatalist, relying on himself and even on Providence. He regarded himself as driven rather than drawn on in his travels, and traversed the world like a railway engine which does not guide itself but is steered by the track.

'I don't follow my path,' he would often say; 'it is my path that follows me.' There is therefore no cause for surprise in the coolness with which he received the applause of the Royal Society; he was above such trivialities, having no pride and still less vanity. The proposal he had made to the President, Sir Francis M — , seemed to him quite simple, and he was not even conscious of the tremendous effect it produced.

After the meeting the doctor was conducted to the Travellers' Club in Pall Mall, where a superb banquet had been prepared in his honour. The size of the dishes served was in keeping with the importance of the guest, and the sturgeon which figured in this sumptuous meal was not more than three inches shorter than Samuel Fergusson himself.

Numerous toasts were drunk, in French wines, to the celebrated travellers who had made themselves illustrious on the soil of Africa. Their healths or memories were toasted in alphabetical order, which is very English: Abbadie, Adams, Adamson, Anderson, Arnaud, Baikie, Baldwin, Barth, Batouda, Beke, Beltrame, du Berba, Bimbachi, Bolognesi, Bolwik, Bolzoni, Bonnemain, Brisson, Browne, Bruce, Brun-Rollet, Burchell, Burckhardt, Burton, Cailliaud, Caillie, Campbell, Chapman, Clapperton, Clotbey, Colomien, Courval, Cumming, Cuny, Debono, Decken, Denham, Desavanchers, Dicksen, Dickson, Dochard, Duchaillu, Duncan, Durand, Duroule, Duveyrier, Erhardt, d'Escayrac de Lauture, Ferret, Fresnel, Galinier, Galton, Geoffrey, Golberry, Hahn, Halm, Harnier, Hecquart, Heuglin, Hornemann, Houghton, Imbert, Kaufmann, Knoblecher, Krapf, Kummer, Lafargue, Laing, Lajaille, Lambert, Lamiral, Lamprière, John Lander, Richard Lander, Lefebvre, Lejean, Levaillant, Livingstone, Maccarthie, Maggiar, Maizan, Malzac, Moffat, Mollien, Monteiro, Morrison, Mungo Park, Neimans, Overweg, Panet, Partarrieau, Pascal, Pearse, Peddie, Peney, Petherick, Pomcet, Prax, Raffenel, Rath, Rebmann, Richardson, Riley, Ritchie, Rochet d'Héricourt,

Rongawi, Roscher, Roppel, Saugnier, Speke, Steidner, Thibaud, Thompson, Thornton, Toole, Tousny, Trotter, Tuckey, Tyrwhitt, Vaudey, Veyssière, Vincent, Vinco, Vogel, Wahlberg, Warrington, Washington, Werne, Wild, and finally, Dr Samuel Fergusson who, by his incredible exploit, was to link up the work of these travellers and complete the chain of African discovery.

2

An article from the Daily Telegraph *— A campaign by learned journals*

The following day, in its issue of January 15, the *Daily Telegraph* published an article in the following terms:

Africa is at last about to yield the secret of her vast solitudes. A modern Oedipus is to give us the key to this enigma which the scientists of sixty centuries have failed to solve. Of old the search for the sources of the Nile, *fontes Nili quærere*, was regarded as a mad project, an unrealisable chimera.

Dr Barth, following as far as the Sudan the track traced by Denham and Clapperton; Dr Livingstone multiplying his daring investigations from the Cape of Good Hope to the shores of the Zambesi; and Captains Burton and Speke, by their discovery of the great lakes of the interior have opened three routes to modern civilisation. Their point of intersection which no traveller has yet succeeded in reaching is the very heart of

12

Africa. It is upon this that all efforts should be concentrated.

Now the work of these bold pioneers of Science is to be taken up again in the audacious scheme of Dr Samuel Fergusson, whose splendid explorations our readers have so often appreciated.

This intrepid discoverer proposes to cross the whole of Africa, from east to west, in a balloon. If we are accurately informed the point of departure of this astonishing journey will be the Island of Zanzibar off the east coast. The point of destination is known only to Providence.

This scheme of scientific exploration was yesterday officially announced to the Royal Geographical Society, and a sum of two thousand five hundred pounds was voted to meet the expenses of the enterprise. We shall keep our readers in touch with this venture which is without precedent in the annals of geography.

As will be imagined, this article caused a tremendous sensation. At first it roused a storm of incredulity. Dr Fergusson was taken to be a purely imaginary being invented by Mr Barnum, who, after having worked the United States, was preparing to 'do' the British Isles. A sarcastic reply appeared in Geneva, in the February number of the *Bulletins de la Société Géographique*, wittily making game of the Royal Geographical Society of London, the Travellers' Club and the prodigious sturgeon. But Herr Petermann, in his *Mitteilungen*, published in Gotha, reduced the Geneva journal to complete silence. Herr Petermann knew Dr Fergusson personally and vouched for the daring of his friend.

Moreover, further doubt soon became impossible. Preparations for the journey were being made in London. The Lyons factories had received an important order for silk for the construction of the balloon. Lastly, the British Government was putting the transport *Resolute*, Captain Pennet, at the doctor's disposal.

At once a thousand voices were raised in encouragement, thousands of congratulations were poured forth. The details of the enterprise were minutely reported in the bulletins of the Royal Geographical Society of Paris. A remarkable article was printed in the *Nouvelles annales des voyages de la géographie, de l'histoire et de l'archéologie* of M. V. A. Malte-Brun, and an exhaustive article published in the *Zeitschrift für allgemeine Erdkunde*, by Dr W. Koner, demonstrated irrefutably the possibility of the voyage, its chances of success, the nature of the obstacles, the immense advantages of air travel. It only condemned the point of departure and suggested for preference Massaua, a small Abyssinian port whence James Bruce had started out in 1768 in search of the sources of the Nile. For the rest it was unstinted in its admiration of Dr Fergusson's dauntless spirit and the heart of triple brass which could conceive and attempt such a journey. The *North American Review* could not see such glory reserved for England without displeasure. It turned the doctor's proposal into a jest and invited him to push forward as far as America while he was so far on the way. In short, among the journals of the entire world there was not a scientific periodical, from the *Journal of Evangelical Missions* to the *Algerian and Colonial Review*, from the *Annals of the Propagation of the Gospel* to the *Church Missionary Intelligence*, which did not describe the event in its every detail.

Considerable wagers were laid in London and throughout England; firstly as to the real or fictitious existence of Dr Fergusson; secondly as to the expedition itself, some holding that it would not be attempted at all, others that it would be carried through; thirdly, on the question of whether it would succeed or not; fourthly, on the probability or improbability of Dr Fergusson's return. Books were made involving enormous sums as though it had been the Derby.

Thus, the eyes of everyone, convinced or sceptical, ignorant or wise, were fixed upon the doctor, who became the lion of the day, though unconscious of his mane. He readily gave exact information about his expedition and was always approachable — the most natural man in the world. More than one bold adventurer presented himself and expressed a desire to share the glory and dangers of his venture, but he refused without giving his reasons. Many inventors of appliances adapted for balloons brought them before his notice. He rejected them all. Whenever he was asked if he had discovered anything in this respect, he invariably refused to commit himself and busied himself more strenuously than ever with the preparations for his journey.

3

*The doctor's friend — Origin of their
friendship — Dick Kennedy in London
— An unexpected and not reassuring
proposal — A not very consoling
proverb — A few words about African
martyrology — Advantages of a balloon
— Dr Fergusson's secret*

Dr Fergusson had a friend; not another self,
not an *alter ego*, for friendship could hardly
exist between two beings completely alike.
But though they possessed distinct qualities,
aptitudes and temperaments, in Dick Kennedy
and Samuel Fergusson there beat but one
heart, a fact which did not trouble them much
— quite the contrary.

This Dick Kennedy was a Scotsman in the
full significance of the word; open, resolute
and dogged. He lived in the little town of
Leith, near Edinburgh, a typical offshoot of 'Auld
Reekie.' He was, on occasion, a fisherman,
but always and everywhere a determined sportsman, which was entirely natural in a son of
Caledonia, however little familiar he may have
been with the mountains of the Highlands.

He was said to be a wonderful shot. Not only could he split bullets on the blade of a knife, but he would cut them into two parts so equal that when they were weighed no appreciable difference could be detected.

Kennedy's face was very reminiscent of that of Halbert Glendinning as he is painted by Walter Scott in *The Monastery*. He was over six feet, graceful and easy in his bearing, and appeared to be endowed with herculean strength. A face deeply tanned by the sun, quick black eyes, a very marked natural bravery; in fact, something good and solid in his whole personality made this Scotsman an attractive figure.

The two friends first met in India, where they both belonged to the same regiment. While Dick was hunting tigers and elephants Samuel was hunting plants and insects. Each could claim to be an expert in his own sphere, and more than one rare plant fell to the doctor which was as well worth winning as a pair of ivory tusks. The two young men never had a chance of saving each other's lives or of rendering each other any service; hence an unshakable friendship. Fate separated them at times, but sympathy always brought them together again.

Since their return to England they had been frequently separated by the doctor's distant expeditions, but whenever he returned he never failed to go and give a few weeks of his company to his Scottish friend. Dick would talk of the past, while Samuel made plans for the future. One looked forward, the other back; hence the restless spirit of Fergusson and the complete placidity of Kennedy.

After his journey to Tibet the doctor went for nearly two years without mentioning fresh explorations. Dick supposed that his traveller's instinct, his thirst for adventure, was dying down. He was delighted. It was bound to end badly one day or another, he thought. Whatever experience one may have of men, one cannot travel with impunity among cannibals and wild beasts. Kennedy therefore urged Samuel to give it up. Besides, he had done enough for science, too much for human gratitude. The doctor was content to meet this suggestion with silence. He remained thoughtful, and then plunged into secret calculations, spending his nights labouring over figures and even experimenting with strange apparatus of which no one could make head or tail. It was felt that some great idea was fermenting in his brain.

'What can he be worrying at now?' pondered Kennedy when his friend had left him in January to return to London. He found out one morning through the article in the *Daily Telegraph*.

'Heaven's mercy!' he cried. 'The fool! The madman! Cross Africa in a balloon! This is the last straw. So this is what he's been brooding over these last two years!'

In place of all these exclamation marks, imagine so many lusty punches on the head, and you will have an idea of the vigour with which the worthy Dick said this. When old Elspeth, the woman to whom he always opened his heart, tried to suggest that it might easily be a hoax, he replied: 'Hang it all! Don't I know the fellow? Isn't it him to the life? Travel through the air! Jealous of the eagles now! No, he won't. I'll put a spoke in his wheel! If there was no one to stop him he'd be off some fine day to the moon.'

The same evening, Kennedy, torn between anxiety and exasperation, took the train at the General Railway Station, and the following day arrived in London. Three-quarters of an hour later a cab set him down at the doctor's little house in Greek Street, Soho. He dashed up the steps and announced his presence by five heavy blows on the door. Fergusson himself opened it.

'Dick?' he said, without betraying much surprise.

'Dick himself,' retorted Kennedy.

'What, you in London in the shooting season, Dick?'

'I'm in London.'

'And what are you here for?'

'To stop a piece of grotesque folly.'

'Folly?' said the doctor.

'Is what this paper says true?' asked Kennedy, holding out his copy of the *Daily Telegraph*.

'Oh, that's what you mean! These papers are very indiscreet. But sit down, Dick, old man.'

'I'm not going to sit down. You actually intend to undertake this journey?'

'I do. My preparations are well ahead, and I — '

'Where are they, these preparations? Let me get at them. Where are they? I'll smash them to pieces.' The worthy Scot was getting very seriously angry.

'Steady, old man,' went on the doctor. 'I can understand your irritation. You think I ought to have told you before about my new plans.'

'New plans, indeed!'

'I've been very busy,' Samuel continued, without heeding the interruption. 'I've had a lot to do. But you needn't worry; I shouldn't have started without writing to you — '

'Writing be hanged — '

'Because I'd thought of taking you with me.'

The Scotsman made a bound which would have done credit to a chamois.

'What!' he yelled. 'Do you want to get us both shut up in Bedlam?'

'I was firmly relying on you, my dear Dick, and picked you out over the heads of many others.'

Kennedy stood thunderstruck.

'When you've listened for ten minutes to what I have to say,' the doctor continued calmly, 'you'll thank me.'

'You're talking seriously?'

'Absolutely.'

'And what if I refuse to go with you?'

'You won't refuse.'

'But what if I do?'

'I shall go alone.'

'Let's sit down,' said the sportsman, 'and talk quietly. Now I know you're not joking it's worth discussing.'

'We'll discuss it over lunch, if you've no objection, old man.'

The two friends sat facing one another over a little table on which was a pile of sandwiches and an enormous tea-pot.

'My dear Samuel,' said the sportsman, 'your plan is madness. It's impossible. It's unheard of, beyond all reason.'

'We'll see, when we've tried.'

'But that's just what we are not going to do; we're not going to try.'

'And why, if you please?'

'The danger, and the obstacles of every kind.'

'Obstacles,' Fergusson answered gravely, 'are created to be overcome, and as for dangers, who has the confidence to think he can avoid them? There's danger everywhere in life. It may be very dangerous to sit at this table or to put your hat on. Besides, what is to happen should be regarded as having happened already, and the future should be regarded like the present, for the future is only the present a little further away.'

'Bah!' said Kennedy, shrugging his shoulders. 'You're still a fatalist!'

'Yes, but in the best sense of the word. Well, don't let us bother our heads about what Fate has up her sleeve for us, and never forget our good old English proverb: 'The man born to be hanged will never be drowned.'' This was unanswerable, but did not prevent Kennedy from producing a number of further arguments, easy to imagine but too long to reproduce here.

'But after all,' he said, after an hour's discussion, 'if you insist on crossing Africa, if you can't be happy unless you do, why not go the ordinary way?'

'Why?' answered the doctor, with spirit. 'Because up to now every attempt has failed. Because from Mungo Park's assassination on the Niger down to Vogel's disappearance in the Wadai; from Oudney's death at Murmur and Clapperton's at Sackatou down to the time when the Frenchman Maizan was cut to pieces; between the murder of Major Laing by the Tuaregs and the massacre of Roscher of Hamburg at the beginning of 1860, the names of many victims have been added to the records of African martyrology. Because to struggle against the elements, against hunger, thirst and fever, against savage animals, and still more savage people, is impossible. Because what can't be done in one way ought to be tried in another. Lastly, because where you can't go through you must go round or over.'

'Passing over would be all right,' Kennedy answered, 'but flying over — '

'Well, what is there to be frightened of?' the doctor continued, completely unmoved. 'You'll admit that the precautions I have taken leave no fear of the balloon falling, so if I do come to grief, I'll be back on land in the same position as an ordinary explorer. But my balloon won't fail me; we needn't think of that.'

'We *must* think of it.'

'Not at all, Dick. I don't intend to leave it

till I get to the West Coast of Africa. With it all is possible; without it I should be back among all the natural dangers and obstacles of such an expedition. With it there will be nothing to fear from either heat, torrents, storms, the simoon, unhealthy climate, wild animals or men. If I'm too hot, I go up; if I'm cold, I come down. If I come to a mountain, I fly over it; a precipice, I cross it; a river, I cross it; a storm, I rise above it; a torrent, I skim over it like a bird. I travel without fatigue and halt without need of rest. I soar over the new cities. I fly with the swiftness of the storm; sometimes near the limit of the air, sometimes a hundred feet above the ground, with the map of Africa unwinding below my eyes in the greatest atlas in the world.'

The excellent Kennedy began to feel excited, and yet the vision raised before his eyes made him dizzy. He regarded Samuel admiringly, but also in fear. He already felt as though he were hovering in space.

'Look here, Samuel. Hold on a bit. Do you mean to say you've found out a way of steering balloons?'

'Rather not, that's utopian — '

'But you're going — '

'Where Providence thinks fit, but in any case from east to west.'

'Why?'

'Because I'm going to rely on the trade winds whose direction is constant.'

'Oh, indeed, that's true,' mused Kennedy. 'Trade winds — yes — at a pinch one can — there's something in that — '

'Something, my good fellow! Why there's everything. The British Government has placed a transport at my disposal. They've also agreed for three or four ships to go and cruise off the West Coast about the time estimated for my arrival. In three months at the outside I'll be at Zanzibar, where I shall inflate my balloon and where we launch her — '

'*We?*' said Dick.

'Have you the shadow of an objection to raise now, Kennedy? Out with it.'

'Objection! I've a thousand. But to take one, tell me: if you intend seeing the country, and going up and coming down as you please, you can't do it without losing gas. So far there's been no way out of that, and that's what has always knocked on the head long journeys through the air.'

'My dear Dick, I'll merely tell you that I shan't lose an atom of gas, not a molecule.'

'And you'll come down when you please?'

'I shall come down when I please.'

'How?'

'That's my secret, old man. Rely on me,

and let my motto be yours: *Excelsior!*'

'All right. *Excelsior!*' answered the sports-man, who didn't know a word of Latin.

But he was fully determined to oppose his friend's departure by every means in his power, so he feigned agreement and settled down to watch. As for Samuel, he went off to supervise his preparations.

4

African Exploration

The aerial course which Dr Fergusson intended to follow had not been chosen at random; his point of departure had been very carefully studied, and it was not without reason that he decided to take off from the island of Zanzibar. This island, situated off the east coast of Africa, is in latitude 6° S., i.e. 430 geographical miles below the Equator. It was from this island that the last expedition, sent *via* the great lakes to discover the sources of the Nile, had recently set out.

But it will be well to indicate what explorations Dr Fergusson hoped to co-ordinate. They were two: that of Dr Barth in 1849, and that of Lieutenants Burton and Speke in 1858. Dr Barth was a native of Hamburg, who obtained permission for his compatriot Overweg and himself to join Richardson's English expedition, Richardson being in charge of a mission into the Sudan. This vast country is situated between lat. 15° and 10° N., so that to reach it, it was necessary to advance over fifteen hundred miles into the interior of Africa. Hitherto this country was only known through the expedition of Denham, Clapperton and Oudney, 1822–24. Richardson, Barth and Overweg, eager to push their investigations still further, reached Tunis and Tripoli, like their predecessors, and got as far as Murzuk, the capital of Fezzan.

They then abandoned their direct line and made a deep detour westward towards Ghat, guided, not without difficulties, by the Tuaregs. After incessant suffering from pillage, vexations and armed attack, their caravan arrived, in October, in the huge oasis of Asben. Here Dr Barth detached himself from his companions, made an excursion to the town of Agades and then rejoined the expedition, which resumed its march on the 12th of December. When it arrived in the province of Damerghu the three travellers separated, and Barth made for Kano, which he reached by dint of patience and the payment of considerable tribute.

In spite of severe fever he left this town on the 7th of March, accompanied by a single servant. The chief objective of his journey was to find Lake Tchad, from which he was still three hundred and fifty miles distant. He therefore turned east and reached the town of Zuricolo, in Bornu, the heart of the great Central Empire of Africa, where he learned of the death of Richardson, who had succumbed to fatigue and privation. He arrived in Kuka, the capital of Bornu, on the banks of the lake, and, three weeks later, on the 14th of April, twelve and a half months after leaving Tripoli, he at last reached the town of Ngourou.

We hear of him leaving again on the 29th of March, 1851, with Overweg, to explore the kingdom of Adamawa, to the south of the lake. He got as far as the town of Yola, a little south of lat. 9° N. This was the extreme southern limit attained by this bold explorer. He returned to Kuka in August, and from there traversed in succession Mandara, Baghirmi and Kanem, his eastern limit being the town of Masena, long. 17° 20′ W.

On the 25th of November, 1852, after the death of Overweg, his last surviving companion, he plunged westward, visited Sokoto, crossed the Niger, and finally reached Timbuktu, where he had to cool his heels for eight long months, subjected by the sheik to persecution, ill-treatment and misery. But the presence of a Christian in the town could be no longer tolerated; the Fellanis threatened to besiege it. The doctor therefore left on the 17th of March, 1854, and fled to the frontier, where he remained thirty-three days in the most complete destitution, returned to Kano in November, and then back to Kuka, whence he rejoined Denham's route after four months' delay. He was back in Tripoli about the end of August 1855, and on the 6th of September returned to London alone. Such was Barth's daring expedition.

Dr Fergusson carefully noted that he had come to a stop in lat. 4° N., long. 17° W. Let us now observe what Lieutenants Burton and Speke accomplished in East Africa.

The various expeditions up the Nile never seemed to have been able to reach the mysterious sources of that river. According to the account given by Doctor Ferdinand Werne, a German, the expedition organised, in 1840, under the auspices of Mehemet Ali, came to a halt at Gondokoro, between lat. 4° and lat. 5° N.

In 1855 Brun-Rollet, a native of Savoy, who had been appointed Sardinian consul in Eastern Sudan in succession to Vaudey, who had just died, started from Khartum, and travelling as Yacoub, trading in gum and ivory, reached Belenia, crossed the fourth parallel and, overcome by illness, returned to Khartum, where he died in 1857.

Neither Dr Peney, head of the Egyptian Medical Service, who in a small steamer reached one degree south of Gondokoro and returned to die of exhaustion in Khartum, nor the Venetian Miani, who, doubling the cataracts south of Gondokoro, reached lat. 2°

N., nor the Maltese merchant, Andrea De Bono, who pushed his expedition up the Nile still farther, seemed able to cross this final limit.

In 1859 M. Guillaume Lejean, placed in charge of a mission by the French Government, went to Khartum, through the Red Sea, and embarked on the Nile with a crew of twenty-one men and twenty soldiers; but he could get no farther than Gondokoro, and was exposed to very serious danger among negroes in open revolt. The expedition commanded by M. d'Escayrac de Lauture also attempted to reach the famous sources. But the same fatal limit always brought the explorers to a standstill. The envoys of Nero had of old reached lat. 9° N.; so that in eighteen centuries there had only been an advance of from five to six degrees, or from 300 to 360 geographical miles.

Several travellers had tried to reach the sources of the Nile from the east coast of Africa. Between 1768 and 1772 the Scotchman Bruce, starting from Massaua, a port of Abyssinia, traversed Tigre, inspected the ruins of Axum, saw the sources of the Nile where they did not exist, and obtained no serious result. In 1844 Dr Krapf, an Anglican missionary, founded a settlement at Mombasa, on the coast of Zanzibar, and, in the company of

the Reverend Rebmann, discovered two mountains three hundred miles from the coast.
These were Kilimandjaro and Kenia, which
recently Messrs von Heuglin and Thornton
have partly climbed. In 1845 the Frenchman
Maizan disembarked alone at Bagamoyo, opposite Zanzibar, and reached Deje la Mbora,
where the chief had him put to death with
cruel torture. In August 1859, the young explorer
Roscher, of Hamburg, setting out with a caravan of Arab merchants, reached Lake Nyasa,
where he was murdered in his sleep. Lastly, in
1857, Lieutenants Burton and Speke, both
officers of the Indian Army, were sent by the
Royal Geographical Society of London to explore
the great African lakes.

They left Zanzibar on the 17th of June and
headed straight towards the west. After four
months of unprecedented suffering, their
baggage stolen and their porters beaten to
death, they arrived at Kazeh, the rendezvous
of traders and caravans, in the heart of the
Moon country. There they obtained valuable
information about the customs, government,
religion, fauna and flora of the country, and
afterwards set out for Tanganyika, the first of
the great lakes, between lat. 3° and lat. 8° S.
This they reached on the 14th of February,
1858, and visited the different tribes inhabiting its banks, for the most part cannibals.

Setting out again on the 22nd of May, they returned to Kazeh on the 20th of June. There Burton, who was in a state of exhaustion, lay ill for several months, during which time Speke made a detour of three hundred miles to the north as far as Lake Ukereue, which he saw on the 3rd of August, but only one end, in lat. 2° 30′ S. He was back in Kazeh on the 25th of August and resumed with Burton the road to Zanzibar, which they reached again in March of the following year. The two intrepid explorers then returned to England and were awarded the annual prize of the Geographical Society of Paris.

Dr Fergusson carefully noted that they had not crossed either lat. 2° S. or long. 29° E.

Thus what remained to be done was to link up Burton and Speke's exploration with that of Dr Barth, which involved covering a distance of more than twelve degrees.

5

Kennedy's dreams — Plural personal pronouns — Dick's insinuations — A trip over the map of Africa — The difference between the two points of a pair of compasses — Expeditions actually in progress — Speke and Grant — Krapf, von Decken and von Heuglin

Dr Fergusson was busily pressing forward the preparations for his departure and personally supervising the construction of his balloon, employing certain devices about which he preserved complete silence. For a long time he had been studying Arabic and various Mandingo dialects. Thanks to his gift for languages he was making rapid progress.

Meanwhile his friend the sportsman never left his elbow. He was doubtless afraid that the doctor would take to the air without saying anything about it. He was still using the utmost persuasion with regard to this subject, but without success, and giving vent to pathetic appeals which had little effect. Dick felt that the doctor was slipping through his fingers.

The poor Scot was indeed to be pitied. He could no longer think of the azure heavens without dark forebodings. In his sleep he felt himself dizzily swaying, and every night he fell from incalculable heights. It must be added that during these terrible nightmares he more than once fell out of bed. On these occasions his first thought was to show Fergusson the bruises on his head.

'A drop of only three feet,' he added good-naturedly; 'certainly not more, and a bruise like this. Just think it out!'

This doleful hint did not disturb the doctor.

'We shan't fall,' he said.

'But if we do?'

'We shan't.'

That was flat; and Kennedy had no reply to make.

What particularly exasperated Dick was that the doctor seemed completely to disregard Kennedy's own personality and to regard him as irrevocably destined to be his companion in the air. There could be no further doubt about this. Samuel abused in an intolerable way the word 'we.'

'*We* are making good headway . . . *We* shall be ready on the . . . *We* shall start on the . . .'

And also the word 'our': '*Our* balloon

36

... *Our* car ... *Our* expedition ... *Our* preparations ... Our discoveries ... *Our* ascents ...'

This made Dick shudder, determined as he was not to go. At the same time he did not want to vex his friend too much. It may even be admitted that without realising it he had quietly had sundry articles of clothing and his best sporting rifles sent from Edinburgh.

One day, realising that the chances of success were, with luck, one in a thousand, he pretended to give way to the doctor's wishes; but in order to postpone the voyage, launched upon a series of widely-varied evasions. He attacked the usefulness of the expedition and its opportuneness ... Was this discovery of the sources of the Nile really necessary? ... Would they really be working for the good of humanity? ... After all, even if the African tribes were to be civilised, would they be any better off? ... Was it certain, moreover, that there was not more civilisation there than in Europe? ... Africa was certain to be crossed sometime or other, and in a less risky manner ... In a month, six months, before the year was out, some explorer would undoubtedly succeed. These insinuations produced the contrary effect to what was intended, and the doctor quivered with irritation.

'Is this what you call friendship, you

traitor? Do you want someone else to get all the glory? Am I to go back on my past? Am I to jib at paltry obstacles? Is this the way you want me to show my gratitude for what the British Government and the Royal Geographical Society have done for me?'

'But — ' went on Kennedy, with whom this conjunction was a habit.

'But,' said the doctor, 'don't you realise that my expedition has to compete with others which are already on the way? Don't you know that fresh explorers are making their way towards the centre of Africa?'

'Yet — '

'Now just listen to me, Dick. Have a look at this map.'

Dick did so with an air of resignation.

'Now make your way up the Nile.'

'Very well,' the Scot replied obediently.

'Go as far as Gondokoro.'

'I've got there.'

And Kennedy realised how easy such a journey is — on the map.

'Take this pair of dividers,' the doctor continued, 'and place one point on that town which the boldest travellers have not been able to get past to any extent worth mentioning.'

'All right, here it is.'

'Now find the Island of Zanzibar, near the coast, lat. 6° S.'

'I've got it.'

'Now follow this parallel until you get to Kazeh.'

'Here we are.'

'Follow the 33rd meridian as far as the end of Lake Ukereue, where Lieutenant Speke came to a stop.'

'I'm there. A little farther and I'll be falling into the lake.'

'Well, do you know what the information given by the natives along the banks justifies us in supposing?'

'I haven't the vaguest idea.'

'That this lake, whose lowest extremity is in lat. 2° 30′ S., must also extend two degrees above the Equator.'

'Really!'

'Now from this northern extremity a water-course runs which cannot help but join the Nile, even if it is not the Nile itself.'

'That's odd.'

'Now place the other point of the dividers on this extremity of Lake Ukereue.'

'Done, my good Fergusson.'

'How many degrees are there between the two points?'

'Not quite two.'

'Do you know how far that is?'

'I don't in the least.'

'Less than one hundred and fifty miles. In

fact, nothing at all.'

'Next to nothing, Samuel.'

'Now, do you know what is happening at this very moment?'

'No; I assure you I do not.'

'Well, this is what is happening. The Royal Geographical Society lays great importance on the exploration of this lake seen by Speke. Under its auspices Lieutenant, now Captain Speke, has been joined by Captain Grant of the Indian Army, and they have placed themselves at the head of a large and heavily subsidised expedition. Their object is to travel up the lake and return as far as Gondokoro. They've received a grant of over five thousand pounds and the Governor of the Cape has lent them native soldiers. They left Zanzibar at the end of October 1860. Meanwhile John Petherick, the British Consul at Khartum, has received from the Foreign Office about seven hundred pounds. He is to fit out a steamer at Khartum, go to Gondoroko, wait there for Speke's expedition and be ready to revictual it.'

'A good idea,' said Kennedy.

'So you see, there's no time to be lost if we intend to have a finger in these explorations. And that's not all. While these men are steadily advancing towards the sources of the Nile, other explorers are boldly pushing into the heart of Africa.'

'On foot?' Kennedy asked.

'On foot,' answered the doctor, disregarding the insinuation. 'Dr Krapf proposes to push west, following the Djob, a river below the Equator. Baron von Decken has identified Mount Kenia and Kilimandjaro, and is heading towards the centre.'

'On foot, too?'

'On foot, too, or else by mule.'

'It's exactly the same thing as far as I'm concerned,' Kennedy replied.

'Lastly,' the doctor went on, 'Herr von Heuglin, the Austrian Vice-Consul at Khartum, has just organised a very important expedition whose first objective is to search for Vogel, the explorer who was sent into the Sudan in 1853 to assist in Dr Barth's work. In 1856 he left Bornu and decided to explore the unknown country stretching between Lake Tchad and Darfur. He has never turned up again. Letters received at Alexandria in 1860 report that he was assassinated by order of the King of Wadai, but other letters sent by Dr Hartmann to the explorers also report that according to the story of a fellah of Bornu, Vogel appears to have been merely held prisoner at Wara, so that all hope is not yet lost. A committee has been formed under the presidency of the Duke Regent of

41

Saxe-Coburg-Gotha. My friend Petermann is secretary, and a national subscription has been raised to defray the expenses of the expedition, to which many distinguished scientists have given their support. Herr von Heuglin left Massaua in June and, while looking for Vogel, he is at the same time to explore all the country between the Nile and Lake Tchad; that is to say, link up Captain Speke's operations with Dr Barth's. Africa will then have been crossed from East to West.'

'Well,' answered the Scot, 'as all this is working out so nicely, what do *we* want to go for?'

Dr Fergusson did not reply but merely shrugged his shoulders.

6

*An incredible manservant — He sees
Jupiter's satellites — Dick and Joe at
variance — Doubt and faith — Weighing
in — Joe in the role of Wellington —
Joe gets half-a-crown*

Dr Fergusson had a manservant who answered
smartly to the name of Joe. He was an excellent fellow, who had devoted himself to his
master's service with absolute competence and
unlimited loyalty, even anticipating his orders
and always carrying them out intelligently. He
never grumbled and his temper was never
ruffled. Had he been created purposely he
could not have been better fitted for his job.
Fergusson relied entirely on him for the details
of his existence, and he was right. Rare and
honest Joe! A servant who would order your
dinner and whose tastes were yours; who would
pack your trunk and forget neither socks nor
shirt; who had possession of your keys and
secrets and never abused his trust!

But on the other hand, what a master the
doctor was for this estimable Joe! With what
respect and confidence he received his

decisions. When Fergusson had spoken, only a fool would have wanted to reply. All he thought was right, all he said wise, all he ordered practical, all he undertook possible, all he achieved admirable. You might have cut Joe in pieces, a job that no doubt would have caused you qualms, without making him change his opinion of his master. And so, when the doctor conceived the plan of crossing Africa by air, Joe regarded it as done; there could be no further obstacles. The moment Dr Fergusson had decided to set out he had as good as arrived at his destination, together with his faithful servant; for the good fellow, without its ever being mentioned, knew well enough that he would be included in the journey. Moreover, he would be of the greatest usefulness by reason of his intelligence and wonderful agility. Had it been necessary to appoint a gymnastic instructor for the monkeys at the Zoological Gardens, themselves pretty nimble, Joe would certainly have had the situation. Jumping, climbing, flying, performing a thousand impossible tricks, were child's play to him.

If Fergusson was the brain of the expedition and Kennedy the arm, Joe would be the hand. He had already accompanied his master on several journeys, and had a smattering of science which he had picked up one way or another; but what specially distinguished him was his good-humoured philosophy and delightful optimism. To him everything seemed easy, logical and natural, and, in consequence, he felt no need to complain. Among other qualities he possessed an amazing power and range of vision. He shared with Moestlin, Kepler's tutor, the rare faculty of being able to distinguish with his naked eye the satellites of Jupiter and to count fourteen stars in the Pleiades, the smallest of which are of the ninth magnitude. This did not make him conceited; he bowed to you very correctly, and when occasion demanded, knew how to make good use of his eyes.

Given this confidence of Joe's in the doctor, it is not surprising that incessant discussions should arise between Kennedy and the worthy servant, all due deference being of course observed. The one was sceptical, the other convinced. One represented clear-sighted prudence, the other blind confidence. The doctor found himself placed between doubt and faith, and it may be said at once that he did not trouble his head about either.

'Well, Mr Kennedy?' Joe would say.

'Well, Joe?'

'The time's getting near. It seems we're setting out for the moon.'

'You mean the Country of the Moon, which isn't quite as far; but set your mind at rest, it's just as dangerous.'

'Dangerous! with a man like Dr Fergusson!'

'I don't want to destroy your illusions, my dear Joe; but what he proposes to do is nothing short of lunacy. He's not going.'

'Not going! So you haven't seen his balloon in Mitchells' workshops?'

'I'd see myself hanged first.'

'You're missing a fine sight, sir; such a beautiful thing, such a lovely car! We shall be very comfortable in it.'

'Are you seriously counting on going with your master?'

'Of course,' Joe replied with conviction. 'I shall go wherever he wants. That would be a nice thing, letting him go alone, after we've been all over the world together! Who'd cheer him up when he was tired? Who'd help him when he wanted to jump over a precipice? Who'd look after him if he was ill? No, sir, Joe will always be at his post by the doctor, or I should say, round the doctor.'

'Good laddie.'

'Besides, you're coming with us,' Joe went on.

'No doubt,' said Kennedy. 'I mean, I'm coming with you to try and stop Samuel, up to the last minute, from committing such a mad trick. I'll even follow him as far as

Zanzibar so that there'll be a friend at hand to put a stop to his idiotic scheme.'

'You won't stop anything at all, sir, begging your pardon. My master's not a crazy fool. He thinks over what he's going to do for a long time, and once he's made up his mind, the devil himself wouldn't turn him.'

'We'll see.'

'Don't you pin any hope to that, sir. Besides, the main thing is that you should come. For a sportsman like you, Africa's a wonderful country; so however you look at it, you won't regret your trip.'

'No, I certainly shan't regret it, especially if this pig-headed fellow gives way to reason.'

'By the way, sir,' said Joe, 'you know that we weigh in today?'

'Weigh in, what do you mean?'

'We three, you and me and the master, will all have to get ourselves weighed, of course.'

'Like jockeys?'

'Yes, sir. But don't worry, sir; you won't have to waste if you are too heavy. They'll take you as you are.'

'I certainly have no intention of being weighed,' said the Scot firmly.

'But, sir, it seems we have to be, for the balloon.'

'Very well, his balloon will have to do without it.'

'Lord, sir! And supposing we couldn't go up because the weights weren't right?'

'By heaven, that's all I ask!'

'Come, Mr Kennedy, my master is coming to fetch us any minute.'

'I shan't go.'

'You wouldn't disappoint him like that.'

'Wouldn't I!'

'All right, sir,' said Joe, laughing; 'you talk like this because he isn't here, but when he says to your face, 'Dick (begging your pardon, sir), Dick, I must know your exact weight,' you'll go, I'll answer for it.'

'I shall not.'

At this moment the doctor re-entered his study where this conversation was going on. He looked at Kennedy, who didn't feel too comfortable.

'Dick,' he said, 'come with Joe. I must know what you both weigh.'

'But — '

'You can keep your hat on. Come along.'

And Kennedy went.

They all three went to Mitchells' work-shops, where a weighing-machine was ready. The doctor had to know the weights of his companions in order to arrange the equilibrium of his balloon. He made Dick get on to the machine, and Dick, without offering any resistance, muttered:

'All right, all right; that doesn't commit me to anything.'

'153 lbs,' said the doctor, writing down the figure in his note-book.

'Am I too heavy?'

'Oh no, sir,' Joe answered; 'besides, I'm light. I'll make up for you.'

So saying, Joe eagerly took Kennedy's place, nearly upsetting the machine in his excitement. He struck the attitude of Wellington trying to imitate Achilles at the entrance to Hyde Park, and was magnificent even without a shield.

'120 lbs,' muttered the doctor, writing it down.

'Ha! Ha!' laughed Joe, beaming with satisfaction. He could never have explained why he laughed.

'My turn,' said Fergusson, and he entered his own weight at 135 lbs.

'The three of us together,' he said, 'don't weigh much over 400 lbs.'

'But if it was necessary to your expedition, sir,' said Joe, 'I could easily get down twenty pounds by not eating.'

'There's no need, Joe,' the doctor answered; 'you can eat as much as you like, and here's half-a-crown to ballast yourself in any way you like.'

7

Dr Fergusson had long been busy with the details of his expedition. It can be imagined that the balloon, that wonderful vehicle destined to carry him through the air, was the object of his constant solicitude.

First of all, in order to avoid giving the balloon too big dimensions, he decided to inflate it with hydrogen, which is fourteen and a half times lighter than air. The gas is easy to produce, and has given the best results in aerostatic experiments.

After very careful calculation, the doctor found that in order to have with him all the things indispensable to his journey and apparatus, he would have to carry a weight of 4000 lbs. He therefore had to find out what would be the lifting force capable of raising this weight and consequently what would be its volume.

A weight of 4000 lbs represents an air displacement of 44,847 cubic feet, which means that 44,847 cubic feet of air weigh, approximately, 4000 lbs. By giving the balloon this capacity of 44,847 cubic feet and filling it, not with air but with hydrogen, which is fourteen and a half times lighter and weighs only 276 lbs, a change of equilibrium is caused amounting to a difference of 3780 lbs. It is this difference between the weight of the gas contained in the balloon and the weight of the air surrounding it that constitutes the lifting force of the balloon.

Yet if he put into the balloon the 44,847 cubic feet of gas we have mentioned, it would be completely filled. Now this would not do, for as the balloon rises into the less dense layers of the atmosphere, the gas contained in it tends to expand, and would soon burst the envelope. It is therefore usual only to fill the balloon up to two-thirds of its capacity. The doctor, however, according to a certain plan known to himself alone, decided to fill his balloon to only one-half of its capacity and, since he had to carry 4447 cubic feet of hydrogen, to double, approximately, the capacity of his balloon.

He designed it in that elongated form which is known to be the best. Its horizontal diameter was fifty feet and the vertical diameter seventy-five.[1] This gave him a spheroid with a capacity in round figures of 90,000 cubic feet.

Had Dr Fergusson been able to employ two balloons his chances of success would have been increased, for, had one happened to break down in the air, he could have thrown out ballast and kept up by means of the other. But it would have been very difficult to handle two balloons when it came to a question of keeping their lifting force equal.

After long reflection, Fergusson, by an ingenious device, obtained the advantages of two balloons without the inconvenience. He constructed two of unequal size and enclosed one within the other. His outer balloon, to which he gave the dimensions already stated, contained inside it a smaller one of the same shape, having a horizontal diameter of only forty-five feet and a vertical diameter of sixty-eight feet. The capacity of this inner balloon was therefore only 67,000 cubic feet. It was to float in the gas surrounding it. A tube connected one balloon with the other and, in case

---

[1] There is nothing extraordinary about these dimensions. In 1784, at Lyons, M. Montgolfier built a balloon with a capacity of 340,000 cubic feet, or 20,000 cubic metres, and succeeded in carrying a weight of 20 tons or 20,000 kilos.

of need, allowed of connection between them.

This arrangement afforded the advantage that, should it be necessary to emit gas in order to come down, the gas of the outer balloon could be emitted first. Should it be necessary to deflate completely, the smaller one would remain intact. The outer envelope could then be removed as an unnecessary burden, and the second balloon, left free, would only offer to the wind the resistance of a half-deflated balloon.

Further, in case of an accident, such as a tear in the outer envelope, the second envelope would remain uninjured.

The two balloons were constructed of twilled taffeta from Lyons, treated with gutta-percha. This resinous substance has the advantage of being completely gas-tight. It is entirely proof against the action of acid or gas. The taffeta at the upper pole of the spheroid, where practically all the strain is concentrated, was of double thickness.

This envelope was capable of retaining the gas indefinitely. It weighed half a pound per nine square feet. Now the surface of the outer balloon having an area of about 11,600 square feet, the envelope weighed 650 lbs. The envelope of the second balloon, with a surface area of 9200 square feet, only weighed 510 lbs, making altogether 1160 lbs.

The net to support the car was made of hemp rope of great strength.

The two tubes were the object of minute care, such as would be given to the steering gear of a ship. The car, circular in form and with a diameter of fifteen feet, was constructed of wicker-work strengthened by a light casing of iron and fitted below with shock-absorbing springs. Its weight, together with that of the net, did not exceed 280 lbs.

In addition, the doctor had four sheet-iron containers constructed of double thickness. They were connected together by pipes, to which taps were fitted. There was also a spiral tube two inches in diameter, ending in two straight pieces of unequal length, the longer measuring twenty-five feet and the other only fifteen. These containers could be packed into the car in such a way as to occupy the minimum of space. The spiral, which was not to be fitted until later, was packed separately, as was also a very powerful Bunsen electric battery. This apparatus was so cleverly contrived that it weighed no more than 700 lbs, even including twenty-five gallons of water in a special container.

The instruments selected for the journey consisted of two barometers, two thermometers, two compasses, a sextant, two chronometers, a theodolite, and an altazimuth for distant and inaccessible objects. The Greenwich Observatory had placed itself at the doctor's disposal. He did not, however, intend to make physical experiments, but merely wanted to determine his direction and the position of the principal rivers, mountains, and towns. He also furnished himself with three carefully tested iron anchors and a ladder of strong light silk, about fifty feet long.

He also calculated the precise weight of his stores, which consisted of tea, coffee, biscuits, salt meat, and pemmican, a preparation combining small volume with great nutritive properties. Apart from an adequate reserve of brandy, he provided two water containers, each having a capacity of twenty-two gallons. The consumption of these various stores would gradually diminish the weight carried by the balloon. For it must be realised that the equilibrium of a balloon in the air is extremely sensitive. The loss of an almost insignificant weight can produce a very appreciable displacement.

The doctor did not forget an awning to cover over a section of the car, nor the blankets which were to compose the sole bedding for the journey, nor the sporting guns, nor his supplies of powder and shot.

Here is a table giving his calculations:

	lbs
Fergusson	135
Kennedy	153
Joe	120
Outer balloon	650
Inner balloon	510
Car and net	280
Anchors, instruments, guns, blankets	190
Tent and sundry gear, meat, pemmican, biscuits, tea	386
Coffee, brandy, water	400
Apparatus	700
Weight of hydrogen	276
Ballast	200
Total	4000

Such were the details of the 4000 lbs which Dr Fergusson proposed to carry. They included only 200 lbs of ballast, 'for emergencies only,' he said, for, thanks to his special device, he was counting on not using it at all.

8

The importance of Joe — The captain of the Resolute — Kennedy's arsenal — Allotment of space — The farewell dinner — Departure on 21st February — The doctor's scientific lectures — Duveyrier and Livingstone — Details of aerial travel — Kennedy reduced to silence

Towards the end of February the preparations were nearly completed. The balloons, one inside the other, were quite ready and had been subjected to a strong pressure of air, which test provided convincing evidence of their strength and of the care taken over their construction.

Joe felt no exhilaration, but was continually running between Greek Street and Mitchells' workshops, always busy, but always beaming and ready to give details of the exploit to anyone who did not ask for them, and, above all, proud to be accompanying his master. I really believe that by showing the balloon, enlarging upon the doctor's ideas and plans, and pointing him out as he stood at the half-open window or walked through the streets, the worthy servant earned a number of half-crowns. One must not blame him, for he surely had the right to make a little out of the admiration and curiosity of his neighbours.

On the 16th of February the *Resolute* dropped anchor off Greenwich. She was a fast propeller-ship of 800 tons, and had undertaken the revictualling of Sir James Ross's last expedition to the Polar regions. Her commanding officer, Captain Pennet, was said to be a pleasant man. He took a special interest in the doctor's journey, which he had followed for a long time. He was rather a scientist than a naval officer, which did not prevent his ship from carrying four guns, but they had never harmed anyone and were only used to produce entirely pacific noises.

The *Resolute*'s hull had been adapted to hold the balloon, which was embarked with the utmost care on the 18th of February. It was stowed in the bottom of the ship in such a way as to preclude any accident. The car and its accessories, such as the anchors, ropes, stores, and water containers, which were to be filled on arrival, were all stowed under Fergusson's supervision.

Ten barrels of sulphuric acid and ten of old

iron for the production of hydrogen were also taken aboard. This quantity was more than was required, but it was necessary to provide against possible loss. The apparatus for manufacturing the gas, consisting of thirty barrels, was stowed at the bottom of the hold.

These various preparations came to an end during the evening of the 18th of February. Two comfortably fitted cabins were ready for Dr Fergusson and his friend Kennedy. The latter, though still swearing that he was not going, went on board with a veritable sporting arsenal: two excellent double-barrelled breech-loading guns and a carbine that would stand any test, from the workshops of Purdey Moore and Dickson of Edinburgh. Armed with such a weapon, the sportsman would have found no difficulty in lodging a bullet in the eye of a chamois at a range of two thousand yards. He had, in addition, two six-chambered Colt revolvers for emergencies. His powder-bag and cartridge-case, his shot and bullets, of which he had a good supply, did not exceed the limit of weight prescribed by the doctor.

The three travellers went on board on the 18th of February, and were received with great deference by the captain and his officers. The doctor maintained most of his usual calm, and was entirely preoccupied with his expedition. Dick was excited but anxious not to show it, Joe exultant and venting his excitement in comic remarks. He at once became the wag of the boatswain's quarters where a place had been reserved for him.

On the 20th a grand farewell dinner was given in honour of Dr Fergusson and Kennedy by the Royal Geographical Society. Captain Pennet and his officers were also invited to this banquet, which was very lively and marked by many complimentary libations. Enough healths were drunk to assure to every guest the life of a centenarian. Sir Francis M — presided with restrained and dignified emotion. To his great confusion, Dick Kennedy had a share in the bacchic good wishes. After drinking to 'the intrepid Fergusson, the glory of England,' they went on to drink to 'the no less courageous Kennedy, his bold companion.' Dick blushed a good deal, and as this was taken for modesty, the applause redoubled. Dick blushed still more.

During dessert a message arrived from the Queen, who presented her compliments to the two travellers and her good wishes for the success of the enterprise. This called forth fresh toasts 'to Her Gracious Majesty.' At midnight, after touching farewells and fervent handshakes, the guests separated.

The *Resolute*'s pinnaces were waiting at

Westminster Bridge. The captain embarked with his passengers and officers, and the swift stream of the Thames bore them towards Greenwich. At one o'clock they were all asleep on board.

The next morning, the 21st of February, at 3 a.m., the furnaces began to roar. At 5 a.m. the anchor was weighed and the *Resolute*'s propeller drove her forward towards the estuary of the Thames. There is no need for us to say that conversation on board turned exclusively on Dr Fergusson's expedition. By his bearing and speech he inspired such confidence that soon, with the exception of the Scotsman, no one questioned the success of his enterprise. During the long unoccupied hours of the voyage the doctor gave a regular course of geography to the officers. These young men were full of enthusiasm for the discoveries made forty years before in Africa. Fergusson told them of the explorations of Barth, Speke, Burton and Grant. He described for them this mysterious country which was entirely given up to scientific investigation. In the north, young Duveyrier was exploring the Sahara, and taking back to Paris the Tuareg chiefs. Two expeditions, inspired by the French Government, were being prepared, which were to make their way from the North to the West, and cross one another at Timbuktu. In the South the indefatigable Livingstone was still going forward towards the Equator, and since March 1862 had been going up the River Rovuma, accompanied by Mackenzie. The nineteenth century would certainly not close before Africa had revealed the secrets that had lain hidden in her breast for six thousand years.

The interest of Fergusson's listeners was especially aroused when he explained to them in detail the preparations for his expedition. They wanted to verify his calculations. They argued, and the doctor entered wholeheartedly into the arguments. What caused general astonishment was the comparatively restricted quantity of provisions he was taking with him. One day, one of the officers questioned the doctor on this point.

'That surprises you?' said Fergusson.

'It certainly does.'

'But how long do you suppose my journey is going to last? Months? You are very much out of it. If it became prolonged we should be lost; we should never come through. You must realise, then, that it is not more than 3500 miles — call it 4000 — from Zanzibar to the Senegal coast. Now reckoning it at 240 miles every twelve hours, which is nothing like the speed of our railways, travelling day and night we should cross Africa in a week.'

'But in that case you'd see nothing; you'd collect no geographical information. You wouldn't even see the country.'

'And so,' the doctor replied, 'if I am master of my balloon and can rise and come down at will, I shall stop wherever I like, especially when the air currents are too strong and threaten to take me out of my course.'

'And you'll find they will,' said Captain Pennet. 'There are hurricanes blowing over two hundred and forty miles an hour.'

'You see,' answered the doctor, 'at a speed like that we should be across Africa in twelve hours. We'd get up at Zanzibar and go to bed at St Louis.'

'But,' went on one of the officers, 'could a balloon travel at such a speed?'

'It has happened,' Fergusson replied.

'And the balloon stood it?'

'A balloon, yes, but what about a man?' Kennedy ventured to interpose.

'And a man, too. For a balloon is always motionless in relation to the surrounding air. It's not the balloon that travels but the air itself. You can light a candle in your car and the flame won't flicker. An aeronaut, if there had been one in Garnerin's balloon, would not have suffered from the speed. Besides, I do not intend to experiment with such speeds, and if I can anchor during the night to some tree or declivity, I shall not fail to do so. After all, we are carrying stores for two months, and there will be nothing to prevent our adept sportsman from supplying us with plenty of game when we alight.'

'Ah, Mr Kennedy, you'll have the chances of a lifetime,' said a young midshipman, looking with envious eyes at the Scot.

'Not to mention the fact,' another went on, 'that your pleasure will bring you great glory in addition.'

'Gentlemen,' answered the sportsman, 'I much appreciate your — er — er — compliments, but — er — er — I have no right to them — '

'What!' came from all sides. 'You're not going?'

'I am not going.'

'You are not going with Dr Fergusson?'

'Not only am I not going with him, but my sole reason for being here is to stop him at the last minute.'

All eyes were turned upon the doctor.

'Don't listen to him,' he replied with his usual calm. 'It's a matter you mustn't discuss with him. At heart he knows perfectly well that he is going.'

'I swear by St Andrew — !' Kennedy cried.

'Don't swear anything, my dear Dick. You've been weighed and measured, and so have your powder, guns and ammunition, so we'll say no more about it.'

And indeed, from that day until the arrival at Zanzibar, Dick kept his mouth shut. He talked neither of that nor of anything else. He maintained complete silence.

9

*Doubling the Cape — The forecastle
— Lectures on cosmography by Professor
Joe — On the steering of balloons — On
the study of atmospheric currents
— Eureka!*

The *Resolute* was steaming rapidly towards
the Cape of Good Hope. The weather continued fine though the sea was growing rougher.
On the 30th of March, twenty-seven days
after they left London, Table Mountain was
seen silhouetted against the horizon. Cape
Town, situated at the foot of an amphitheatre
of hills, could be made out through marine
glasses, and soon the *Resolute* dropped anchor
in the harbour. But the captain was only stopping to coal. This was done in one day, and
the ship proceeded south to double the southern extremity of Africa and enter the Mozambique
Channel.

This was not Joe's first sea-voyage, and he
had not taken long to make himself at home
on board. His straightforwardness and good
temper made him universally popular. A large
share of his master's fame was reflected upon

him. He was listened to like an oracle and made no more mistakes than anyone else might have done. And so, while the doctor was conducting his course of description in the officers' quarters, Joe held the forecastle and yarned in his own sweet way; a course, incidentally, that has been followed by the greatest historians of all time.

His subject was naturally aerial travel. Joe found difficulty in making some of the more sceptical spirits swallow the idea of the expedition, but once this was accepted, the imagination of the sailors, stimulated by Joe's account, began to regard nothing as impossible. The brilliant narrator convinced his audience that the expedition would be followed by many others; it was only the beginning of a long series of superhuman adventures.

'You see, you fellows, once a man has started this kind of travel, he can't get on without it; so, on our next expedition, instead of going sideways we'll go straight up higher and higher.'

'That's good,' said one astonished listener. 'Then you'll get to the moon.'

'The moon!' Joe retorted. 'Bless my soul, that's much too ordinary. Everybody goes to the moon. Besides, there's no water there and you'd have to take a big lot of stores, and even bottles of air if you wanted to breathe.'

'Is there any gin there?' asked a sailor who was very partial to that beverage.

'There's nothing else, mate. No, no moon for us. We're going to have a trip among those pretty stars, those jolly old planets my master's often told me about. We're going to start off with a trip to Saturn — '

'The one with the ring?' asked the quartermaster.

'Yes, a wedding ring. But they don't know what's happened to his wife.'

'What, you're going as high as that?' exclaimed a cabin-boy in amazement. 'Your master must be the devil himself.'

'The devil? He's too good for that.'

'And what next after Saturn?' asked one of the less patient of his audience.

'After Saturn? Oh, well, we'll have a look at Jupiter. That's a funny place, now, where a day is only nine and a half hours long. A good place for loafers, and the year lasts twelve years, which is nice for people who've only six months to live. It gives them a bit longer.'

'Twelve years?' the boy exclaimed.

'Yes, sonny. So in that country you'd still be drinking your mother's milk and that old fellow of fifty or so would still be a kid of four and a half.'

'Would you believe it!' cried the whole

forecastle as one man.

'It's the absolute truth,' said Joe with conviction. 'But what can you expect? If you will persist in hanging on to this world you'll never learn anything; you'll stay a lot of ignorant sailors. Come and have a look at Jupiter and you'll see. And you've jolly well got to keep your weather eye open up there, some of those satellites are nasty customers!'

They laughed, but they half-believed him, and he talked to them about Neptune, where sailors are sure of a rousing reception, and Mars, where the soldiers monopolise the pavement, which after a bit becomes intolerable. As for Mercury, that was an ugly place, full of thieves and shopkeepers so alike, that it was difficult to distinguish one from another. And, lastly, he gave them a really charming picture of Venus.

'And when we get back from this expedition,' he went on, 'they'll give us the Southern Cross shining up there in God's buttonhole.'

'And you'll certainly deserve it!' the sailors replied.

And so the long evenings in the forecastle were spent in cheerful conversation, while the doctor's instructive talks pursued their course elsewhere. One day the conversation turned to the steering of balloons, and Fergusson was asked to give his views on this subject.

'I don't believe,' he said, 'that it will ever be possible to steer balloons. I know all the methods that have been tried or suggested. Not one has succeeded, not one is practicable. You will understand that I have had to study this question, which is, of course, of great interest to me, but I've failed to solve the problem with the data that the present state of mechanical science makes available. It would be necessary to invent a motor of extraordinary power and incredible lightness. And, in addition, it will be impossible to resist any considerable air current. Up to now effort has been most concentrated on steering the car rather than the balloon, which is a mistake.'

'But there's a close relationship between a balloon and a ship; and a ship can be steered,' someone replied.

'Oh no,' Dr Fergusson replied, 'the density of air is infinitely less than that of water; and besides, the ship is only half-immersed, while a balloon is completely enveloped in the atmosphere and does not move relatively to the surrounding air.'

'So you think aeronautics has spoken its last word?'

'No; indeed not! We shall have to find some other way, and if we can't steer a balloon we shall have to find out how to keep it in favourable atmospheric currents. As one gets up higher these become much more uniform and are constant in their direction. They're no longer influenced by the valleys and mountains which score the earth's surface, and, as you know, that is the principal cause of both the changes of the wind and the irregularity of its strength. Once these zones are determined, the balloon will merely have to enter the currents that suit it.'

'But in that case,' interposed Captain Pennet, 'in order to reach them you'd have to keep going up and down. There's the real difficulty, my dear doctor.'

'And why, captain?'

'Well, I grant you, the difficulty will only arise in the case of long journeys, not on short trips.'

'For what reason, may I ask?'

'Because you can only rise by throwing out ballast, and only come down by letting out gas, and if you go on doing that, your stores of gas and ballast will soon run out.'

'My dear Pennet, that's the whole point, the whole difficulty science has to overcome. The point is not to steer balloons but to move them up and down without losing gas, which is the life-force, the blood and the soul, so to speak, of a balloon.'

'You're right, my dear doctor, but this difficulty has not been overcome yet. This method has not yet been discovered.'

'I beg your pardon. It has.'

'By whom?'

'By me.'

'You!'

'You can rest assured that otherwise I should not have risked this voyage across Africa in a balloon. I should have run out of gas in twenty-four hours.'

'But you said nothing of this in England.'

'No; I didn't want to start a public argument. There seemed no point in that. I made my preliminary experiments in secret, and was entirely satisfied, so there was no need to make any more.'

'Indeed! And may one ask, my dear Fergusson, what your secret is?'

'It's this, gentlemen, and it's very simple.'

The attention of the audience was strained to the utmost, and the doctor quietly went on as follows.

10

Preliminary trials — The doctor's five containers — The gas

'Many attempts have been made, gentlemen, to rise and drop at will in a balloon without loss of gas or ballast. A French aeronaut, M. Meunier, proposed to achieve this object by means of compressed air. Dr van Hecke, a Belgian, using planes and paddles, developed a vertical force which in most cases would have been inadequate. The practical results obtained by these methods were negligible.

'I therefore made up my mind to approach the question more directly. To begin with, I do away entirely with ballast, except for emergencies, such as the breakdown of my apparatus or the need to rise instantly in order to avoid some unexpected obstacle.

'My method of rising and descending consists merely in expanding or contracting the gas contained in the envelope of the balloon by changing the temperature; and this is how I do it.

'You saw me bring on board with the car several containers the purpose of which was unknown to you. There are five of them. The first contains about twenty-five gallons of water, to which I add a few drops of sulphuric acid to increase its conductivity. I then decompose it by means of a powerful Bunsen battery. Water, as you know, is made up of two parts hydrogen and one part oxygen. Separated by the battery, the oxygen is collected from its positive pole in a second container, while a third, fitted above the second and of double its capacity, takes the hydrogen coming from the negative pole.

'These two containers are connected with a fourth by means of taps, the bore of one of which is double that of the other. This container is called the mixing chamber, for it is there that the two gases, separated by the decomposition of the water, mix. The capacity of this chamber is about forty-one cubic feet, and the upper part is fitted with a platinum tube to which a tap is fixed. You will realise, gentlemen, that the apparatus I am describing to you is purely and simply an oxy-hydrogen burner, the temperature of which is greater than that of a blacksmith's forge.

'That being clear, I will pass on to the second part of the apparatus. From the lower part of my balloon, which is hermetically closed, project two tubes a little distance apart. One begins in the middle of the upper layers of the hydrogen, the other among the lower. At intervals these two tubes are fitted with strong rubber joints which allow them to give to the swaying of the balloon. They both reach as far as the car where they enter a cylindrical chamber which is called the heating chamber, and is closed at its two extremities by strong discs. The pipe from the lower part of the balloon enters this cylinder through the lower disc, after which it becomes a spiral, the coil stretching to the full height of the cylinder. Before emerging again, this spiral passes through a small cone the convex base of which, shaped like a skull-cap, bulges downwards. To the apex of this cone is fitted the second pipe, which, as I have explained, connects with the lower part of the balloon.

'The convex base of the cone is of platinum to prevent its melting under the action of the heating chamber, which is situated at the bottom of the iron case, inside the spiral, so that the flame just touches the base of the cone.

'You know, gentlemen, the principle of a furnace for the central heating of a house. You know how it works. The air of the rooms is forced through the pipes and returned at a higher temperature. What I have just described to you is nothing more or less than a central heating furnace.

'Now, what actually happens? When the heating apparatus is lit, the hydrogen in the spiral and convex cone is heated and rises rapidly through the pipe leading to the upper part of the balloon. A vacuum is formed below which draws down the gas from the lower parts. This, in its turn, is heated and is constantly being replaced. In this way a very rapid flow of gas takes place through the pipes and spiral, the gas being continually drawn from the balloon and returning to it after being heated.

'Now gases expand by of their volume per degree of temperature. If, therefore, I increase the temperature by 18 degrees, the volume of the hydrogen in the balloon will be increased by or 1674 cubic feet. It will thus displace 1674 additional cubic feet of air, and this will increase its lifting force by 130 lbs. This, then, is tantamount to throwing out the same weight of ballast. If I increase the temperature by 180 degrees, the gas will increase in volume by, will displace 16,740 additional cubic feet, and the lifting force will increase by 1300 lbs.

'You see, gentlemen, I can easily obtain considerable variations in the conditions of equilibrium. The volume of the balloon has been so calculated that when it is half-inflated it will displace a weight of air exactly equal to that of the envelope, the hydrogen and the car together with all its passengers and accessories. Up to this point of inflation it is in exact equilibrium in the air, neither rising nor dropping.

'To rise, I raise the gas to a temperature higher than that of the surrounding air by means of my burner, obtaining a greater pressure and increasing the dilation of the balloon, which rises in proportion as I expand the hydrogen. Coming down is, of course, effected by diminishing the heat of the furnace and lowering the temperature. Rising, therefore, will generally be much more rapid than descending, but that is an advantage, as I shall never need to come down rapidly, whereas a quick ascent will be necessary to clear obstacles. The dangers are below, not above.

'Moreover, as I have already told you, I am taking a certain amount of ballast, which will allow me to rise even quicker still, should that prove necessary. My emission pipe, situated near the top of the balloon, becomes nothing more than a safety-valve. The balloon always retains its full charge of hydrogen, and the variations of temperature that I bring about in the enclosed gas are of themselves sufficient to allow me to rise or drop.

'There's just one thing, gentlemen, that I should like to add as a practical detail. The combustion of hydrogen and oxygen at the top of the furnace produces only steam. I have therefore fitted the lower part of the iron cylinder with an escape-valve functioning at less than two atmospheres' pressure. Consequently, as soon as the steam develops this pressure, it is automatically released.

'And now for some exact figures. 25 gallons of water decomposed into its constituent elements give 222 lbs of oxygen and 28 lbs of hydrogen. This represents, at atmospheric pressure, 2050 cubic feet of oxygen and 4100 cubic feet of hydrogen, making 6150 cubic feet of the mixture. The tap of my furnace when fully open can pass 27 cubic feet an hour, with a flame at least six times as strong as that of a large street lamp. On an average, then, to maintain an ordinary altitude, I shall not burn more than 9 cubic feet per hour. My 25 gallons of water therefore represent for me 683 hours of travel in the air, or rather more than 26 days. But, as I can come down when I like and replenish my supply of water on the way, my journey could be prolonged indefinitely.

'That is my secret, gentlemen. It is simple and, like all simple things, cannot fail to succeed. Expansion and contraction of the gas in the balloon; such is my method, and it involves no cumbersome planes or engines. A furnace to produce the changes of temperature, a chamber to heat the gas: these are neither cumbersome nor heavy. I think, then, that I have provided myself with all the essential conditions for success.'

With these words Dr Fergusson brought his discourse to a conclusion and was heartily applauded. There were no objections to his scheme. Everything had been foreseen and solved.

'All the same,' said the captain, 'it may be dangerous.'

'And what if it is?' the doctor answered quietly. 'So long as it's practicable.'

11

Arrival at Zanzibar — The British consul — Threatening attitude of the inhabitants — The island of Koumbeni — The rain-makers — Inflation of the balloon — Departure on the 8th April — Final farewells — The Victoria

A constantly favourable wind had hastened the progress of the *Resolute* towards her destination. The navigation of the Mozambique Channel was performed in particularly calm conditions. The sea-journey augured well for the journey by air. Everyone was looking forward to the arrival and to giving the final touches to Dr Fergusson's preparations. At last the ship came in sight of the town of Zanzibar, which is situated on the island of the same name, and at 11 a.m. on the 15th of April she dropped anchor in the harbour.

The island of Zanzibar belongs to the Imam of Muscat, an ally of France and England, and is beyond doubt his finest colony. The harbour is used by a large number of ships from neighbouring countries. The island is separated from the African coast by a channel which is not more than thirty miles wide at its widest point. Zanzibar carries on a large trade in gum, ivory, and especially ebony, for the town is the great slave-market where all the booty captured in the wars in which the chiefs of the interior are constantly engaged is collected. This traffic also extends over the whole east coast as far north as the Nile, and Monsieur G. Lejean has seen the trade openly carried on under the French flag.

The moment the *Resolute* arrived, the British consul at Zanzibar came on board to place himself at the disposal of the doctor, of whose plans he had been informed through the European newspapers of the month before. Up to this time, however, he belonged to the large army of sceptics.

'I had doubts,' he said, as he shook hands with Samuel Fergusson, 'but now I'm convinced.'

He offered the hospitality of his own house to the doctor, Dick Kennedy, and, of course, the worthy Joe. Through him the doctor was able to acquaint himself with the letters received from Captain Speke. The latter and his companions had suffered terribly from hunger and bad weather before reaching Ugogo. They were only advancing with extreme difficulty and did not think that they would be able to send any more news through for some time.

'These are the dangers and trials we intend to avoid,' said the doctor.

The baggage of the three travellers was transferred to the consul's house and preparations were made for unshipping the balloon on to the beach of Zanzibar. There was a favourable site near the signalling mast, adjoining an enormous erection which would have protected it against the east wind. This great tower, shaped like a barrel standing on end, and beside which the Heidelberg tun would have looked like a mere cask, was used as a fort, and on its platform Beloutchis, armed with lances, were lounging about like a collection of chattering loafers.

When it came to unshipping the balloon, however, the consul was warned that the population of the island would oppose this by force. There is nothing blinder than the rage of fanatics. The news of the arrival of a Christian who was to rise into the air was received with fury. The negroes, who were more excited than the Arabs, regarded the project as an attack on their religion. They imagined that it was an attempt against the sun and moon. These two astral bodies are objects of worship in Africa, so it was resolved to oppose such a sacrilegious expedition.

Hearing of this attitude, the consul

discussed the situation with Dr Fergusson and Captain Pennet. The latter had no intention of giving way to threats, but his friend persuaded him to listen to reason.

'We shall, of course, get the better of them in the end,' he told him. 'The Imam's garrison would even come to our assistance at a pinch. But, my dear captain, an accident might easily happen. It would not require much to do an irreparable injury to my balloon, and then the trip would be hopelessly compromised. So we must act with great caution.'

'But what can we do? If we land on the African coast, we shall come up against the same difficulties. What are we to do about it?'

'Nothing could be simpler,' the consul replied. 'Look at those islands the other side of the harbour. Land your balloon on one of those, surround yourselves with a cordon of sailors, and you'll run no risks.'

'Splendid,' said the doctor, 'and we'll be able to get on with our preparations undisturbed.'

The captain gave in to this advice and the *Resolute* headed for the island of Koumbeni. During the morning of the 16th of April the balloon was safely placed in the middle of a clearing of the great woods that cover the island. Two masts eighty feet high were erected eighty feet apart. A combination of pulleys fitted to the ends of these enabled the balloon to be lifted by means of a cross-rope. It was completely deflated. The inner balloon was attached to the top of the outer so that it would be lifted at the same time. To the lower extremity of each balloon were fitted the two pipes for supplying the hydrogen.

The day of the 17th was spent in setting up the apparatus for producing the gas. This consisted of thirty casks in which the sulphuric acid, diluted with water, was decomposed by means of iron. The hydrogen, having been washed on the way, passed into a huge central cask and then through the pipes into the two balloons. In this way each balloon received the exact amount of gas required. The operation consumed 1,866 gallons of sulphuric acid, 16,050 lbs of iron and 966 gallons of water.

The work was begun during the following night, at about 3 a.m., and lasted about eight hours. In the morning the balloon, in its net, was swaying gracefully above the car, which was held down by a large number of sacks filled with earth. The expansion apparatus was mounted with great care, and the pipes projecting from the balloon were fixed to the cylinder. Anchors, ropes, instruments, rugs, tent, guns, all had to be stowed in their appointed places in the car. The supply of water was brought from Zanzibar. The 200 lbs of ballast were divided into fifty bags and placed in the bottom of the car, but within easy reach.

These preparations lasted until 5 p.m., and meanwhile sentries kept a constant look-out round the island, and the *Resolute*'s boats patrolled the channel. The negroes continued to give vent to their anger by means of yells, grimaces and contortions. The witch-doctors dashed about between the various groups, inflaming their excitement, and a few fanatics attempted to swim out to the island but were easily driven back. Then the witch-doctors, the 'rain-makers,' who claim to control the clouds, summoned the hurricanes and 'stone showers' (hail) to their aid. To do this they gathered leaves from all the different species of trees that grow in the country, boiled them over a slow fire, and meanwhile slaughtered a sheep by driving a long needle into its heart. But in spite of these rites the sky remained clear and the sheep and grimaces were wasted.

The negroes now abandoned themselves to frenzied orgies, making themselves drunk with 'tembo,' a potent liquor drawn from the coconut palm, or with a very strong beer called 'togwa.' Their singing, devoid of any distinguishable melody, but with a very regular rhythm, continued far into the night.

About six in the evening the travellers assembled at a farewell dinner given by the captain and his officers. Kennedy, whom they had given up questioning, was heard to mutter a few words, but no one caught what he said. He never took his eyes off the doctor. Altogether this was a gloomy meal. The imminence of the supreme moment filled the minds of all with anxious thoughts. What had fate in store for these bold venturers? Would they ever be restored to the circle of their friends? Would they ever again sit at their own firesides? If their means of transport happened to fail them, what would become of them among these savage races, in these unexplored regions, in the heart of these vast wastes? Such were the thoughts, hitherto only transient and little heeded, that invaded their over-excited imaginations. Dr Fergusson, still as cool and impassive as ever, chatted about one thing and another, but it was in vain that he tried to drive off this infectious depression: he met with no success.

As there was fear of some sort of demonstration against the persons of the doctor and his companions, they all three slept aboard the *Resolute*. At 6 a.m. they left their cabins and made for the island of Koumbeni. The balloon was gently swaying to the east wind. The sacks of earth which held it down were replaced by a score of sailors. Captain Pennet and his officers had come to watch the solemn departure. Just at this moment Kennedy went straight up to the doctor, took his hand and said:

'It's settled that I'm coming, Samuel?'

'Quite settled, old man.'

'I've done all in my power to stop this expedition?'

'Everything.'

'Then I have an easy conscience as far as that's concerned, and I'm coming with you.'

'I knew you would,' the doctor answered, an expression of emotion passing rapidly over his face.

The moment for the final farewells had arrived. The captain and his officers warmly shook hands with their intrepid friends, not forgetting the worthy Joe, who was full of pride and delight. All present were anxious to grip the doctor's hand.

At 9 a.m. the three men took their places in the car. The doctor lit his burner and forced the flame so as to produce heat rapidly. A few minutes later the balloon, which was hovering over the ground in perfect equilibrium, began to rise. The sailors had to pay out the ropes that were holding her. The car rose about twenty feet.

'My friends,' shouted the doctor, standing

up between his two companions and raising his hat, 'let us christen our airship by a name that will bring her luck; let us call her the *Victoria!*'

A tremendous cheer went up: 'Long live the Queen! Hurrah for England!'

At this moment the lifting force of the balloon increased enormously. Fergusson, Kennedy and Joe called a last farewell to their friends.

'Let go!' cried the doctor. And the *Victoria* rose rapidly into the air, while the four guns of the *Resolute* thundered in her honour.

12

Crossing the straits — Mrima
— Kennedy's remarks and a suggestion
from Joe — A recipe for coffee —
Usaramo — The unhappy Maizan
— Mount Duthumi — The doctor's
maps — A night over a nopal

The air was clear, the wind moderate. The *Victoria* climbed almost vertically to a height of 1500 feet, indicated by a drop of not quite two inches in the column of the barometer. At this height a more decided current carried the balloon in a southwesterly direction. What a magnificent panorama unrolled itself below the eyes of the explorers! The island of Zanzibar was displayed in its entirety, its deeper colour causing it to stand out as though on a huge relief map; the fields looked like samples of various coloured stuffs, and the forests and jungle like small clumps of trees. The inhabitants of the island had the appearance of insects. The cheers and shouts gradually faded away and the gunfire of the ship alone shook the lower folds of the balloon.

'How beautiful it all is!' exclaimed Joe, breaking the silence for the first time. He received no reply. The doctor was busy watching the variations of the barometer and noting the different details of the ascent. Kennedy's eyes were inadequate to take in all he wanted to see. The rays of the sun came to the assistance of the furnace. The tension of the gas increased and the *Victoria* attained a height of 2500 feet. The *Resolute* now looked like a pinnace, and the African coast could be traced to westward by a long line of foam.

'You're very quiet,' said Joe.

'We're looking,' the doctor answered, pointing his glasses towards the continent.

'I can't help talking.'

'Go ahead, Joe. Talk as much as you like.'

Joe broke into a succession of ono-matopœic sounds. A torrent of 'ohs,' 'ahs' and 'eehs' poured from his lips.

While they were passing over the sea the doctor thought it wise to maintain the height they had reached. It enabled him to command a wider view of the coast. The thermometer and barometer, hanging under the half-open tent, could be readily observed. A second barometer placed under cover was to be used for the night watches. In two hours the *Victoria*, now moving at rather more than eight miles an hour, was drawing near to the coast.

The doctor decided to come down a little. He lowered the flame of the furnace and the balloon descended to 300 feet.

He found that they were above Mrima, as this part of the East African coast is called. It was edged by a thick border of mangroves, the thick roots of which, exposed to the waves of the Indian Ocean, were left exposed, for the tide was out. The dunes which had once formed the coast-line swelled up against the horizon, and Mount Nguru stood up sheer to the north-west.

The *Victoria* passed close to a village which the doctor recognised from the map as Faole. The whole population had turned out, and howled with rage and fear. Arrows were vainly shot at the monster of the air soaring majestically above all this impotent fury. The wind was blowing them south, but this did not worry the doctor, as it would enable him to follow the route taken by Captains Burton and Speke. Kennedy had by now become as talkative as Joe and the two exchanged ejaculations of admiration.

'A bit better than travelling by coach,' said one.

'Or steamer,' replied the other.

'I don't know that I think much of railways either,' went on Kennedy. 'I like to see where I'm going.'

'What price balloons!' said Joe. 'You don't feel as if you were moving and the scenery slides along under you to be looked at.'

'What a view! Splendid! Perfect! Like dreaming in a hammock.'

'What about some lunch, sir?' said Joe, whose appetite had been sharpened by the fresh air.

'Good idea, Joe.'

'It won't take long to cook; some biscuit and tinned meat.'

'And as much coffee as you like,' added the doctor. 'You can borrow a little heat from my furnace; there's plenty to spare and it might save the danger of a fire.'

'That would be pretty awful,' Kennedy answered. 'It's like hanging under a powder-magazine.'

'Not at all,' said Fergusson; 'and even if the gas did get on fire, it would burn gradually and we should come down, which would be a nuisance. But don't worry; our balloon is quite gas-tight.'

'Well, in that case, let's have something to eat,' said Kennedy.

'Here you are, gentlemen,' said Joe; 'and while I'm having mine I'll go and make you some coffee which I think you'll find extra special.'

'It's a fact,' said the doctor, 'that among his thousand virtues Joe has an extraordinary gift for preparing that delicious beverage. He uses a mixture of various ingredients which he has always kept a secret from me.'

'Well, sir. As we're in the open I can let you into the secret. It's only a mixture of equal parts of mocha, bourbon and rio-nunez.'

A few minutes later three steaming cups were served to crown a substantial lunch which was seasoned by the good-humour of the company, and afterwards each man returned to his post of observation. The landscape was remarkable for its extreme fertility. Narrow, winding paths were hidden under a vaulting of foliage. The balloon passed over fields of ripe tobacco, maize and barley. Here and there stretched vast fields of rice with its straight stems and purplish flowers. Sheep and goats could be seen penned in large enclosures raised on piles to protect them from the leopards. A luxuriant vegetation covered this rich soil. In many villages the sight of the balloon roused fresh clamour and bewilderment, and Dr Fergusson prudently kept out of range of arrows. The inhabitants, gathered round their groups of huts, continued for a long time to hurl their vain imprecations after the balloon.

At noon the doctor, consulting his map, reckoned that he was over the district of Usaramo. The balloon seemed to gambol over the masses of coco-nut palms, papaws and cotton-trees. Joe took this vegetation for granted the moment he knew he was in Africa. Kennedy saw hares and quails simply asking to be shot; but it would have been waste of powder in view of the impossibility of retrieving the game. Travelling at a rate of twelve miles per hour, the aeronauts soon found themselves in long. 38° 20′ E., above the village of Tunda.

'That's the place,' said the doctor, 'where Burton and Speke were attacked by virulent fever and thought for a moment that it was all up with their expedition. Though they weren't far from the coast, fatigue and privations were already making themselves seriously felt.' In fact, a malaria hung perpetually over this country and even Dr Fergusson could only avoid it by lifting his balloon above the miasmas which the hot sun drew from the damp earth. Every now and again they caught sight of a caravan resting in a kraal, awaiting the cool of the evening to resume its march. These kraals are large plots of ground surrounded by hedges and jungle, affording shelter for travellers not only against wild beasts but also against the marauding tribes of the country. The natives could be seen running away in all directions at the sight of the balloon. Kennedy wanted to get a closer look at them, but

Fergusson refused to listen to this suggestion.

'The chiefs are armed with muskets,' he said, 'and our balloon would offer too easy a target.'

'Would a bullet hole bring us down, sir?' asked Joe.

'Not immediately, but the hole would soon develop into a big rent through which all the gas would soon escape.'

'Well, let's keep away from the brutes. I wonder what they think of us flying through the air like this. I'm sure they'll want to worship us.'

'We'll let ourselves be worshipped then, but from a distance. That's always an advantage. Look, the country's changing. There aren't so many villages and no more mangroves. They don't grow in this latitude. The country is getting hilly and it looks as though we are coming near the mountains.'

'As a matter of fact, I think I can see some over there,' said Kennedy.

'To westward — those are the first chains of the Urizaras, probably Mount Duthumi, behind which I hope to spend the night. I'll turn up the flame, for we shall have to keep at a height of five or six hundred feet.'

'That's a great idea of yours, sir,' said Joe, 'it's so easy to work. Just turn a tap and the thing's done.'

'That's better,' said the Scotsman when the balloon had lifted. 'The glare of the sun on that red sand was getting unbearable.'

'What fine trees!' cried Joe. 'Of course they're what you'd expect, but they really are fine specimens. It would only take a dozen of them to make a forest.'

'Those are baobabs,' Dr Fergusson answered. 'Look! That one must have a girth of a hundred feet. It might have been at the foot of that very tree that Maizan, the Frenchman, died in 1845, for we're over the village of Deje la Mhora into which he ventured alone. He was captured by the chief of this country and tied to the trunk of a baobab, after which the bloodthirsty nigger cut his tendons one by one, while the tribe chanted their war-song. He then cut his throat a little way, stopped to sharpen his knife that had become rather blunted, and then tore off the wretched man's head before the neck had been cut through. The poor fellow was twenty-six years old.'

'And France has not demanded vengeance for the crime?' Kennedy asked.

'France put in a claim. The Sultan of Zanzibar did all he could to capture the murderer, but without success.'

'I vote we don't stop,' said Joe. 'We'll go up higher, sir, if you take my advice.'

'I'm quite ready to do so, Joe, especially as

that's Mount Duthumi standing up ahead of us. If my reckoning is correct, we shall be over it before seven.'

'We're not going to travel by night, are we?' asked Kennedy.

'No more than we can help. If we take precautions and keep a good look-out we shall be able to without risk; but it's not enough just to cross Africa, we want to see it.'

'So far we've had nothing to complain of, sir. It's the best cultivated and most fertile country in the world instead of being a desert. Now we know how much good geography is.'

'Wait, Joe, wait. We'll see before long.'

About half-past six in the evening, the *Victoria* was directly in front of Mount Duthumi. To cross it, they would have to rise to over 3000 feet, to do which the doctor had only to raise the temperature by 18° Fahrenheit. Kennedy pointed out the obstacles that had to be cleared, and the *Victoria* sailed just over the mountain.

At 8 p.m. they were running down the opposite slope, which was less abrupt. The anchors were thrown out of the car and one, catching the branches of a huge nopal, established a firm hold. At once Joe slid down the rope and made it fast. The silk ladder was lowered and he climbed back again briskly. The balloon remained almost motionless in the lee of the mountain. The evening meal was prepared and the travellers, their appetites stimulated by their journey through the air, made a big hole in their stores.

'How far have we come today?' asked Kennedy.

The doctor took a reckoning on the moon and consulted the excellent map which served as his guide, and which was taken from the *Atlas der neuesten Entdeckungen in Afrika*, published at Gotha by his learned friend Petermann, who had presented him with a copy. This atlas could be used for the whole of the doctor's journey, for it gave Burton and Speke's route to the Great Lakes, Dr Barth's discoveries in the Sudan, Lower Senegal according to Guillaume Lejean, and the Niger delta as surveyed by Dr Baikie.

Fergusson had also provided himself with a work which contained in one volume all the information that had been acquired about the Nile. This was called *The Sources of the Nile*, and was a general survey of the basin of that river and of its main stream, with the history of Nilotic discovery by Charles Beke, D.D. He also possessed an excellent map published in *Bulletins of the London Royal Geographical Society*, so that no area already discovered was likely to baffle him.

Measuring on his map with his dividers, he

found that their latitudinal route had covered two degrees or 120 miles in a westerly direction. Kennedy observed that the route was southerly, but the doctor did not mind this as he was anxious, as far as possible, to follow the tracks of his predecessors.

It was decided to divide the night into three watches so that each might take his turn in guarding the other two. The doctor was to take the watch beginning at nine, Kennedy that beginning at midnight, and he in his turn was to be relieved by Joe at 3 a.m. Kennedy and Joe therefore wrapped themselves up in their blankets, lay down under the awning and slept soundly while Dr Fergusson kept watch.

13

*Change in the weather — Kennedy
attacked by fever — The doctor's
medicine — Travel by land — The
Imenge basin — The Rubeho Mountains
— Six thousand feet up — A halt by day*

The night was calm, but when he woke up on
Saturday morning Kennedy complained of
lassitude and the shivering of fever. The
weather was changing. The sky, covered with
thick clouds, seemed to be gathering for rain.
Zungomero is a dreary country, where it rains
continually except, perhaps, for a fortnight in
January. It was not long before heavy rain
began to pour down upon the travellers.
Below them the roads cut out by *nullahs*, a
sort of intermittent torrent, became impassable, especially as they were also overgrown
with thorny shrubs and gigantic creepers. The
emanations of sulphuretted hydrogen mentioned by Captain Burton could be distinctly
detected.

'According to Burton,' the doctor said, 'and
he's right, it smells as though a corpse were
concealed in every thicket.'

'Beastly country,' answered Joe, 'and I don't think it's done Mr Kennedy any good spending the night here.'

'As a matter of fact, I have a pretty bad touch of fever,' said the Scot.

'There's nothing surprising about that, old man. We're in one of the unhealthiest districts in Africa. But we're not going to stop long. Let's make a start.'

Joe skilfully freed the anchor and climbed back up the ladder into the car. The doctor quickly expanded the gas and the *Victoria* set off again before a stiffish breeze. Nothing was to be seen in the pestilent mist except a very occasional hut, but soon the appearance of the country changed. It often happens in Africa that an unhealthy area is of quite small dimensions and borders on districts which are perfectly salubrious. Kennedy was obviously very unwell, the fever sapping his natural energy.

'This is no place to be ill in,' he said, wrapping himself up in his blanket and lying down under the awning.

'Have a little patience, Dick, and you'll soon be well again,' Dr Fergusson replied.

'Look here, Samuel, if you've got anything in your medicine-chest that might put me right, give me some at once. I'll swallow it with my eyes shut.'

'I've something better than that, old man. I'm going to give you a cooling draught that will cost you nothing.'

'What is it?'

'It's quite simple. I'm just going to rise above those clouds which are swamping us and get away from this pestilent atmosphere. Give me ten minutes to expand the hydrogen.'

Before the ten minutes were up the travellers were above the rain zone.

'Wait a bit, Dick, and you'll feel the effects of the pure air and sunshine.'

'Well, that is a cure!' said Joe. 'It's wonderful!'

'No. It's quite natural.'

'Oh, yes, I suppose it's natural enough, sir.'

'I take Dick where the air is better, as they always do in Europe. Just as, if we were at Martinique, I should send him to the Piton Mountains to escape yellow fever.'

'Why, this balloon's a perfect paradise,' said Kennedy, already feeling more comfortable.

'At any rate, it takes us there, sir,' Joe answered solemnly.

It was strange to see masses of cloud now piled up under the car. They rolled over one another and formed a confused mass of light as they reflected the rays of the sun. The *Victoria* reached a height of four thousand feet. The thermometer registered an appreciable drop in the temperature. The earth was no longer visible. Some fifty miles to westward the Rubeho Mountains raised their glistening crests. These mountains bound the country of Ugogo in long. 30°20′. The wind was blowing at twenty miles an hour, but the travellers had no sensation of their speed. They felt no swaying and were not even conscious that they were moving.

Three hours later the doctor's prediction was realised. Kennedy's fever had left him and he lunched with a good appetite.

'That beats sulphate of quinine hollow,' he said with relief.

'This is certainly the place I shall retire to in my old age,' said Joe.

About 10 a.m. the atmosphere cleared. A great hole appeared in the clouds and the earth once more came into view. The *Victoria* was dropping imperceptibly towards it as Dr Fergusson sought a current which might carry them more to the north-eastward. He found one six hundred feet above the ground. The country became broken, even mountainous. Zungomero faded away to the east together with the last coco-nut palms of that latitude. Soon the crests of mountains stood out more sharply. Peaks rose here and there. It was necessary to keep a constant look-out for the sharp cones which seemed to start up without warning.

'We're among the breakers,' said Kennedy.

'Don't worry, Dick, we shan't run aground.'

'It's a fine way of travelling, all the same!' Joe broke in.

The doctor was indeed handling his balloon with wonderful skill.

'If we had had to march over that waterlogged country,' he said, 'we should have had to plough through the foul mud. Since leaving Zanzibar half our pack animals would have died of fatigue. We should be looking like ghosts and feeling desperate. We should have had constant struggles with our guides and porters, and no protection against their savagery. Damp, unbearable, crushing heat by day, and by night often intolerable cold; bitten by flies with mandibles that would go through the thickest canvas and drive men mad; not to mention the wild animals and savage tribes.'

'I'm in no hurry to try it,' Joe answered simply.

'I'm not exaggerating in the least,' Dr Fergusson continued, 'for travellers who have been daring enough to venture into these countries tell stories that would make your blood curdle.'

About eleven o'clock they crossed the

Imenge basin. The tribes scattered over the hills vainly threatened the *Victoria* with their weapons. At length they reached the last undulations before the Rubehos which form the third and highest chain of the Usagara Mountains. The travellers took careful note of the geographical conformation of the country. The three ranges, of which the Duthumis form the first stage, are separated by immense longitudinal plains. These lofty ridges take the form of rounded cones between which the earth is strewn with stray boulders and rocks. The steepest declivity of these mountains faces the coast of Zanzibar, while the eastern slopes are merely tilted plateaus. The low-lying areas are covered with black rich soil, where vegetation is very vigorous. Various water-courses make their way eastward to join the Kingani, amid huge clumps of sycamores, tamarinds, calabash-trees and palmyras.

'Look,' said Dr Fergusson. 'We're getting near the Rubehos. In the native language the name means 'passage of the wind.' It will be wise to cross the sharp ridges at a good height. If my map is right we ought to go up to over five thousand feet.'

'Shall we often have to go as high as that?'

'No, only very seldom. The African mountains are not very high compared with the peaks of Europe and Asia. But in any case, the

Victoria would have no difficulty in clearing them.'

The gas quickly expanded under the action of the heat, and the balloon lifted very considerably. The expansion of the hydrogen, moreover, presented no danger, as the enormous capacity of the balloon was only three-quarters filled. The barometer, by a drop of nearly eight inches, indicated a rise of six thousand feet.

'Is this going to last long, sir?' asked Joe.

'The atmosphere surrounding the earth extends to a height of six thousand fathoms,' replied the doctor. 'With a big balloon one might go far. MM. Brioschi and Gay-Lussac did, but after a time they began to bleed at the mouth and ears. The air was not breathable. Some years ago two other bold Frenchmen, MM. Barral and Bixio, also ventured very high, but their balloon tore — '

'And they fell?' Kennedy asked sharply.

'Certainly. But as wise men fall, without hurting themselves.'

'Well, gentlemen,' said Joe, 'you may be able to fall like that, but I'm only an ignorant man and I'd rather stop at a reasonable height. It doesn't do to be ambitious.'

At six thousand feet the density of the air had already appreciably diminished. Sound carried badly, and it was more difficult for them to make themselves heard. Sight became blurred, and the eye could only distinguish large masses and that vaguely; men and animals became quite invisible; roads looked like strips of tape and lakes like ponds. The doctor and his companions felt that they were in abnormal conditions. An atmospheric current of tremendous velocity was sweeping them over arid mountains on whose summits great patches of snow startled the eye, and their convulsed appearance indicated some Neptunian labour of the world's first days. The sun shone in the zenith, pouring its rays vertically upon these barren crests. The doctor made a careful sketch of the mountains, which consist of four distinct ridges running almost in a straight line, the most northerly being the longest.

Soon the *Victoria* descended the opposite slope of the Rubehos, skirting a ridge covered with trees of very dark-coloured foliage. Then came the crests and ravines of the sort of wilderness which precedes the Ugogo district. Lower still stretched yellow plains burnt and cracked, and strewn here and there with saline plants and thorny shrubs. A few thickets which later gave place to forests adorned the horizon. The doctor came close to the ground and the anchors were dropped, one of them soon catching the branches of an enormous sycamore.

Joe slid quickly down the tree and carefully made fast the anchor. The doctor kept his furnace going to give the balloon sufficient lift to hold her in the air. The wind had dropped almost instantly.

'Now,' said Fergusson, 'take a couple of guns, Dick, one for yourself and one for Joe, and see if between you you can't get us a few good slices of antelope for dinner.'

'Rather,' cried Kennedy. 'Come on, Joe.'

He climbed over the side of the car and went down. Joe had slid down from branch to branch and was stretching himself while he waited. The doctor, relieved of the weight of his companions, was now able to put out his furnace.

'Don't go and fly away, sir!' Joe cried.

'Don't worry, Joe; I'm firmly fixed. I'll get my notes up to date. Good hunting, and be careful. From up here I shall be able to overlook the country round about, and if I see anything the slightest bit suspicious, I'll fire a carbine. That will be the signal for return.'

'Right ho!' Kennedy replied.

14

*The gum-tree forest — The blue antelope
— The signal to return — An unexpected
attack — Kanyemi — A night in the
air — Mabunguru — Jihoue la Mkoa
— Water-supplies — Arrival at Kazeh*

The country, with its clayey soil, arid, parched
and cracked by the heat, looked a wilderness.
Here and there were to be seen the tracks of
caravans, whitened bones of men and animals
half gnawed away and scattered together in
the dust. After walking for about half an hour,
Dick and Joe, keeping a sharp look-out and
their fingers held to the triggers of their guns,
plunged into a forest of gum-trees. They did
not know what they might meet with. Without
being an expert shot, Joe knew how to handle
a gun.

'It does you good to walk again, sir, and yet
the going is none too good,' he said as he
stumbled among the bits of quartz with which
the ground was strewn.

Kennedy signed to his companion to be
silent and to halt. They had to manage
without a dog and, agile as Joe might be, he

could not be expected to have the nose of a spaniel or greyhound. In the bed of a torrent where a few pools of water still stagnated a group of ten antelopes were drinking. The graceful animals seemed to scent danger and showed signs of uneasiness. After each drink they would raise their pretty heads quickly and, with their sensitive nostrils, sniff the air coming to them from their pursuers.

Kennedy skirted some trees while Joe stood motionless. When he came within range he fired. The antelopes vanished in the twinkling of an eye, but one stag fell, hit behind the shoulder, and Kennedy dashed towards his prey. It was a blaubok, a splendid animal of a pale bluish-grey, the belly and the inside of the legs pure white.

'That was a lucky shot,' cried Kennedy. 'This is a very rare species of antelope and I hope I'll be able to preserve his skin.'

'Why, sir, how could you?'

'Why not? Look what a splendid skin.'

'But Dr Fergusson will never allow the extra weight.'

'You're right, Joe. But it's annoying to have to leave such a splendid animal like this.'

'Like this? No, we won't do that, sir. We'll get all the nourishment out of it we can, and if you'll allow me, I'll deal with it as if I was the warden of the Honourable Company of

Butchers in London.'

'Go ahead, Joe, but you know, as a hunter I'm as good at eating a bit of game as at shooting it.'

'I'm quite sure of that, sir, so perhaps you'd make an oven with three stones. There's lots of dead wood, and once you get them glowing I shall only be a few minutes.'

'I won't be a minute,' Kennedy replied, and at once set about building his fire, which a few minutes later was blazing.

Joe had cut a dozen cutlets from the antelope and the tenderest pieces from the fillet, which were soon transformed into a savoury grill.

'This will please Dr Fergusson,' said the Scotsman.

'Do you know what I'm thinking about, sir?'

'The job you're doing, I expect; your grill!'

'No, sir, I'm thinking what we should look like if we couldn't find the balloon again.'

'What an idea! Are you expecting the doctor to desert us?'

'No; but supposing his anchor broke away?'

'Impossible. Besides, the doctor could easily bring his balloon down again; he's pretty good at handling her.'

'Supposing the wind carried him off and he couldn't get back to us?'

'Oh, shut up, Joe; your suppositions aren't at all amusing.'

'Well, sir, everything that happens in this world is natural, and as anything may happen, we ought to be ready for anything — '

At this moment a shot rang out.

'What's that?' said Joe.

'My carbine. I recognised its report.'

'A signal!'

'We're in danger.'

'Perhaps he is,' cried Joe.

'Come on.'

The two men quickly picked up their bag and went back the way they had come, following their own footprints. The thickness of the foliage prevented them from seeing the *Victoria*, which could not be far away. Then came a second shot.

'He's in a hurry,' said Joe.

'Yes. There's another.'

'It sounds to me as though he was defending himself.'

'Come on!' and they ran as fast as their legs would carry them.

When they reached the end of the wood the first thing they saw was the *Victoria* still in position and the doctor in the car.

'What's wrong?' asked Kennedy.

'Good God!' cried Joe.

'What is it?'

'Over there. Niggers attacking the balloon.'

Indeed, in the distance there appeared a band of about thirty men hustling one another, gesticulating, shrieking and leaping about at the foot of the sycamore. A few had climbed into the tree and were already among the highest branches. The danger seemed immediate.

'It's all up with the master,' cried Joe.

'Come, Joe, keep calm and look out. We hold the lives of four of those blackguards in our hands. Come on.' When they had run about a mile a fresh gunshot sounded from the car. It hit a tall ruffian who was swarming up the anchor-rope. A lifeless body fell from branch to branch and remained hanging twenty feet from the ground, its arms and legs dangling in the air.

'Great Scott!' said Joe, stopping. 'What's holding the fellow up?'

'What's it matter?' replied Kennedy. 'Run, man, run!'

'Oh, I see, sir,' cried Joe, bursting into a guffaw of laughter. 'It's his tail. It must be a monkey. Why, they're only monkeys after all.'

'That's worse than men,' Kennedy replied as he dashed into the middle of the shrieking band. It was a troop of pretty fearsome baboons, ferocious, cruel and horrible to look at with their dog-like snouts, but a few shots were enough for them and the grimacing horde made off, leaving several victims on the ground. In an instant Kennedy seized the ladder. Joe climbed into the sycamore and freed the anchor. The car came down to him and he got in without difficulty. A few minutes later the *Victoria* was rising in the air and heading eastward before a moderate wind.

'What a battle!' said Joe.

'We thought you were being attacked by natives.'

'Luckily they were only monkeys,' the doctor replied.

'From the distance there's little difference, old man.'

'Nor near to, either,' Joe replied.

'In any case,' Fergusson went on, 'the attack might have been serious. If they'd shaken the anchor loose, who knows where I might have got to?'

'What did I tell you, Mr Kennedy?'

'You were right, Joe. But in addition to being right you were also at that moment cooking some antelope steaks, and it made me hungry to watch you.'

'It would,' the doctor replied; 'antelope's flesh is delicious.'

'You can judge for yourself, sir. Dinner is served.'

It was now four o'clock in the afternoon. The *Victoria* ran into a stronger air-current, the ground rose imperceptibly, and soon the barometer registered a height of 1500 feet above sea-level. The doctor was forced to buoy the balloon up by a considerable expansion of the gas and the burner was working continually. About seven o'clock the *Victoria* was soaring over the Kanyemi basin. The doctor immediately recognised this great stretch of cultivated land, stretching for ten miles, with its villages buried among baobab and calabash-trees. It contains the residence of one of the sultans of Ugogo, where civilisation is perhaps less primitive — the people do not sell the members of their own families quite so frequently, but animals and people all live together in the round, roofless huts that look like haystacks.

After Kanyemi the country became arid and rocky, but half an hour later, in a fertile valley not far from Mdaburu, the vegetation became as vigorous as ever again. As evening came on the wind dropped and the atmosphere seemed to fall asleep. The doctor vainly tried different levels in search of a breeze, and when he saw the whole of Nature at rest he decided to spend the night in the air and, as a precaution, rose about a thousand feet. The *Victoria* hung motionless.

The night, splendid with stars, came down in silence.

Dick and Joe stretched themselves out on their peaceful couches and slept soundly during the doctor's watch. At midnight he was relieved by the Scotsman.

'If anything in the slightest degree unusual happens, wake me,' he said; 'and, above all, don't take your eyes off the barometer. It's our compass.'

The night was cold, the temperature being nearly 27 degrees lower than the previous day. The darkness awoke the nightly concert of the animals, driven from their lairs by hunger and thirst; the soprano of the frogs mingling with the howls of the jackals, while the sonorous bass of the lions provided a foundation to the harmonies of this living orchestra.

When he returned to his post in the morning, Doctor Fergusson consulted his compass and noticed that the wind had shifted during the night. The *Victoria* had drifted some thirty miles to the north-eastward during the last two hours or so. She was now passing over Mabunguru, a rocky district strewn with boulders of beautifully polished cyanite, and broken by rocks shaped like a camel's hump. Conical tors, like the rocks of Karnak, stood out of the ground like Druidical dolmens; many bones of elephants and buffaloes lay bleaching here and there. The trees were few, apart from some dense woods to eastward, which sheltered occasional villages.

About seven o'clock, a circular rock appeared, about two miles across, and shaped like an enormous turtle-shell.

'We're on the right track,' said the doctor; 'there's Jihoue la Mkoa, where we're going to halt for a few minutes. I want to get a fresh supply of water for my furnace. Let's look for somewhere to anchor.'

'There aren't many trees about,' Kennedy replied.

'Let's try, anyhow,' said Joe; 'over with the anchors.'

Gradually losing her lift, the balloon slowly neared the ground. The anchor-ropes ran out and one anchor caught a fissure in the rock, bringing the *Victoria* to a standstill. It must not be imagined that the doctor could completely extinguish his burner during a halt. The equilibrium of the balloon had been calculated at sea-level, but the country had been continually rising, and at a height of six or seven hundred feet the balloon would have had a tendency to drop to a lower level than that of the ground. It was therefore necessary to maintain a certain expansion of the gas. Only in an absolute calm would the doctor have allowed the car to rest on the ground, in which case the balloon, relieved of a considerable weight, would have kept in the air without the help of the burner.

The maps showed immense lakes on the western slopes of the Jihoue la Mkoa. Joe set off alone with a cask that would hold about ten gallons and had no difficulty in finding the place he wanted, not far from a little deserted village, where he filled his cask and was back again in less than three-quarters of an hour. He had seen nothing of special interest except, perhaps, the huge footprints of an elephant; he even nearly fell into one of these in which a half-eaten carcass was lying. But he brought back a kind of medlar which the monkeys were eating greedily. The doctor identified it as the fruit of the 'mhenbu,' a tree growing in great abundance in the eastern part of Jihoue la Mkoa. Fergusson was waiting for Joe with a certain amount of impatience, for even a short stay in these inhospitable regions always filled him with anxiety. The water was shipped without difficulty, for the car was almost on a level with the ground. Joe then loosed the anchor and climbed nimbly up to his master's side. The latter at once increased the flame and the *Victoria* resumed her voyage through the air.

She was at this time about a hundred miles from Kazeh, an important settlement in the

African interior, which, thanks to a breeze from the south-east, the travellers had hopes of making in the course of the day. They were travelling at about fourteen miles per hour. The handling of the balloon became somewhat difficult. It was impossible to rise without a big expansion of the gas, for the level of the country was, on the average, about three thousand feet. As the doctor preferred, so far as was possible, not to force the expansion, he followed very skilfully the windings of a fairly rapid slope and skimmed over the villages of Thembo and Tura Wels. The latter forms part of Unyamwezi, a magnificent country where the trees attain enormous dimensions, especially the cactus which is gigantic.

About two o'clock, in splendid weather and under a burning sun which stifled the slightest breath of air, the *Victoria* was hovering over the town of Kazeh, about three hundred and fifty miles from the coast.

'We left Zanzibar at nine in the morning,' said the doctor, consulting his notes, 'and in two days our circuitous route has brought us nearly five hundred geographical miles. Burton and Speke took four and a half months to do the same distance.'

15

*Kazeh — The noisy market — The
Victoria sighted — The wagangas —
Sons of the Moon — The doctor's walk
— Population — The royal tembe —
The sultan's wives — Royal dissipation
— Joe worshipped — How they dance in
the Country of the Moon — Two moons
in the sky*

Kazeh, an important settlement in Central
Africa, is not a town; there is, in fact, no town
in the interior. It is only a collection of six
huge excavations. Within these are enclosed
dwellings and slave-huts with little courts and
carefully cultivated gardens. Onions, sweet
potatoes, aubergines, water-melons and delicious mushrooms grow there in great
abundance.

Unyamwezi is the Moon Country at its
best, the fertile and luxuriant park of Africa.
In its centre is the district of Unyamyembe, a
delightful place where a few families of the
Omani, of pure Arab origin, live in idleness.
They have long trafficked with Central Africa
and Arabia in gums, ivory, calico and slaves.

Their caravans cross these equatorial regions in every direction. They still go to the coast in search of articles required for the life of luxury and pleasure led by the wealthy merchants who, surrounded by women and servants, live in this delightful country the most peaceful and placid life that can be imagined. All day long they recline on couches, laughing, smoking and sleeping.

Around these excavations are native dwellings, vast market-places and fields of cannabis and datura, splendid trees and cool shade; such is Kazeh. It is also the general rendezvous of caravans; those coming from the south with their slaves and loads of ivory, and those from the west carrying cotton and beads to the tribes of the Great Lakes. In the markets, therefore, there is perpetual excitement, an indescribable pandemonium made up of the shouts of the porters, the din of drums and trumpets, the neighing of mules, the braying of donkeys, the singing of women, the screaming of children, with the whip-cracks of the jemadars (head-men of caravans) giving the beat for this pastoral symphony. In attractive disorder are displayed brilliantly-coloured stuffs, ivories, rhinoceros' horns, sharks' teeth, honey, tobacco and cotton. The strangest bargains are conducted, in which the value of each object depends solely on the desires it excites.

Suddenly all the excitement, movement and noise ceased. The *Victoria* had just been sighted in the sky, hovering majestically, and gradually dropping straight down. Men, women, children, slaves, merchants, Arabs and niggers all vanished, taking cover in the *tembes* and huts.

'My dear Samuel,' said Kennedy, 'if we go on producing an effect like this, we shan't find it easy to establish business relations with these people.'

'But there's one bit of business which would be easy enough,' said Joe, 'and that would be to go down quietly and pinch some of the more valuable goods, without bothering our heads about the merchants. It would be worth doing.'

'Steady,' answered the doctor. 'These natives were frightened at first, but superstition or curiosity will soon bring them back.'

'Do you think so, sir?'

'We'll see. But it will be just as well not to get too close. The *Victoria* is not armoured, so there's no protection against bullets or arrows.'

'Are you thinking, then, of trying to talk with these natives, Samuel?'

'Why not? If it can be done,' answered the doctor. 'In a place like Kazeh there must be

Arab merchants a little more educated and less uncivilised than the rest. I remember Burton and Speke had nothing but praise for the hospitality of the inhabitants of the town, so we may as well try.'

The *Victoria* had been almost imperceptibly nearing the ground. They threw out one of the anchors, which caught the crest of a tree near the market-place. The whole population at this very moment emerged from their holes, sticking out their heads cautiously. Several *wagangas*, distinguishable by their ornaments of conical shells, came forward boldly. These were the local magicians. At their belts they carried little black gourds, smeared with fat, and various devices used in the practice of magic, all of typically medical dirtiness. Gradually a crowd collected round them, including women and children; the drums did their utmost to drown one another, hands were clapped together and arms stretched out towards the sky.

'That's their way of worshipping,' said Doctor Fergusson.

'Unless I'm mistaken, we're going to be called upon to play an important rôle.'

'All right, sir, get on with it.'

'It's quite likely, my dear Joe, that you are about to become a god.'

'Well, sir, that doesn't worry me, and I rather like the smell of incense.'

At this moment one of the magicians, a *myanga*, made a sign, and all the tumult died down into perfect silence. He addressed some words to the travellers but in an unknown language. Doctor Fergusson, who could not understand what was said, tried at random a few words of Arabic, and was at once answered in the same tongue. The orator burst out into a tremendous harangue in very ornate language, which was attentively listened to by the crowd. The doctor at once realised that the *Victoria* had been taken for the Moon herself who had graciously come down to the town with her three sons, an honour which would never be forgotten in this, her favourite land.

The doctor replied with great dignity that every thousand years the Moon toured her realm, as she liked to show herself more closely to her worshippers. He begged them, therefore, to put themselves at their ease and to use her divine presence as an opportunity for making known their needs and desires.

The wizard replied in his turn that the sultan, the *mwani*, who had been an invalid for many years, solicited the aid of heaven and invited the Sons of the Moon to visit him. The doctor communicated the invitation to his companions.

'And you really mean to visit this negro king?' Kennedy asked.

'Certainly. These people seem friendly and the weather is calm; there's not a breath of wind; so we have nothing to worry about as far as the *Victoria* is concerned.'

'But what will you do?'

'Set your mind at rest, old man. A little medicine will pull me through.' Then, addressing the crowd: 'The Moon, taking pity on the beloved sovereign of the children of Unyamwezi, has entrusted to us the charge of healing him. Let him prepare to receive us.'

The shouting, singing and demonstrations redoubled in vigour, and the vast swarm of black heads were once more set in motion.

'And now, my friends,' said Doctor Fergusson, 'we must be ready for anything. We may at any moment be forced to make a bolt for it. Dick, therefore, will remain in the car and keep the necessary lift with the furnace. The anchor is firmly fixed. There's nothing to be afraid of. I'm going down and Joe will come with me, but he will remain at the foot of the ladder.'

'What! you're going to see this cut-throat alone?' exclaimed Kennedy.

'What!' cried Joe, 'you're not going to let me come with you?'

'No! I'm going alone. These good people imagine that their great goddess the Moon has come to visit them. I'm protected by superstition, so don't worry, and each of you stay at the post I have assigned.'

'Since you insist — ' said the Scot.

'Keep an eye on the gas expansion.'

'Right ho!'

The shouts of the negroes grew louder still. They were energetically invoking celestial intervention.

'Just look,' said Joe. 'Surely they're taking rather a high line with their good moon and her mighty sons.'

Armed with his portable medicine chest, the doctor landed, preceded by Joe. The latter, solemn and dignified as the occasion demanded, sat down at the foot of the ladder with his legs crossed under him in the Arab fashion, and part of the crowd gathered round him in a respectful circle. Meanwhile Doctor Fergusson, accompanied by the blare of musical instruments and by religious dances, deliberately approached the royal *tembe*, which was situated some way outside the town. It was about three o'clock in the afternoon and the sun was shining brilliantly, which was the least it could do under the circumstances. The doctor walked with dignity, surrounded by the *wagangas*, who

126

controlled the crowd. He was soon joined by the natural son of the sultan, quite a well-set-up young man who, in accordance with the custom of the country, was the sole heir to his father's possessions, to the exclusion of the legitimate children. He prostrated himself before the Son of the Moon, who raised him to his feet with a gracious gesture.

Three-quarters of an hour later the excited procession, following shady paths cut through the luxuriant vegetation, reached the sultan's palace, a square building called *Ititenya*, on the slope of a hill. A kind of veranda formed by the overhanging thatched roof surrounded the exterior, supported by wooden pillars upon which there had been some attempt at carving. The walls were ornamented with long lines of reddish clay, intended to portray the forms of men and serpents; the latter, of course, being the more successful. The roof of this dwelling did not rest immediately upon the walls, so that the air could circulate freely. For the rest, there were no windows and little in the way of doors.

Dr Fergusson was received with great ceremony by the guards and favourites, men of high birth called *wanyamwezis*, the purest breed of the Central African populations, strong and vigorous, well-built and of fine bearing. Their hair, divided into a large number of little plaits, fell on to their shoulders, and their cheeks were striped from forehead to mouth with black or blue scars. From their ears, which were horribly distended, hung wooden discs and resin ornaments. They were dressed in brilliantly-dyed stuffs. The soldiers were armed with assegais, bows with barbed arrows poisoned with the juice of the euphorbia, cutlasses, *simes* (a long sabre toothed like a saw), and small battle-axes.

The doctor entered the palace, where, in spite of the sultan's illness, the clamour, already terrific, redoubled as he entered. On the lintel of the door he noticed the tails of hares and the manes of zebras hanging as talismans. He was received by the whole troop of the sultan's wives to the harmonious music of the *upatu* (a kind of cymbal made from the bottom of a copper pot) and the crash of the *klindo* (a drum five feet high, hollowed out of a tree trunk), which two virtuosi were attacking with their fists.

Most of the women were very pretty. They laughed and smoked *thang* in great black pipes. Their well-formed figures were draped in long gracefully-hanging robes, and they wore kilts of calabash fibre fastened at the waist. Six of them, and these were not the least gay of the company, were set apart from the rest as they were under sentence of cruel torture. On the death of the sultan they were to be buried alive at his side to distract his eternal solitude.

Doctor Fergusson, who had taken all this in at a glance, approached the bedside of the sovereign. There he saw a man of about forty years of age, wrecked by debauchery of every kind, and with whom there was obviously nothing to be done. His malady, which had lasted for years, was nothing more than chronic drunkenness. The royal rake had practically lost consciousness, and all the ammoniac in the world could not have set him on his legs again.

During the doctor's solemn examination of the patient the favourites and women knelt in an attitude of reverence. With a few drops of strong cordial the doctor put a brief spark of life into the torpid body. The sultan moved, and this sign of life in what for some hours had seemed a corpse was received by a further redoubling of the shouting in the doctor's honour. The latter, who had had enough of it, waved aside his over-demonstrative admirers and left the palace. It was six o'clock in the evening.

During his absence Joe waited patiently at the foot of the ladder, the crowd meanwhile showing him the greatest respect. As a true

Son of the Moon he resigned himself to this. For a divine being he looked a good fellow, showing himself approachable, even familiar towards the young African women, who never tired of gazing at him and kept up a friendly conversation.

'Worship away, ladies; keep it up,' he said. 'I'm not such a bad sort of cove, even though I am the son of a goddess.'

Propitiatory gifts were offered him, such as are usually deposited in the *mzimus* or fetish huts. These consisted of ears of barley and *pombe*. Joe felt called upon to taste this kind of strong beer, but his palate, though broken to wine and whisky, could not stand the potency of this beverage. He pulled a terrible face which the spectators took for a pleasant smile. Then, mingling their voices in a drawling melody, the girls executed a solemn dance around him.

'Dancing, are you? All right. I'm not going to be outdone. I'll show you one of our dances.' And he broke into a dizzy jig, twirling, leaping, dancing with his feet, knees and hands, throwing himself into amazing contortions and impossible postures and indulging in incredible grimaces, all of which gave the natives an extraordinary impression of the way gods dance in the moon. The Africans, however, who are as imitative as monkeys, soon began to mimic his extravagances. Not a single gesture or posture escaped them. It became a hustling, excited pandemonium, of which it would be impossible to convey even a slight idea. When the ball was at its height, Joe caught sight of the doctor hastily forcing his way through the shrieking, abandoned crowd.

This produced a strange reaction. Had the sultan been clumsy enough to die under the treatment of his celestial physician? Kennedy, from his look-out, saw the danger but did not realise its cause. The balloon, responding to a considerable expansion of the gas, was straining at her moorings, eager to take flight.

The doctor reached the foot of the ladder. A superstitious fear still held the crowd and prevented them from indulging in any violence. He quickly climbed up the rungs, followed nimbly by Joe.

'We haven't a minute to spare,' said the doctor. 'Don't bother to loose the anchor. We'll cut the rope. Follow me.'

'But what's the matter, sir?' asked Joe as he climbed into the car.

'What's up?' said Kennedy, carbine in hand.

'Look,' answered the doctor, pointing to the horizon.

'Well?' asked Kennedy.

'Well! The moon!'

Indeed, red and imposing against the azure background, the moon was rising like a globe of fire. There she was, and there, too, was the *Victoria*. Either there were two moons or these strangers were nothing but impostors, adventurers, false gods. Such had naturally been the reflections of the crowd; hence the reaction.

Joe could not restrain a great guffaw of laughter. The inhabitants of Kazeh, realising that their prey was slipping through their fingers, uttered long-drawn howls; bows and muskets were levelled against the balloon.

But, just then, one of the magicians made a sign and the weapons were lowered. Climbing into the tree he tried to seize the rope and bring the machine to the earth. Joe dashed forward, an axe in his hand.

'Shall I cut?' he asked.

'Wait,' replied the doctor.

'But this nigger — ?'

'We may be able to save our anchor, and I should like to. There'll still be time to cut.'

The magician, having climbed the tree, put in such good work that he managed, by breaking a few branches, to free the anchor which, answering to the strong pull of the balloon, caught the magician between the legs and, astride this unexpected hippogriff, he set off for the regions of the air. When they saw

132

one of their *wagangas* flying through space, the amazement of the crowd was tremendous.

'Hurray!' shouted Joe, as the *Victoria*, impelled by her lifting force, leapt upwards at terrific speed.

'He's all right,' said Kennedy, 'a little trip won't do him any harm.'

'Shall we drop him off, sir?' Joe asked.

'Steady, Joe,' replied the doctor. 'We'll let him gently down, and I expect his trip will do a good deal to enhance his reputation as a magician among his contemporaries.'

'They're quite capable of making a god of him,' said Joe.

The *Victoria* had reached a height of about a thousand feet. The negro was frenziedly clinging to the rope in silence, his eyes starting out of his head with terror and astonishment. A light west wind was driving the balloon away from the town. Half an hour later the doctor, seeing that the country was now deserted, lowered the flame of the furnace and came down. When he was twenty feet from the ground the negro came to a rapid decision. Throwing himself off, he fell on his feet and made off towards Kazeh, while the balloon, suddenly relieved of his weight, rose once more in the air.

16

Signs of a storm — The Country of the Moon — The future of the African continent — The machine that will bring about the end of the world — The landscape in the setting sun — The fire zone — A night of stars

'That's what comes of pretending to be sons of the moon without her permission,' said Joe. 'She nearly got us into a nasty mess. I suppose, sir, you didn't do anything to damage her reputation with your medicine?'

'By the way,' asked Kennedy, 'what sort of a fellow was this sultan?'

'An old tippler on his last legs. He won't be much missed. But the moral is that glory is ephemeral, and it doesn't do to acquire too strong a taste for it.'

'Well, never mind,' Joe replied. 'I was getting on famously, being worshipped and playing the god in my own way. But it can't be helped. The moon came up, and all red, which shows she wasn't pleased with us.'

During the course of this conversation, in which Joe discussed the moon from an entirely novel point of view, the sky to the northward was becoming heavy with great clouds, lowering and sinister. A brisk wind, which they encountered three hundred feet from the ground, drove the *Victoria* north-north-east. The azure vault above them was clear but the atmosphere felt oppressive. About eight in the evening the travellers were in long. 32°40′ E., lat. 4° 17′ S. The atmospheric currents, under the influence of the approaching storm, were driving them along at a rate of thirty-five miles an hour. Below them, the undulating fertile plains of Mfuto swept past. It was a splendid sight, which the travellers watched with admiration.

'We're in the heart of the Moon Country,' said the doctor. 'It has kept the name given to it in antiquity, doubtless because the moon has always been worshipped here. It really is a wonderful country and it would be hard to find finer vegetation.'

'If it was near London it would be unnatural, but very nice,' said Joe. 'Why are all the beautiful things only to be found in such wild countries?'

'But how do we know that some day this country may not become the centre of civilisation?' the doctor answered. 'The nations of the future may come here when the land in

Europe is no longer able to feed the inhabitants.'

'Do you really think that?' asked Kennedy.

'Certainly, old man. Think of the march of history, the successive migrations of the nations, and you'll come to the same conclusion. Asia was the cradle of the world, wasn't she? For about four thousand years she was continually bringing forth fruit, and then, when stones covered the ground that once yielded the golden crops we read of in Homer, her children left her exhausted, shrivelled lap. Next we see them pouring down upon Europe, then young and vigorous, and Europe has been suckling them for two thousand years. Already, however, her fertility is becoming exhausted, her productive faculties are diminishing every day. All these new diseases that are every year attacking the agricultural products, these ruined harvests, insufficient supplies, all this is a certain sign of flagging vitality and approaching exhaustion. Already the people are beginning to flock to the generous breasts of America as to a source, not inexhaustible, but as yet unexhausted. That continent will in her turn grow old, her virgin forests will fall under the axe of industry, her soil will weaken through trying to respond to the excessive demands made upon it. Where two harvests were gathered yearly, hardly one will force itself through the tired soil. When that time comes, Africa will offer to the new races the treasures accumulated in her breast for centuries. Irrigation and scientific agriculture will cleanse this climate, now fatal to foreigners. These scattered waters will unite in a single bed to form a navigable artery, and this world over which we are soaring, more fertile, richer, more virile than the rest, will become some great kingdom where discoveries will be made greater even than steam and electricity.'

'Really, sir, I'd like to see that,' said Joe.

'You've been born too early, Joe.'

'Besides,' said Kennedy, 'the time when industry gets a grip of everything and uses it to its own advantage may not be particularly amusing. If men go on inventing machinery they'll end by being swallowed up by their own machines. I've always thought that the last day will be brought about by some colossal boiler heated to three thousand atmospheres blowing up the world.'

'And I bet the Yankees will have had a hand in it,' said Joe.

'Quite likely,' the doctor replied. 'But don't let us get carried away by these discussions. Let us be content to admire this splendid Country of the Moon while we have the chance.'

The sun, glancing its last rays beneath the piled-up mass of cloud, was touching with a crest of gold everything that stood out in any way from the ground. Gigantic trees, tall shrubs, even the moss clinging to the soil, all caught this flood of light. The land, which was slightly undulating, swelled up here and there to form small conical hills, but there were no mountains in sight. Dense thickets, impenetrable hedges and thorny jungles divided the clearings in which numerous villages were to be seen, and which were surrounded by enormous euphorbias as by a natural wall in which the coralliform branches of the shrubs were tangled together.

Soon the Mlagarasi, the principal tributary of Lake Tanganyika, began to wind beneath these masses of foliage and absorb the many streams caused by the swelling of mountain torrents through the melting of the snows or by the overflowing of pools sunk in the clayey surface of the soil. From the air it gave the impression of a network of cascades pouring over the whole western part of the country.

Great humped animals were grazing in the lush meadows, being at times completely hidden by the tall grass. The forests from which fragrant scents arose had the appearance of vast bouquets, but in these bouquets lions, leopards, hyenas and tigers lurked, seeking shelter from the heat of the late afternoon. Now and again an elephant would sway the crests of the thickets, and the cracking of the trees before his ivory tusks could be heard.

'What a hunting country!' Kennedy exclaimed enthusiastically. 'You'd only have to let off a gun in any direction you liked and you'd be bound to hit something worth having. Couldn't we have a try?'

'No, old man. It's getting dark and we're in for a stormy night. In these parts the ground is like a huge electric battery and the storms are terrific.'

'You're right, sir,' said Joe. 'The heat is stifling and there's not a breath of wind. It makes you feel as if something is going to happen.'

'The whole atmosphere is charged with electricity,' replied the doctor. 'Every living creature reacts to this peculiar state of the air that comes before a storm, and I confess I never felt it as much as I do now.'

'Wouldn't it be a good idea to get down, then?' asked Kennedy.

'On the contrary, Dick, I'd much rather get up higher. The only thing I'm afraid of is that we might be swept out of our course in the cross-currents.'

'Don't you intend to hold on to the course

we've been following since we left the coast?'

'If possible,' the doctor answered, 'I shall steer more directly north for seven or eight degrees. I want to get up towards the supposed latitude of the Nile sources. We might pick up some traces of Speke's expedition or even Heuglin's caravan. If my reckoning is correct, we are now in long. 32° 40', and I should like to make straight across the Equator.'

'Just look!' cried Kennedy. 'Look at those hippopotamus sneaking out of the water; and those are crocodile. You can hear them gasping for breath.'

'They're suffocating,' said Joe. 'There's a lot to be said for travelling like this. You can snap your fingers at all that nasty vermin. Look, sir; look, Mr Kennedy! Just look at those animals running, in packs. There must be a couple of hundred of them. They're wolves.'

'No, Joe, those are wild dogs. They're a tough breed and will even attack lions with impunity. They are the most terrible thing a traveller can meet with. He would be torn to pieces at once.'

'Well, you won't catch me trying to muzzle them,' the worthy fellow replied. 'After all, if they're made like that, I suppose we mustn't blame them.'

Little by little a hush came over the world

under the influence of the oncoming storm. It was as though the air had lost its capacity to convey sound. Like a room muffled with hangings, the atmosphere had lost all resonance. The crested stork, red and blue jay, the mocking-bird and flycatchers, vanished into the great trees. All Nature revealed symptoms of an imminent cataclysm. At 9 p.m. the *Victoria* was hanging motionless over Msene, a large group of villages that could hardly be distinguished in the gloom. Now and again the glinting of a stray beam of light on the murky water showed the presence of a regular system of dykes, and in a final glow could be seen the dark and placid shape of palms, tamarisks, sycamores, and the gigantic euphorbias.

'I'm suffocating,' said the Scotsman, laboriously trying to fill his lungs with the rarefied air. 'We're not budging an inch. Let's go down.'

'But what about the storm?' asked the doctor with some anxiety.

'If you're afraid of being carried off by the wind it seems to me it's the only thing to do.'

'The storm may not burst tonight,' said Joe. 'The clouds are very high.'

'That's one of my reasons for not trying to rise above them. We should have to go very high. We should lose sight of the ground and shouldn't know whether we were making any way, or in which direction.'

'Make up your mind, Samuel. There's no time to lose.'

'It's a nuisance, the wind dropping,' said Joe. 'It might have blown us away from the storm.'

'It certainly is a pity, my friends,' replied the doctor, 'for the clouds are a danger for us. They contain cross-currents which may involve us in a tornado, and lightning that may set us on fire. On the other hand, if we made fast to a tree the force of the wind might dash us to the ground.'

'What's to be done, then?'

'We must keep the *Victoria* in an intermediary zone between the dangers of the earth and those of the sky. We've plenty of water for the furnace, and we've lost none of our ballast. If necessary I shall use it.'

'We'll keep watch with you,' said Kennedy.

'No, my friends. Stow away the stores and go to bed. I'll wake you if necessary.'

'But hadn't you better get some sleep yourself, sir, as there's no danger yet?'

'No, thanks, Joe. I'd rather keep a look-out. We're not moving, and unless something fresh happens we shall be in the same spot tomorrow morning.'

'Good-night, sir.'

'Good-night, if possible.'

Kennedy and Joe lay down under their rugs and the doctor was left alone in the immensity of space. Meanwhile the dome of clouds was lowering imperceptibly and the darkness became intense. The black vault of the night enveloped the earth as though to crush it. Suddenly a sharp, swift, stabbing flash of lightning striped the darkness. Before the rent had closed again a terrific peal of thunder shook the depths of the sky.

'Wake up!' shouted Fergusson; and the two sleepers, already roused by the tremendous din, were ready to carry out his orders.

'Let's drop,' said Kennedy.

'No. The balloon wouldn't stand it. We must rise before these clouds break and the wind gets up.' And he vigorously increased the flame of the burner in the spiral.

Tropical storms develop with a rapidity in keeping with their violence. A second flash tore the clouds and was immediately followed by a score of others. The sky was scored with electric flashes which hissed under great drops of rain.

'We're late,' said the doctor. 'Now we shall have to pass through a zone of fire with our balloon full of inflammable gas.'

'Get down to earth! Get down to earth!' Kennedy went on repeating.

'The risk of being struck would be about the same, and we should soon get torn to pieces in the branches of the trees.'

'We're rising, sir.'

'Quicker, quicker still!'

In this part of Africa, during the equatorial storms it is a common thing to count thirty or thirty-five flashes per minute. The sky is literally ablaze and there is no pause between the peals of thunder. The wind was unleashed with terrific violence in the torrid air. It twisted the incandescent clouds about like a bellows fanning the blaze. Dr Fergusson kept his burner going at full strength. The balloon dilated and rose. On his knees in the middle of the car, Kennedy was holding on to the ropes of the tent. The tossing of the balloon made him giddy. Great hollows were blown in the envelope of the balloon into which the wind drove with its full force, the silk cracking under the pressure. With a deafening roar a sort of hail battered down upon the *Victoria*, which however continued to rise, the lightning sparking off her surface in fiery tangents. She was in the heart of the storm.

'God help us!' said Fergusson. 'We're in His hands and He alone can save us. We must be ready for anything, even fire. We shan't drop too suddenly, perhaps.'

The doctor's voice scarcely reached his

companions, but they could see his calm face in the light of the flashes. He was watching the play of the lightning on the net of the balloon. The *Victoria* was whirling and tossing but still rising. Quarter of an hour later she had passed above the lightning zone. The electric display could be seen below her like a vast cluster of fireworks hanging from the car. This was one of the finest spectacles that Nature has to offer. Below, the storm, and above, the starry sky, tranquil, silent and impassive, with the moon pouring her peaceful light upon the raging clouds. Dr Fergusson consulted his barometer and found it showed a height of twelve thousand feet. It was 11 p.m.

'By God's mercy we're safe,' he said. 'All we have to do now is to keep at this level.'

'That was awful,' Kennedy replied.

'At any rate, it gave a little variety to the trip,' said Joe, 'and I'm glad to have seen a thunderstorm from above. It was a fine sight.'

17

The Mountains of the Moon
— An ocean of verdure

About six in the morning (Monday) the sun rose, the clouds scattered, and a pleasant breeze gave freshness to the early day. The fragrant earth reappeared to the eyes of the travellers. The balloon, twisting on her axis amid the cross-currents, had scarcely drifted from her former position. Allowing the gas to contract, the doctor came down in search of a wind that would carry him in a more northerly direction. For a long time he searched in vain; he was being carried to the westward, within sight of the celebrated Mountains of the Moon which enclose the extremity of Lake Tanganyika in a semicircle. Their almost unbroken outline stood out against the faint blue of the sky like a natural barrier to keep explorers out of the centre of Africa. A few isolated peaks bore traces of perpetual snows.

'We are now in unexplored country,' said the doctor. 'Captain Burton went very far west, but was unable to reach these famous mountains. He even denied their existence, which was affirmed by Speke, his companion. He makes out that Speke imagined them. In our case, at any rate, there can be no doubt about them.'

'Are we going to cross them?' Kennedy asked.

'No, if God is good. I hope to find a favourable wind that will take us towards the Equator. If necessary, I'll wait and anchor the balloon like a ship in a contrary wind.'

But what the doctor was hoping for was not long in coming. After trying different levels, the *Victoria* ran north-west at a moderate speed.

'Now we're on the right course,' he said, consulting his compass, 'and only two hundred feet up, so we shall be in a good position to view this new ground. When Speke was making for Lake Ukereue he took a course due north from Kazeh but farther to the east than ours.'

'Are we going on like this long?' asked Kennedy.

'Possibly. What we're trying to do is to veer towards the sources of the Nile, and we have more than six hundred miles to go before we come to the farthest point reached by the explorers from the north.'

'And we aren't going to land, not even to

stretch our legs?' asked Joe.

'Oh, yes, we are. For one thing, we shall have to be careful with our stores, and you, Dick, will have to keep us supplied with fresh meat on the way.'

'You've only to say the word, Samuel.'

'We shall also have to renew our supply of water. For all we know, we may be carried off into districts where there is no water. We can't be too careful.'

At noon the *Victoria* was in long. 29° 15′ E., lat. 3° 15′ W. She passed the village of Uyofu, the northern extremity of Unyamwezi, with Lake Ukereue, as yet invisible, on her beam.

The tribes living near the Equator seem a little more civilised. They are governed by absolute monarchs with unlimited powers. Their most compact settlement constitutes the province of Karagwah. It was decided among the three travellers that they would land at the first favourable place they came to. They would make a considerable halt and carefully overhaul the balloon. The flame of the burner was lowered and the anchors, which had been dropped overboard, soon began to brush the tall trees of a huge plain. From the height at which they were, it appeared to be covered with smooth turf, but in reality the grass was seven or eight feet tall.

The *Victoria* skimmed over this without touching it, like a gigantic butterfly. There was no obstacle in sight. It was like an ocean of green without a breaker.

'We may go on like this for a long time,' said Kennedy. 'I see no signs of a tree to which we could make fast. There doesn't seem much chance of any shooting after all.'

'Wait a bit, old man, you couldn't go shooting in grass taller than yourself. We'll find a place in time.'

The crossing of this green, almost transparent sea, undulating gently in the breeze, made very pleasant travelling. The car cut its way through the waves of tall grass, from which every now and again flocks of brilliantly-coloured birds would burst out, uttering shrill cries of joy. The anchors trailed through the lake of flowers, leaving a furrow which closed up behind them like the wake of a ship. Suddenly a sharp shock was felt. An anchor must have caught a rocky fissure hidden under the long grass.

'She's got a hold,' said Joe.

'All right. Out with the ladder,' Kennedy answered.

Before these words were out of his mouth a trumpeting cry rent the air, and the following remarks, punctuated with exclamations, came from the travellers:

'What's that?' 'A curious noise!' 'Hello, we're off again!' 'The anchor's broken loose!'

'No, it's still holding,' said Joe, who was pulling on the rope. 'It's the rock that's moving!'

There was a tremendous commotion in the grass and soon a long, sinuous shape emerged.

'A snake!' said Joe.

'A snake!' cried Kennedy, cocking his carbine.

'No,' said the doctor, 'it's an elephant's trunk.'

'Great Scott,' said Kennedy, bringing his gun to his shoulder.

'Half a minute, Dick. Wait.'

'He's towing us,' said Joe.

'Yes,' said the doctor, 'and in the right direction.'

The elephant was making good headway and soon reached a clearing where his whole shape was revealed. From his enormous size the doctor saw that he was a splendid male with two cream-coloured tusks, beautifully curved and probably eight feet long. Between these the anchor was firmly wedged. With his trunk the animal was making frantic efforts to rid himself of the rope by which he was attached to the car.

'Gee up! Get along!' shouted Joe, overjoyed

and doing what he could to urge forward this strange steed. 'Here's a new way of travelling. No horses for us. An elephant, if you please!'

'But where's he taking us to?' asked Kennedy, waving his carbine, which he was itching to use.

'Where we want to go, my dear Dick. Have a little patience.'

Joe went on shouting and urging the animal forward. All at once it broke into a fast gallop, throwing its trunk from right to left, its heavy lurches shaking the car. Axe in hand, the doctor stood by to cut the rope should it become necessary, though he was anxious not to lose the anchor until the last possible moment. They travelled behind the elephant for about an hour and a half, the animal showing no signs of fatigue. These huge beasts can trot a long way and are found to cover long distances from day to day, like whales, which are similar in bulk and speed.

'It's like harpooning a whale,' said Joe. 'This is just what the whalers do.'

But a change in the conformation of the country forced the doctor to change his method of locomotion. A dense wood of camaldores came in sight about three miles to the northward. It became necessary to cut loose from their tug. Kennedy was therefore called upon to stop the elephant. He raised his carbine but was not in a favourable position for a sure shot. His first, aimed at the animal's head, flattened itself out as if it had struck a sheet of armour-plating. The animal seemed in no way disturbed. At the noise of the report it quickened its pace, and swept along like a horse in full gallop.

'The devil!' said Kennedy.

'There's a thick head for you!' said Joe.

'We'll try a few elongated bullets behind the shoulder,' replied Dick, carefully loading his rifle, and he fired. The animal emitted a terrible roar and went on faster than ever.

'Come, sir,' said Joe, 'I'll have to help or we shan't get the job over.' And two bullets pierced the animal's flank. It halted, threw up its trunk, and then dashed off again at full speed, making for the wood. Its huge head swayed from side to side and the blood began to flow freely from its wounds.

'Keep it up, sir!' said Joe.

'And fire as fast as you can,' added the doctor. 'We're only a few hundred yards from the wood.' Ten more shots followed. The elephant took a tremendous bound forward, the car and balloon cracking as though the whole thing were coming to pieces. The lurch caused the doctor to drop his axe, which fell to the ground.

The situation was now a terrible one. There

was no hope of unlashing the rope under the present strain, and the travellers' pocket-knives were useless to cut it. The balloon was being dragged rapidly towards the wood, when the animal received a bullet in the eye as it was raising its head. It stopped and hesitated, then its knees gave way and its flank was exposed to the carbines.

'In the heart,' said Kennedy, firing for the last time. The elephant uttered a roar of distress and agony, stood erect again for a moment, waving its trunk, then fell with its full weight upon one of its tusks, which snapped. It was dead.

'He's broken his tusk!' cried Kennedy. 'The ivory would be worth forty guineas a hundredweight.'

'All that?' said Joe, dashing down the ladder.

'We can't help it, old man,' replied Doctor Fergusson. 'We're not ivory traders, and we haven't come here to make our fortunes.'

Joe examined the anchor, which was still firmly fixed in the undamaged tusk. Fergusson and Kennedy jumped to the ground and the half-deflated balloon hovered over the animal's body.

'What a splendid beast!' cried Kennedy. 'What a size! I've never seen an elephant this size in India!'

'That's very likely, Dick. The elephants of Central Africa are the finest in the world. Men like Anderson and Canning have hunted them so vigorously round the Cape that they are moving towards the Equator, where we'll see herds of them.'

'Meanwhile,' said Joe, 'I hope we shall get a taste of this one. I'll guarantee to serve you an appetising meal off it. Perhaps Mr Kennedy will go off shooting for an hour or two while Dr Fergusson has a look at the balloon and I get on with the cooking.'

'That's a good arrangement,' said the doctor. 'Do just what you like.'

'As far as I'm concerned,' said Kennedy, 'I shall take advantage of the two hours' leave Joe has been kind enough to allow me.'

'Yes, I should. But don't run any risks, and don't go far away.'

'You needn't worry,' Kennedy replied, as he shouldered his gun and plunged into the wood. Joe set to work. He first made a hole about two feet deep in the ground and filled it with the dry branches which covered the ground and which had been torn off by the passage of the elephant, whose track could be distinctly traced. When the hole was filled, he piled up the wood to a height of two feet and set fire to it. Then, turning to the elephant, which had fallen not fifty yards from the wood, he skilfully cut off the trunk, which was two feet thick at its upper extremity. From this he selected the tenderest part and added one of the spongy feet. These, indeed, are the tit-bits, like the hump of the bison, the paw of the bear, or the snout of the boar. When the bonfire had been completely consumed and the ashes cleared away, the hole in the ground was very hot. The flesh, encased in aromatic leaves, was placed at the bottom of this improvised oven and covered with the hot ashes. Joe then built a second bonfire over the top, and when the wood was burned away again the meat was cooked to a turn. Taking it out of the oven, Joe placed it on some fresh leaves and laid the meal in the centre of a splendid stretch of smooth turf. He next brought biscuits, brandy and coffee, and drew some fresh, clear water from a neighbouring stream. The feast thus arranged was pleasing to the eye, and Joe thought, without undue pride, that it would be even more pleasing to the palate.

'Travel without getting tired and without danger,' he repeated to himself, 'punctual meals, living in a hammock; what more could a man want? And to think Mr Kennedy didn't want to come!'

Dr Fergusson, for his part, undertook a minute examination of the balloon. It did not seem to have suffered any harm from the strain that had been put upon it. The silk and gutta-percha had stood it wonderfully. Measuring the present height of the balloon above the ground and calculating the lift, he was delighted to see that he had lost no hydrogen. So far the envelope was intact.

It was only five days since the travellers had left Zanzibar. The pemmican was still untouched, and the stores of biscuits and tinned meats were enough for a long journey. The water, then, was all that required replenishment. The pipes and spiral seemed in perfect order and, thanks to the rubber joints, had given to every oscillation of the balloon. When he had completed his examination of the balloon the doctor got his log up to date, and made a very successful drawing of the surrounding country, with the long plain stretching as far as the eye could reach, the forest of camaldore and the balloon hanging motionless over the body of the elephant.

When two hours had elapsed Kennedy returned with a string of fat partridges and a leg of oryx, a sort of gemsbok, one of the most agile species of antelope. Joe took charge of this addition to their provisions.

'Dinner is served,' he announced impressively, shortly afterwards. And the three travellers sat down simply on the green sward. The foot and trunk of the elephant were declared to be excellent. As always, they toasted England, and for the first time the aroma of choice Havanas lent its fragrance to the air of this delightful country. Kennedy ate, drank and talked enough for four. He was quite carried away and solemnly proposed to his friend that they should take up their abode in the forest, build a wigwam of branches and found a dynasty of African Robinson Crusoes. The proposal did not meet with approval, although Joe proposed himself for the position of Friday.

The country seemed so peaceful and deserted that the doctor decided to spend the night on land. Joe built a cordon of fires, an essential precaution against wild animals, for hyenas and jackals, attracted by the smell of elephant flesh, were prowling in the vicinity. Several times Kennedy had to fire his carbine at over-bold visitors, but in the end the night passed without any untoward incident.

18

The Karagwahs — Lake Ukereue —
A night on an island — The Equator
— Crossing the lake — The falls —
View of the country — The sources of
the Nile — Benga Island — Andrea
Debono's signature — The British flag

At five o'clock the following morning the
preparations for the departure were begun.
With the axe, which he had been lucky
enough to recover, Joe cut the elephant's
tusks, and the *Victoria*, free once more,
carried the travellers north-west at a speed of
eighteen miles an hour. The doctor had taken
a careful reckoning of his position the
previous evening by means of the stars. He
was in lat. 2° 40′, about 160 miles below the
Equator. He passed over numerous villages
without paying any attention to the outcry
their appearance provoked, noting the conformation of these places by summary glances
below. They crossed the Rubemhe range,
the slopes of which are almost as sheer as the
peaks of Usagara, and later, at Tenga, came to
the first foothills of the Karagwahs, which,

according to the doctor, originate in the Mountains of the Moon. Thus the ancient legend which held these mountains to be the cradle of the Nile was near the truth, for they border Lake Ukereue, which is supposed to be the reservoir of the great stream.

From Kafuro, the great merchant centre of the country, they at last caught sight, on the horizon, of the long-sought lake of which Speke had caught a glimpse on the 3rd of August, 1858. The doctor felt a thrill. He had almost attained one of the chief goals of his expedition and, his glass to his eye, he did not miss a wrinkle of this mysterious country, which he saw as follows:

Below him the land was, in general, sterile, only a few ravines showing signs of cultivation. Dotted with cone-shaped hills of moderate height, the ground flattened out as it neared the lake. The rice-fields gave place to fields of barley, and the plantain flourished from which the wine of the country is made, as also the *mwani*, a wild plant used for coffee. A collection of circular huts roofed with flowering thatch constituted the capital of Karagwah.

They could clearly distinguish the amazed faces of the inhabitants, a fairly handsome race of yellowish-brown complexion. Women of extraordinary bulk dragged themselves about the plantations, and the doctor caused his companions considerable surprise when he told them that this corpulence, which is greatly favoured, is obtained by a compulsory régime of curdled milk.

At noon the *Victoria* was in lat. 1° 45′ S., and at one o'clock the wind drove her over the lake. This lake was named Victoria Nyanza (Nyanza means lake) by Captain Speke. At this place its breadth might have been ninety miles. At its southern extremity the captain found a group of islands which he called the Bengal Archipelago. Pushing his survey as far as Muanza on the east bank, he was well received by the sultan. He made a survey of this part of the lake but was unable to obtain a boat to cross it or to visit the large island of Ukereue, a very populous island governed by three sultans and at low tide forming a peninsula.

The *Victoria* began to cross the lake farther north, to the great regret of the doctor, who would have liked to make a sketch of its lower contours. The banks, bristling with thorny shrubs and tangled creepers, were literally buried under myriads of mosquitoes of a light brown colour. The district must have been both uninhabitable and uninhabited. Herds of hippopotamus could be seen wallowing in the forests of reeds or diving beneath the whitish waters of the lake. Seen from above, the lake extended westward to such a distant horizon that it might have been a sea, the distance between the banks being so great that no communication was possible; moreover the storms are strong and frequent, for this elevated and exposed basin is at the mercy of the winds.

The doctor had some difficulty in holding his course and had fears of being carried eastward, but fortunately he found a current that bore him due north, and at 6 p.m. the *Victoria* made a small deserted island twenty miles from the bank, in lat. 0° 30′ S., long. 32° 52′ E. They managed to moor to a tree and, the wind dropping as night came on, they rode quietly at anchor. There could be no question of landing, for here, as on the banks of the lake, the ground was covered with a thick cloud of millions of mosquitoes. Joe even returned from the tree covered with bites, but was not perturbed as he found this behaviour very natural on the part of the mosquitoes. The doctor, however, less optimistic, paid out as much rope as possible, to get away from these merciless insects which had begun to rise with a disquieting hum. He confirmed Captain Speke's estimate of the height of the lake above sealevel: 3750 feet.

'Here we are, then, on an island,' said Joe,

scratching himself desperately.

'It wouldn't take us long to explore it,' said Kennedy, 'and except for these friendly insects there's not a living creature to be seen.'

'The islands scattered over the lake,' said Dr Fergusson, 'are really nothing more than the summits of submerged hills, but we're lucky to have found a refuge here, for the shores of the lake are inhabited by fierce tribes; so get a good night's sleep, for we're going to have a calm night.'

'Aren't you going to sleep too, Samuel?'

'No. I shouldn't sleep a wink. I have too much to think about. Tomorrow, my friends, if the wind is favourable, we'll bear straight to northward and perhaps we may discover the sources of the Nile, the secret that has so far baffled everybody. I couldn't sleep while we are so near.'

Kennedy and Joe, who were less troubled by scientific preoccupations, soon fell into a deep sleep, while the doctor kept watch.

On Wednesday the 23rd of April, the *Victoria* got under way at four in the morning, under a grey sky. The darkness lingered over the waters of the lake, which were veiled in a dense fog, but soon a strong wind swept this away. For some minutes the *Victoria* drifted about in various directions and finally bore away due north. Dr Fergusson clapped his hands with delight.

'This is the way we want to go,' he cried. 'If we don't see the Nile today, we shall never see it. We are now crossing the Equator, entering our own hemisphere.'

'Oh!' cried Joe. 'Do you really think this is the Equator, sir?'

'In this very place, Joe.'

'In that case, begging your pardon, sir, oughtn't we to drink its health at once?'

'We might drink a glass of grog,' the doctor answered, laughing. 'Your methods of cosmography have their points.'

Accordingly they celebrated the *Victoria*'s crossing of the line. She was moving swiftly. To westward could be seen the low-lying coast, broken by a few hills, and beyond, the higher plateaus of Uganda and Usoga. The wind became very strong, nearly thirty miles an hour. The waters of the lake lashed themselves into foam like the waves of a sea; and from the movement of the water the doctor saw that the lake must be of great depth. One or two clumsy boats were all the craft they sighted during their rapid crossing.

'This lake,' said the doctor, 'is from its high situation obviously the natural reservoir of the rivers of East Africa. The rain replenishes it with the water evaporated from its tributaries. It seems to me certain that it is the source of the Nile.'

'We shall soon see,' replied Kennedy.

About nine o'clock the west bank closed in. It was thickly wooded and seemed deserted. The wind shifted a little towards the east, and they were able to catch a glimpse of the other shore. It curved in such a way as to form a very wide angle at the extremity of the lake (lat. 2° 40' N.). High mountains raised their barren peaks at this end of the lake, and between them a deep and winding gorge gave passage to a turbulent torrent. While attending to the handling of his balloon Dr Fergusson examined the country with an eager eye.

'Look, my friends!' he cried. 'The stories of the Arabs were correct. They spoke of a river by which Lake Ukereue poured its waters northward. That river exists and we are following it. It flows at about the same pace as we are travelling. This little stream gliding away below our feet will certainly merge into the waves of the Mediterranean. It's the Nile!'

'It's the Nile!' echoed Kennedy, who was becoming infected with the doctor's enthusiasm.

'Hurrah for the Nile!' cried Joe, who was always ready to cheer anything that pleased him.

In places huge rocks stemmed the course of

this mysterious river. The water foamed, forming rapids and cataracts, which confirmed the
doctor's prophecies. From the surrounding
mountains many torrents poured down, foaming as they fell; there were hundreds of them.
Scattered all over the ground thin threads of
water trickled, joined one another and raced
towards this nascent stream which, as it absorbed
them, became a large river.

'That must be the Nile,' the doctor
repeated with conviction. 'The origin of its
name has been as eagerly sought by scholars
as the origin of its waters. It has been traced
to Greek, Coptic and Sanskrit; but, after all, it
doesn't matter since it has at last been forced
to reveal its sources.'[1]

'But,' said Kennedy, 'how are we to
establish the identity of this river with that
seen by the explorers from the north?'

'We shall have proofs certain, irrefutable
and infallible,' replied Fergusson, 'if the wind
keeps favourable for another hour.'

The mountains divided, giving place to
numerous villages, fields of sesame, durra and
sugar-cane. The tribes of this district seemed

---

[1] A Byzantine scholar took Neilos to be an
arithmetical symbol, N representing 50, E 5, I
10, L 30, O 70, S 200, which gives the number
of days in a year.

165

excited and hostile, more inclined to anger than worship, and regarded the travellers as foreigners, not as gods. They seemed to feel that by discovering the sources of the Nile the Europeans were robbing them of something. The *Victoria* had to be kept out of musket range.

'It will be difficult to make fast here,' said the Scotsman.

'Well, so much the worse for the niggers,' Joe answered. 'They won't get the benefit of our conversation.'

'I'll have to go down in any case,' the doctor answered, 'even if it's only for a quarter of an hour. Otherwise I shan't be able to confirm the results of our expedition.'

'Is it unavoidable, Samuel?'

'Yes, we shall have to go down, even if it means shooting.'

'I shan't mind that,' answered Kennedy, fondling his carbine.

'Whenever you like, sir,' said Joe, getting ready for the fray.

'It won't be the first time that science has been pursued weapon in hand,' answered the doctor. 'The same thing happened in the case of a French scientist in the mountains of Spain when he was measuring the earth's meridian.'

'Don't worry, Samuel. Trust your two guards.'

'Are we ready, sir?'

'Not yet. As a matter of fact, we're going to rise a bit first, to see the exact configuration of the country.'

The hydrogen was expanded and in less than ten minutes the *Victoria* was soaring at a height of 2500 feet. From this level they could distinguish a complicated tangle of rivers flowing into the bed of the main stream. Others flowed into it from the hills and fertile plains to the west.

'We're less than nineteen miles from Gondokoro,' said the doctor, pointing to his map, 'and less than five from the point reached by the explorers from the north. We must drop cautiously.'

The *Victoria* came down more than two thousand feet.

'Now, my friends, be ready for anything.'

'We're ready,' replied Dick and Joe.

'Good!'

The *Victoria* was soon following the bed of the river at a height of hardly a hundred feet. The Nile was three hundred feet wide at this place and the natives in the villages along both banks became tremendously excited. On reaching the second parallel the river forms a sheer cascade about ten feet high and consequently impassable.

'That's certainly the fall reported by

Debono,' cried the doctor.

The river bed widened and became dotted with many islands, which Dr Fergusson eagerly scanned. He seemed to be looking for a landmark he had not yet seen. As some natives in a boat approached below the balloon, Kennedy greeted them with a shot which, though it did not hit them, forced them to turn back and make for the shore as fast as they could.

'A pleasant voyage,' Joe shouted to them. 'If I were in their place I shouldn't risk coming back. I'd be jolly frightened of a monster that spits out lightning whenever it likes.'

But suddenly Dr Fergusson seized his glass and trained it on an island lying in the middle of the stream.

'Four trees,' he cried. 'Look over there!' Indeed, four isolated trees rose from the end of the island.

'That's Benga. It must be,' he added.

'Well, what about it?' Dick asked.

'That's where we come down, if God is kind.'

'But it looks inhabited, sir.'

'Joe's right. Unless I'm mistaken I can see a score of natives collected there.'

'We'll soon make them run,' said Fergusson.

'Let's get at it,' replied Kennedy.

The sun was in the zenith. The *Victoria*

drew near the island. The negroes, who were of the Makado tribe, uttered fierce cries, one waving his hat of bark. Kennedy took it as a target, fired, and the hat flew in pieces. There was a general rout, the natives plunging into the river and swimming across it. From both banks came a hail of bullets and arrows, but with no danger to the balloon, whose anchor had caught a rocky cleft. Joe slid to the ground.

'The ladder!' cried the doctor. 'Follow me, Kennedy.'

'What are you going to do?'

'Come along down. I want a witness.'

'I'm with you.'

'Keep a good look-out, Joe.'

'Don't worry, sir. I'll see to everything.'

'Come along, Dick,' said the doctor, jumping to the ground. He led his companion towards the group of rocks rising from the extremity of the island. There he searched for some time, hunting about amongst the thorns and scratching his hands till the blood ran. Suddenly he seized the Scotsman's arm.

'Look!' he said.

'Letters!' cried Kennedy.

Indeed, two letters appeared on the rock, clearly carved:

A.D.

'A. D.,' the doctor went on; 'Andrea Debono. The initials of the traveller who got nearest to the sources of the Nile.'

'That's unanswerable, Samuel.'

'Are you convinced now?'

'It's the Nile. There can be no doubt about it.'

The doctor took a last look at these precious initials, and took a careful sketch of their shape and dimensions.

'Now,' he said, 'back to the balloon!'

'We'll have to be quick. There are some natives getting ready to cross back.'

'It doesn't matter now. If only the wind will take us north for a few hours we shall reach Gondokoro and shake hands with our countrymen.'

Ten minutes later the *Victoria* was majestically pursuing her course, while Dr Fergusson celebrated his success by unfurling the Union Jack.

19

The Nile — Trembling Mountain
— Memories of home — Arab stories
— The Nyam Nyam — Joe's reflections
— The Victoria severely tested — Balloon
ascents — Madame Blanchard

'What course are we following?' Kennedy asked, seeing his friend consult the compass.

'N.N.W.'

'Good Lord! but that's not north!'

'No, Dick, but I think we're going to have some difficulty in reaching Gondokoro. I'm sorry, but in any case we've linked up the eastern explorations with the northern, so we mustn't grumble.'

The *Victoria* was gradually leaving the Nile behind.

'One last look at this impassable latitude which has baffled the boldest travellers,' said the doctor. 'These will be the unruly tribes reported by Petherick, D'Arnaud, Miani and young Lejean, to whom we owe the best work on the Upper Nile.'

'Then do our discoveries agree with the prophecies of science?' asked Kennedy.

'Entirely. The sources of the White Klver, the Bahr-elAbiad, run into a lake as big as a sea, and it is this lake which gives birth to the river. No doubt poetry will suffer. Men liked to ascribe a celestial origin to this king of rivers. The ancients called it Ocean and almost believed that it flowed directly from the Sun. But one must give way from time to time before the teaching of Science. There may not always be scientists, but there will always be poets.'

'There are some more waterfalls,' said Joe.

'They are the Falls of Makedo, in the third parallel. Nothing could be more accurate. What a pity we couldn't have followed the course of the Nile for a few hours.'

'And over there, ahead of us,' said Kennedy, 'I can see the top of a mountain.'

'It is Logwek, the Trembling Mountain of the Arabs. All this country has been explored by Debono, who passed through it under the name of Latif Effendi. The tribes near the Nile are enemies and wage war to the death upon one another. You can imagine the dangers he had to face.'

The wind was now bearing the *Victoria* to the north-westward. To avoid Mount Logwek it was necessary to seek another current.

'My friends,' the doctor said to his two companions, 'we are now beginning to cross

Africa in real earnest. Up to now we have been chiefly following the trail of our predecessors. Now we are about to launch into the unknown. Are we ready to face it?'

'Rather,' cried Dick and Joe together.

'Off we go, then, and Heaven prosper us.'

At 10 p.m., after crossing ravines, forests, and scattered villages, the travellers reached the side of Trembling Mountain and passed along its gentle slopes. On this memorable 23rd of April they had, after running for fifteen hours before a strong wind, covered a distance of over 315 miles. But this part of the journey had left upon them a melancholy impression. Complete silence reigned in the car. Was Dr Fergusson absorbed in his discoveries? Were his companions reflecting on this crossing of unknown regions? These thoughts were no doubt partly responsible, but with them were mingled poignant memories of England and distant friends. Joe alone maintained his good spirits, and thought it quite natural that the homeland should be no longer there the moment it was absent. However, he respected the silence of the other two.

At 11 p.m. the *Victoria* moored abreast of Trembling Mountain.[1] The travellers ate a

---

[1] Tradition says that it trembles whenever a Mussulman sets foot upon it.

substantial meal and fell asleep in turn, taking the watch in succession.

The following morning they wakened with brighter thoughts. The weather was beautiful and the wind blowing in their favour. Breakfast, much enlivened by Joe, put a final touch to their good humour. The district they were traversing was of vast dimensions, stretching from the Mountains of the Moon to those of Darfur, and so about the size of Europe.

'We are now crossing what is supposed to be the kingdom of Usoga,' said the doctor. 'Geographers have claimed that there used to exist in the centre of Africa a huge depression, a vast central lake. We'll see if there's any appearance of truth in this.'

'But how did they arrive at this idea?' asked Kennedy.

'Through the stories told by the Arabs. These people are great storytellers, perhaps too much so. Travellers arriving at Kazeh or the Great Lakes saw slaves from the central districts, questioned them as to their country, put together a number of these stories and reduced them to a theory. Beneath it all there is always some grain of truth and, you see, they were not deceived as to the origin of the Nile.'

'Nothing could be more accurate,' replied Kennedy.

'It is upon these documents that the sketch-maps have been based. I intend to set our course by one of them and, if necessary, correct it.'

'Is all this region inhabited?' asked Joe.

'Without a doubt, and unpleasantly so.'

'I thought as much.'

'These scattered tribes are included in the general name of Nyam Nyams, which is merely onomatopœic, and reproduces the sound of mastication.'

'That's good,' said Joe; 'nyam! nyam!'

'My dear Joe, if you were the immediate cause of this onomatopœia you wouldn't find it quite so good.'

'What do you mean, sir?'

'That these people are said to be cannibals.'

'Is that true?'

'Quite true. It was also said that they possessed tails like animals, but it was soon discovered that these appendages belonged to the skins they wore.'

'Well, at any rate, a tail is a good thing for driving off mosquitoes, sir.'

'That may be, Joe, but this can be put down as a fable, like the dogs' heads attributed to certain tribes by the explorer, Brun-Rollet.'

'Dogs' heads? Useful for barking and not a

bad thing for a cannibal.'

'One thing that has unfortunately been reported is the ferocity of these tribes and their avidity for human flesh, which they hunt down passionately.'

'I hope they won't show too much keenness for mine,' said Joe.

'Listen to that,' said Kennedy.

'It's this way, Mr Kennedy. If I've got to be eaten in case of need, I'd like it to be to your advantage or my master's. But as for providing food for these niggers, bless me, I'd rather die.'

'All right, Joe,' said Kennedy. 'That's understood. We shall rely on you when the time comes.'

'At your service, gentlemen.'

'Joe talks like this,' remarked the doctor, 'to make us pamper him and fatten him up.'

'Perhaps,' Joe answered. 'Men are selfish animals.'

During the afternoon the sky was hidden by a warm mist that rose from the ground. This made it almost impossible to distinguish anything on the earth, so at about five o'clock the doctor, afraid of running upon some unexpected mountain peak, gave the signal to halt. The night passed without any accident, but the intense darkness made it necessary to keep a doubly sharp look-out. Throughout the morning of the following day the monsoon blew with extreme violence. Wind drove into the lower cavities of the balloon, hurling to and fro the appendix through which the expansion pipes passed. These had to be made fast with ropes, a task which Joe carried out with great skill. At the same time he ascertained that the orifice of the balloon was still hermetically closed.

'That's doubly important for us,' said Dr Fergusson. 'In the first place, we avoid losing precious gas and, in addition, it prevents our leaving around us an inflammable trail which might end by setting us on fire.'

'That would be awkward,' said Joe.

'Should we be dashed to the ground?' asked Kennedy.

'No, not dashed; The gas would burn quietly and we should come down gradually. Such an accident did happen to a French aeronaut, Madame Blanchard. She set fire to her balloon by letting off fireworks, but she did not fall and would probably not have been killed if her car had not struck a chimney, from the top of which she was thrown to the ground.'

'It's to be hoped nothing of the sort will happen to us,' said Kennedy. 'Up to now our journey has not struck me as dangerous, and I see no reason why we should not reach our goal.'

'Nor I, old man. Besides, accidents have always been caused by the carelessness of the aeronaut or the faulty construction of the balloon. Moreover, out of several thousand ascents there have not been twenty fatal accidents. As a rule, landing and rising from the ground are the most dangerous parts of the business. But we can't afford to neglect any precautions.'

'It's lunch-time, sir,' said Joe. 'We'll have to be satisfied with tinned meat and coffee until Mr Kennedy can manage to get us a nice piece of venison.'

20

*The bottle out of the sky — Fig-palms
— Mammoth trees — The tree of war
— Winged horses — A battle between
two tribes — A massacre — Divine
intervention*

The wind became violent and irregular. The *Victoria* was blown about in all directions, now northward, now southward, and met with no regular current.

'We're moving very fast without making much headway,' said Kennedy, noting the oscillations of the compass needle.

'We're doing at least ninety miles an hour,' said Fergusson. 'Lean your head out and see how quickly the country is sliding away below us. Look at that forest dashing at us.'

'It's already a clearing,' replied Kennedy.

'And the clearing a village,' Joe put in a few moments later. 'Those niggers look pretty astonished.'

'And very natural,' answered the doctor. 'When they first saw balloons, the French peasants used to fire, taking them for monsters of the air, so it's permissible for a

Sudan negro to open his eyes pretty wide.'

'Good Lord!' said Joe, while the *Victoria* was skimming over a village, a hundred feet from the ground. 'If I may, sir, I'll throw down an empty bottle. If it reaches them whole they'll worship it, and if it breaks they'll use the pieces as charms.'

So saying, he threw out a bottle, which was, of course, shattered into a thousand pieces. The natives dashed out of their round huts, shouting loudly. A little later Kennedy exclaimed: 'Just look at that strange tree. The top part is of a different species from the bottom.'

'Well,' said Joe. 'Here's a country where the trees grow on top of one another.'

'It's only a fig trunk on which a little vegetable loam has been spread,' replied the doctor. 'One fine day the wind blew a palm seed into it, and the palm has grown just as it would in a field.'

'A great idea,' said Joe. 'I'll try it in England. It would look well in the London parks, besides being a way of getting more fruit trees. You could have gardens one on top of the other. The people with small gardens would like it.'

At this moment the *Victoria* had to be lifted to clear a forest of trees over three hundred feet high, a kind of banyan, hundreds of years old.

'What splendid trees,' cried Kennedy. 'I know no finer sight than these ancient forests. Just look, Samuel.'

'These banyans are indeed of extraordinary height, Dick; and yet there would be nothing surprising about them in the American forests.'

'Do you mean to say there are trees taller than these?'

'What are called 'mammoth trees' are certainly taller. In California they have found a tree measuring four hundred and fifty feet, higher than the tower of the Houses of Parliament or even the Great Pyramid in Egypt. At its base the trunk had a circumference of a hundred and twenty feet, and the concentric layers of wood showed that it was over four thousand years old.'

'Well, sir, in that case there's nothing to be surprised at. Anyone four thousand years old ought to be a good size.'

But during this conversation the forest had already given place to a large collection of huts, arranged in a circle round an open space in the centre of which a single tree stood. When he saw it Joe exclaimed:

'Well, if that tree has been producing flowers like those for four thousand years, it hasn't much to be proud of,' and he pointed to a gigantic sycamore, whose trunk was completely buried beneath a mass of human bones. The flowers Joe spoke of were freshly-cut heads, hanging from knives stuck into the bark.

'The war-tree of the cannibals,' said the doctor. 'The Indians remove the scalp, the Africans the entire head.'

'A matter of fashion, then,' said Joe.

But already the village with the bleeding heads was vanishing on the horizon. Another, farther on, afforded a spectacle no less repulsive. Corpses half-eaten away, skeletons crumbling into dust, and human limbs scattered over the ground, had been left for the hyenas and jackals to feed upon.

'Those are probably the bodies of criminals. It is the custom in Abyssinia to leave them to the mercy of the wild animals, which finish them off at their leisure after tearing their throats with their teeth.'

'After all, it's not much more cruel than the stake,' said the Scotsman. 'Messier, that's all.'

'In the southern parts of Africa,' the doctor went on, 'they merely shut the criminal up in his own hut, with all his livestock and perhaps his family, set fire to it and burn the lot together. That's what I call cruelty; but I agree with you, Kennedy, even if the gibbet is less cruel, it is just as barbarous.'

With his excellent sight, of which he made such good use, Joe reported some flocks of carnivorous birds soaring over the horizon.

'They're eagles,' exclaimed Kennedy, after looking at them through his glass, 'splendid birds, and they're flying as fast as we are.'

'Heaven preserve us from being attacked by them,' said the doctor. 'They're more dangerous to us than wild beasts or savage tribes.'

'Pooh!' retorted Kennedy; 'a few shots would soon scatter them.'

'I'd rather not have to rely on your skill, old man. The silk of our balloon wouldn't hold out against a peck from one of those. Luckily, I think the birds are more frightened by our balloon than attracted.'

'I've got an idea, sir,' said Joe. 'I'm full of ideas today. How would it be to harness some live eagles to our car and let them drag us through the air?'

'The idea has already been seriously considered,' the doctor replied, 'but I don't think it would be workable with such spirited birds.'

'They could be trained,' Joe said. 'Instead of bits they could be guided by eye-pieces to stop them from seeing. By covering one eye you could make them turn to right or left, and by covering both they could be stopped.'

'You must allow me to prefer a favourable wind to your harnessed eagles, Joe. It costs less for upkeep and is more reliable.'

'As you like, sir, but I stick to my idea.'

It was noon. For some time the *Victoria*'s pace had been more moderate. The country was still passing below them, but less rapidly. Suddenly shouts and the sharp whizz of arrows reached the travellers' ears. Leaning over, they saw upon the open plain a sight which might well stir them. Two tribes were engaged in a furious battle; clouds of arrows were flying through the air. The combatants, busy killing one another, did not notice the *Victoria*. About three hundred men were struggling in a tangled mass. Most of them, wallowing in the blood of the wounded, presented a hideous spectacle.

When they caught sight of the balloon there was a pause. Then the pandemonium redoubled and some arrows were loosed against the car, one flying so close that Joe caught it in his hand.

'Let's get up out of range,' cried Fergusson. 'No risks. We can't afford them.'

The mutual massacre continued with axe and assegai. As soon as an enemy fell to the ground his adversary would at once cut off his head. The women, mingling with the tumult, picked up these bleeding heads and piled them up at either end of the battlefield, often fighting among themselves for possession of the hideous trophy.

'What a ghastly scene!' exclaimed Kennedy in profound disgust.

'They're nasty fellows,' said Joe. 'If they were only in uniform they'd be just like other warriors the world over.'

'I feel a desperate itch to intervene in the fight,' continued the Scotsman, brandishing his carbine.

'No, no,' the doctor replied sharply. 'Let's mind our own business. Who are you to play the part of Providence, when you don't even know who's right and who's wrong! Let's get away from it as quickly as possible. If our great leaders could get a bird's-eye view like this of their exploits they might lose their taste for blood and conquest.'

The chief of one of these savage armies was distinguishable by his athletic build, combined with herculean strength. With one hand he would plunge his lance into the serried ranks of his enemies and with the other open up great gaps with his axe. Once he hurled away his blood-stained assegai, threw himself upon a wounded man, cut off his arm at a single blow, picked it up and, raising it to his mouth, bit into it with his teeth.

'Pah!' said Kennedy. 'The swine! I can't

stand any more of this,' and the warrior fell backwards with a bullet in his forehead.

With his fall a deep stupor took possession of his men. This supernatural death struck terror into them, at the same time putting fresh life into their enemies, and in a second the battlefield was deserted by half the combatants.

'Let's get up and look for a breeze that will get us away,' said the doctor. 'This makes me feel sick.'

But he was not in time to avoid seeing the victorious tribe hurl themselves upon the dead and wounded and fight among themselves over the still warm flesh, which they devoured greedily.

'Pah!' said Joe. 'How disgusting!'

The *Victoria* rose as the gas expanded. The howling of the delirious horde followed them for a few moments, but at length, borne southward, they left the scene of carnage and cannibalism behind them. The ground then became broken with numerous watercourses flowing eastward and doubtless joining those tributaries of Lake Nu, or of the Gazelle River, about which M. Guillaume Lejean has furnished such curious details. With the fall of night the *Victoria* anchored, in long. 27° E., lat. 4° 20′ N., after a journey of one hundred and fifty miles.

21

*Strange noises — A night attack
— Kennedy and Joe in a tree — Two
shots — 'Help! Help!' — An answer in
French — The plan of rescue*

The night grew very dark. The doctor had
been unable to recognise the country. He
had moored to a strong, tall tree, whose vague
bulk he could hardly distinguish in the darkness. As his habit was, he took the nine o'clock
watch, and at midnight Kennedy came to
relieve him.

'Keep a keen look-out, Dick.'

'Has anything happened?'

'No. But I thought I heard strange sounds
below us. I'm none too sure where the wind
has brought us, and a little extra caution can
do no harm.'

'You must have heard the cries of the wild
beasts.'

'No. This seems quite different. In any case,
don't fail to wake us at the slightest alarm.'

'You needn't worry about that.'

After listening attentively once more, the
doctor, hearing nothing, threw himself down

on his blanket and was soon asleep. The sky was covered with thick clouds, but not a breath disturbed the air. The *Victoria*, held by a single anchor, made no movement. Kennedy, leaning his elbow on the side of the car so as to be in a position to keep an eye on the burner, gazed into the still darkness. He searched the horizon and as happens to uneasy or expectant minds, he thought from time to time that he could distinguish vague lights. Once, even, he thought he could clearly see one some two hundred yards away, but it was only a flash, after which he saw nothing further. Probably it was merely one of those imaginary flashes that appear to anyone who gazes into deep darkness. Kennedy reassured himself and was once more relapsing into his vague contemplation when a sharp hissing noise broke the silence.

Was it the cry of some animal or bird of the night? Was it from human lips? Kennedy, realising the full gravity of the situation, was on the point of awakening his companions, but he told himself that in any case the men or animals, whichever it was, were out of reach. He inspected his weapons and with his night-glass once more searched the space around him. Soon he thought he could make out vague forms gliding towards the tree below.

By the light of a moonbeam which filtered like a flicker of lightning between two clouds, he distinctly saw a group of individuals moving in the darkness. The adventure with the apes came back to his mind. He placed his hand on the doctor's shoulder. The latter awoke instantly.

'Hush!' said Kennedy. 'Whisper.'

'Has something happened?'

'Yes. Wake Joe.'

As soon as Joe had got up, Kennedy related what he had seen.

'Some more of those beastly monkeys?' said Joe.

'Possibly. We must take precautions.'

'Joe and I,' said Kennedy, 'will go down into the tree by the ladder.'

'And meanwhile,' the doctor put in, 'I'll fix things so that we can get away quickly.'

'Right, oh!'

'Come along, sir,' said Joe.

'Don't use your weapons except as a last resource,' said the doctor. 'We don't want to advertise our presence here.'

Dick and Joe replied with a nod. They lowered themselves noiselessly towards the tree and took up their position on a fork of strong branches in which the anchor was fixed. For some minutes they remained silent and motionless among the foliage. Hearing a rustle against the bark, Joe seized Kennedy's arm.

'Do you hear?'

'Yes. It's getting nearer.'

'Suppose it's a snake? That hiss you heard — '

'No. There was something human about it.'

'I'd rather have savages,' Joe muttered to himself. 'These reptiles give me the creeps.'

'It's getting louder,' Kennedy said a few moments later.

'Yes. It's coming up, climbing.'

'Watch this side, I'll see to the other.'

'All right.'

They were sitting on a main branch which grew straight out of the centre of one of those huge trees called baobabs. The darkness, increased by the density of the foliage, was intense, but Joe, leaning towards Kennedy's ear and pointing to the lower part of the tree, said: 'Niggers!'

A few whispered words reached the two men. Joe raised his rifle.

'Wait,' said Kennedy.

Some savages had indeed climbed into the baobab. They were coming up from all sides, gliding along the branches like snakes, mounting slowly but surely. They could be distinguished by the smell of their bodies smeared with rancid fat. Soon two heads came into sight, on a level with the branch upon which Kennedy and Joe were sitting.

'Now!' said Kennedy. 'Fire!'

The double report rang out like thunder and died away amid cries of pain. In an instant the whole horde had vanished. But through the howls they had heard a strange, unexpected and impossible cry. A human voice had distinctly cried in French: 'Help! Help!'

Dumbfounded, Kennedy and Joe swung themselves up into the car with all speed.

'Did you hear?' the doctor asked them.

'We did. It's incredible. 'Help! Help!''

'A Frenchman in the hands of these ruffians!'

'A traveller.'

'A missionary, perhaps.'

'Poor devil,' cried Kennedy, 'they are murdering him, or torturing him.'

The doctor tried in vain to hide his emotion.

'There's no doubt about it,' he said. 'A wretched Frenchman has fallen into the hands of these beasts. We can't go without doing all we can to save him. When he heard our shots he must have realised that unhoped-for help was at hand, providential intervention. We won't destroy this last hope. Do you agree?'

'We do, Samuel, and we are at your orders.'

'Let's think it out, and as soon as it's light

we'll try to rescue him.'

'But how are we going to get rid of these beastly niggers?' asked Kennedy.

'I feel sure, from the way they bolted,' said the doctor, 'that they don't know what firearms are, so we ought to make the most of their fright. But we can't act before it's light, and we shall have to make our plans according to the lie of the ground.'

'The poor wretch can't be far off,' said Joe. 'I — '

'Help! Help!' came the voice again, weaker this time.

'The swine!' cried Joe, shaking with indignation. 'But suppose they kill him in the night?'

'Do you hear, Sam?' Kennedy broke in, seizing the doctor's arm. 'Suppose they kill him in the night?'

'It's not likely. These savage races kill their prisoners in the daylight. They must have the sun.'

'How would it be,' said the Scot, 'if I took advantage of the dark to try and creep up to the poor fellow?'

'I'll come with you, sir.'

'Wait a minute! Wait a minute! The idea does you credit, but you'd be exposing us all and would only be doing still more harm to the man you're trying to save.'

'How?' asked Kennedy. 'These niggers are

terrified, scattered. They won't come back.'

'Dick, I beg of you, do what I say. I'm acting for the safety of us all. If you happened to be taken by surprise it would be all up.'

'But this poor fellow waiting, hoping! No answer. No one coming to help him. He must be thinking his senses have deceived him, that he heard nothing — '

'We can reassure him,' said Dr Fergusson, and, standing up in the darkness and using his hands as a megaphone, he shouted loudly in French: 'You, there, whoever you are! Don't worry. There are three friends here looking after you.'

A terrible roar answered him, doubtless drowning the prisoner's reply.

'He's being murdered, or going to be,' cried Kennedy. 'All we've done is to hasten his death. We must act.'

'But how, Dick? What can we do in this darkness?'

'Oh, if only it was light!' sighed Joe.

'And supposing it were?' the doctor asked in a strange tone.

'Nothing simpler, Samuel,' replied the Scot. 'I'd go down and scatter the scum with a carbine.'

'And you, Joe?' asked Fergusson.

'I'd be more careful, sir. I'd give the prisoner a sign to escape in a special direction.'

'And how would you do that?'

'With this arrow I caught. I'd stick a note on it, or I could simply shout, for these niggers wouldn't understand.'

'None of these plans would work, my friends. The chief difficulty would be for the poor fellow to get away, even supposing he evaded his guards. As for your idea, Dick, old man, if you were very bold and took advantage of the fear our guns produced, your plan might succeed. But if it failed, it would be all over with you and we should have two to save instead of one. No, we must have all the chances on our side. We must try something else.'

'But we'll have to look sharp,' replied Kennedy.

'Perhaps,' Fergusson answered, emphasising the word.

'Do you know a way of breaking the darkness, sir?'

'Who knows, Joe?'

'Oh! If you could do that, I'd say you were the wisest man in the world.'

The doctor was silent for a few moments, lost in thought. His two companions watched him eagerly. The extraordinary situation had worked them up to a high pitch of excitement. Soon Fergusson went on: 'This is my plan. We have two hundred pounds of ballast left, for we haven't used any. We'll suppose this man, who is obviously exhausted by suffering, weighs the same as one of us. That would leave us about sixty pounds for a quick rise.'

'What are you getting at?' asked Kennedy.

'This, Dick. It's clear, if I reach the prisoner and throw out ballast equal to his weight, I shan't affect the equilibrium of the balloon; but then, if I want to rise quickly to get away from these negroes, I shall have to use something more drastic than the burner. Now, by throwing out this surplus of ballast at the given moment, I'm certain of rising very rapidly.'

'That's clear.'

'Yes, but there is one disadvantage; when I want to come down later I shall have to loose a quantity of gas in proportion to the excess of ballast I've dropped. But gas is precious. However, we can't grudge its loss when it's a question of a man's life.'

'You're right, Samuel. We must sacrifice anything to save him.'

'Come on, then, put those sacks round the edge of the car so that they can be thrown out by a single push.'

'But the darkness?'

'It will hide our preparations and we can deal with it when we're ready. Be careful to have all the guns ready to hand. We may need them. The carbine gives us one shot, the two guns four, the two revolvers twelve. That makes seventeen, which could be fired off in a quarter of a minute. But perhaps we shan't need to make all this din. Are you ready?'

'Aye, aye, sir!' Joe answered.

The sacks were set in position, the guns placed ready.

'Good,' said the doctor. 'Keep an eye on everything. Joe, you be ready to throw out the ballast, and you, Dick, to get hold of the prisoner; but don't do anything till I give the word. Now, Joe, you go down and loose the anchor and come back as quick as you can.'

Joe slid down the rope and was back a few seconds later. Set free, the *Victoria* floated almost motionless in the air. Meanwhile the doctor assured himself that there was enough gas in the mixing chamber to feed the burner if required, without having to use the Bunsen battery for a time. He removed the two conducting wires which were used to decompose the water, then, rummaging in his valise, took out two pieces of carbon, sharpened to a point, and fixed one to the end of each wire. His two companions watched him without understanding, but did not speak. When the doctor had finished his preparations he stood up in the middle of the car, took the pieces of carbon, one in each hand, and brought the two points together. With an intolerable glare, an intense and dazzling ray was produced between the two carbon points. A vast sheet of electric light literally tore through the blackness of the night.

'Oh! sir!' said Joe.

'Don't speak,' said the doctor.

22

*The sheet of light — The missionary
— He is picked up by the light from the
balloon — A Lazarist priest — Little
hope — Medical attention — A life of
self-denial — Passing a volcano*

Fergusson directed his powerful ray towards different points of space and brought it to a standstill over a place whence cries of terror could be heard. His two companions peered down eagerly. The baobab over which the *Victoria* hung almost motionless rose from the centre of a clearing. Among fields of sesame and sugar-cane they could see some fifty low, conical huts, round which a swarm of men were clustered. A hundred feet below the balloon stood a stake, at the foot of which lay a human creature, a young man of thirty at most, half-naked, with long black hair, emaciated, and covered with blood and wounds, his head hanging on his chest like Christ's on the Cross. His hair, cut close over the crown of his head, still showed where his tonsure had been.

'A missionary! A priest!' cried Joe.

'Poor wretch!' said Kennedy.

'We'll save him, Dick,' said the doctor. 'We'll save him.'

The crowd of negroes, seeing the balloon like a huge comet with a blazing tail, were seized with a terror that can easily be understood. Hearing their cries, the prisoner raised his head. A swift light of hope came into his eyes and, without too clear an idea of what was happening, he stretched his hands towards these unexpected helpers.

'He's alive!' cried Fergusson. 'Thank God. The brutes are scared out of their lives. We'll get him. Are you ready?'

'Yes, Samuel.'

'Joe, put out the burner.'

The doctor's order was carried out. A hardly perceptible breeze gently moved the *Victoria* over the prisoner and at the same time she gradually dropped as the gas contracted. For about ten minutes she remained floating in a sea of light. Fergusson directed his beams upon the crowd. The natives, panic-stricken, gradually vanished into the huts until the space round the stake was left empty. The doctor was right in relying on the fantastic apparition of the *Victoria* pouring rays of light into the intense darkness. The car drew near the ground, but meanwhile some of the bolder among the negroes, realising that their victim was about to escape them, returned, shouting. Kennedy picked up his gun, but the doctor told him not to fire.

The priest, on his knees and without the strength to stand, was not even tied to the stake, his weakness making this unnecessary. The moment the car was almost touching the ground, Kennedy threw aside his gun, seized the priest round the body and hauled him into the car. At the same moment Joe pushed out the two hundred pounds of ballast. The doctor was expecting to rise with extreme rapidity but, contrary to his expectation, the balloon, after rising three or four feet from the ground, hung motionless.

'What's holding us?' he cried in a tone of fear.

Some of the savages ran up, uttering fierce cries.

'Oh!' cried Joe, leaning over. 'One of these brutes is hanging to the bottom of the car.'

'Dick,' cried the doctor, 'the water container!'

Dick divined his friend's thought and, raising one of the water containers, which weighed over a hundred pounds, he threw it overboard. The *Victoria*, suddenly relieved of this weight, leapt three hundred feet into the air, amid the roars of the savages, who saw their prisoner escaping in a dazzling shaft of light.

'Hurrah!' cried the doctor's two companions.

Suddenly the balloon took another leap, which brought her to a height of a thousand feet.

'What's that?' asked Kennedy, who was almost thrown off his feet.

'Nothing. Only that blackguard letting go,' Fergusson replied calmly.

Joe, leaning over quickly, was in time to watch the savage twist through the air with outstretched arms and dash himself to pieces on the ground. The doctor then separated the two electric points and the darkness once more became profound. It was 1 a.m. The Frenchman, who had swooned, at last opened his eyes.

'You're safe,' the doctor told him.

'Safe,' he answered in English, with a sad smile. 'Saved from a cruel death. My brothers, I thank you. But my days are numbered, my hours even, and I have not long to live.' And the exhausted missionary again fell back, unconscious.

'He's dying!' cried Dick.

'No, no,' Fergusson answered, leaning over him, 'but he's very weak. Lay him under the tent.'

They gently stretched the poor emaciated body, covered with scars and still bleeding wounds which showed where iron and fire had done their cruel work. The doctor made some lint with his handkerchief and placed it on the wounds, after washing them. These attentions he carried out with the skill of an expert; then, taking a cordial from his medicine-chest, he poured a few drops on to the priest's lips. The man feebly closed his blistered mouth and with difficulty summoned strength to say: 'Thank you. Thank you.'

The doctor saw that he needed absolute rest. He closed the curtains of the tent and returned to take command of the balloon. Allowing for the weight of the new occupant, the *Victoria* had been lightened by nearly one hundred and eighty pounds, and so kept up without any help from the burner. With the first rays of daylight a current of air drove her gently west-north-west. Kennedy went to take a look at the sleeping priest.

'I hope we'll be able to save this man who has been sent to us. Do you think there's any chance?' he said.

'Yes, Dick, with care. This air is so pure.'

'How he must have gone through it!' said Joe with feeling. 'You know he had to be braver than us to go alone among these people.'

'That's quite true,' Kennedy answered.

Throughout the day the doctor would not allow the poor man's sleep to be disturbed. It lasted long, broken only by a few murmurs of pain, which made Fergusson feel anxious. Towards evening the *Victoria* came to a standstill in the darkness, and during the night, while Joe and Kennedy took turns by the sick man's side, Fergusson watched over the safety of them all The next morning the *Victoria* had drifted very little westward. The day dawned clear and splendid. The invalid was able to speak to his new friends more distinctly. The curtains of the awning were raised and he breathed the fresh morning air with satisfaction.

'How do you feel?' Fergusson asked.

'A bit better, I think,' he replied. 'But so far, my friends, I have only seen you in a dream. I can scarcely realise what has happened. Who are you, that you may not be forgotten in my last prayer?'

'We're English travellers,' the doctor replied. 'We're trying to cross Africa in a balloon, and on the way we've had the good luck to save you.'

'Science has its heroes,' said the missionary.

'But religion has its martyrs,' the Scotsman added.

'You're a missionary?' Fergusson asked.

'I'm a priest of the Lazarist Mission. Heaven has sent you to me. Heaven be praised. The sacrifice of my life was accomplished. But you come from Europe. Speak to me of Europe, of France. I have had no news for five years.'

'Five years alone among these savages!' exclaimed Kennedy.

'They are souls to be brought back,' said the young priest. 'Ignorant wild brothers whom religion alone can teach and civilise.'

Dr Fergusson, in response to the missionary's request, talked to him for a long time about France. The man listened, and tears poured from his eyes. He took the hands of the three men in turn in his own, which were burning with fever. The doctor made him several cups of tea, which he drank with enjoyment, and he then had sufficient strength to raise himself a little and smile at finding himself being carried through the clear air.

'You are brave travellers,' he said, 'and you will succeed in your audacious enterprise. You will see again your relations, your friends, your country — '

The young priest then grew so weak that he had to lie down again. A state of prostration lasting several hours kept him as though dead in Fergusson's arms, who could not restrain his emotion as he felt his life ebb away. Were they then so soon to lose this man they had snatched from death? He again dressed the dreadful wounds of the martyr, and had to sacrifice the greater part of his supply of water to cool his burning lips. He lavished upon him the tenderest and wisest care. In his arms the sick man gradually took a fresh hold on life and won back at least feeling. The doctor patched together his story from his halting words.

'Speak your own language,' he said. 'I understand it and it will be less tiring for you.'

The missionary was a poor young man from the village of Aradon, in the centre of Brittany. His earliest instincts had drawn him towards an ecclesiastical career. To this life of self-denial he desired to add the life of danger by entering the order of the mission founded by Saint Vincent de Paul. When he was twenty years old he left his country for the inhospitable shores of Africa whence, gradually overcoming obstacles and facing privations, marching forward and praying, he came among the tribes inhabiting the banks of the tributaries which flow into the Upper Nile. For two years his religion was rejected, his zeal misconstrued, his charity flouted. He remained a prisoner of one of the cruellest tribes of Nyambarra, the victim of persistent

205

ill-treatment. But still he went on, teaching and praying. This tribe having been dispersed and himself left for dead after one of those battles so frequent between one tribe and another, instead of retracing his steps he pursued his evangelical pilgrimage. The most peaceful times he enjoyed were when he was taken for a madman. He had made himself familiar with the language of these districts, and he taught the Catechism. In short, for two more long years he traversed these barbarous regions, driven on by the superhuman strength that comes from God. For the last year he had been living with the Nyam Nyam tribe that is called Barafri, one of the most savage. When the chief died a few days before, the death was ascribed to the influence of the missionary, and it was decided to put him to death. His torture had lasted forty hours and, as the doctor had supposed, he was to die at noon. When he heard the shots, Nature carried the day. He shouted for help, and when a voice from the sky brought him words of encouragement, he thought he was dreaming.

'I don't regret this life which is leaving me. My life is God's,' he said.

'There's still hope,' the doctor replied. 'We are with you. We'll save you from death as we have saved you from torture.'

'I do not ask so much of Heaven,' replied the priest with resignation. 'Blessed be God, who has given me, before I die, the joy of pressing the hands of a friend and hearing the language of my country.'

The missionary weakened again. The day passed thus between hope and fear, Kennedy being deeply moved and Joe trying to keep his eyes averted. The *Victoria* made little headway, and the wind seemed to be sparing its precious burden.

Towards evening Joe sighted a great light in the west, which in more northern regions they would have taken to be the aurora borealis. The sky seemed on fire. The doctor examined the phenomenon attentively.

'It must be a volcano in eruption,' he said.

'But the wind is driving us directly on to it,' said Kennedy.

'Well, we shall clear it at a comfortable height.'

Three hours later the *Victoria* was over mountainous country. Her exact position was lat. 4°42' N., long. 24°15' E. Ahead of her a blazing crater was pouring out torrents of molten lava, and hurling great masses of rock to an enormous height. Streams of liquid fire poured down in dazzling cascades. It was a magnificent sight, but betokened danger, for the wind, remaining constant, was driving the balloon persistently towards this fiery atmosphere. As it was impossible to evade the obstacle, it would have to be cleared. The burner was heated to its utmost limit and the *Victoria* reached 6000 feet, leaving between the volcano and herself a distance of more than 1800 feet

From his bed of pain the dying priest could see this burning crater throwing out thousands of dazzling flames with a deafening roar.

'What a beautiful sight!' he said. 'How infinite is God's power — even in terrible manifestations!'

The stream of burning lava covered the sides of the mountain with a veritable carpet of flame. The lower slopes shone in the darkness; a torrid heat rose to the car and Dr Fergusson was anxious to escape with all speed from the dangerous situation.

About 10 p.m. the mountain had become merely a glowing point on the horizon and the *Victoria* was quietly pursuing her way on a lower level.

23

Joe angry — Death of a good man — The vigil by the body — The burial — The blocks of quartz — Joe's hallucination — Precious ballast — Discovery of the auriferous mountains — Beginning of Joe's despair

A magnificent night spread over the earth. The priest relapsed into a state of peaceful coma.

'He won't come round,' said Joe. 'Poor young fellow; not thirty!'

'He will die in our arms,' said the doctor in despair. 'His breathing is growing even weaker still, and I can do nothing to save him.'

'The blackguards!' exclaimed Joe, who was given to occasional sudden outbursts of temper. 'And to think that this good priest could still think of words to pity them, find excuses for them, forgive them!'

'Heaven has given him a splendid night, Joe; perhaps his last. He won't suffer much now, and his death will be like falling into a peaceful sleep.'

The dying man uttered a few halting

words. The doctor drew close to him. The sick man's breathing became laboured. He was asking for air. The curtains were completely drawn back, and he drew in with enjoyment the light breath of this transparent night. The stars showered upon him their twinkling rays and the moon wrapped him in a shroud of white.

'My friends,' he said weakly, 'I'm going. May God, who rewards the righteous, bring you safe to port. May He pay for me my debt of gratitude.'

'Don't give in yet,' Kennedy answered. 'It's only a passing weakness. You're not going to die. Could anyone die on a beautiful summer night like this?'

'Death has come,' replied the missionary. 'I know it. Let me face it. Death, the beginning of eternal things, is only the end of earthly cares. Raise me to my knees, my brothers, I beg of you.'

Kennedy lifted him. It was pitiable to see his nerveless limbs give way beneath him.

'God, have pity upon me,' cried the dying missionary.

His face was radiant. Far above the earth, whose joys he had never known, in this night which shed upon him its gentlest radiance, on this road of Heaven towards which he was rising as in a miraculous ascension, he seemed already to have entered upon a new existence. His last gesture was a final benediction to his new friends. Then he fell back into the arms of Kennedy, whose face was bathed in tears.

'Dead!' said the doctor, bending over him. 'Dead!' and with a common impulse the three friends fell on their knees in silent prayer.

'Tomorrow morning,' Fergusson went on a little later, 'we'll bury him in this African soil upon which his blood has been shed.'

During the rest of the night the body was guarded in turn by the doctor, Kennedy and Joe, and not a word disturbed the religious silence. All were in tears.

The following day the wind was blowing from the south and the *Victoria* made her way rather slowly over a vast mountain plateau. Here could be seen extinct craters, there uncultivated ravines. Not a drop of water on any of these gnarled craters. Piles of rock, stray blocks of stone, grey marl-pits, everything indicated complete sterility.

About noon the doctor, in order to bury the body, decided to come down in a ravine amid gigantic rocks of primitive formation. The surrounding mountains would act as a shelter and allow him to bring his car to the ground, for there was no tree to which he could make fast. But as he had explained to

Kennedy, owing to the loss of ballast at the time of the priest's rescue he could now only descend by losing a proportional quantity of gas. He therefore opened the valve of the outer balloon. The hydrogen escaped and the *Victoria* sank gently towards the ravine.

As soon as the car touched ground the doctor closed the valve. Joe leapt out, keeping one hand on the outer edge of the car while with the other he picked up a number of stones, which soon compensated for his own weight. He was then able to use both hands, and in a short time had piled over five hundred pounds of stone into the car. The doctor and Kennedy were then able to alight in their turn. The *Victoria* was in equilibrium, her lifting force counteracted.

Nor was it necessary to use a great quantity of stone, for the blocks picked up by Joe were extremely heavy, a fact which attracted Fergusson's attention. The ground was strewn with quartz and porphyritic rocks.

'What a strange thing!' the doctor mused.

Meanwhile Kennedy and Joe went off a few yards to select a site for the grave. It was intensely hot in this ravine, shut in as it was in a sort of furnace. The midday sun poured down vertically its burning rays. They first had to clear the ground of the fragments of rock which covered it, after which a grave was dug of sufficient depth to prevent the body being scratched up by wild animals. The corpse of the martyr was reverently laid in the grave. The grave was filled and large fragments of rock were arranged over it in the form of a tombstone.

Meanwhile the doctor remained motionless, deep in thought. He did not hear the call of his companions, and did not go with them to shelter from the heat of the day.

'What are you thinking of, Sam?' asked Kennedy.

'This strange contrast in Nature, this odd freak of chance. Do you know in what soil this self-denying man, this man, poor of heart, has been buried?'

'What do you mean, Sam?' his friend asked.

'This priest who had taken the vow of poverty is now resting in a gold mine.'

'A gold mine!' exclaimed the two others.

'A gold mine,' the doctor replied calmly. 'These blocks that you are trampling under foot like worthless stones are mineral of great purity.'

'It's impossible, impossible!'

Joe repeated.

'You wouldn't have to search long in these fissures of schist before you found large nuggets.'

Joe hurled himself like a madman upon the scattered fragments, and Kennedy was not long in following his example.

'Steady, Joe, my good fellow,' said his master.

'That's all very well, sir, but — '

'What! a philosopher like you.'

'Well, sir, no philosophy would hold out against this.'

'Come, think a little. What's the use of all this wealth to *us*? We can't take it away.'

'Not take it away?'

'It's a bit heavy for our car. I even hesitated to tell you about the discovery. I was afraid you'd be disappointed.'

'What!' said Joe. 'Leave all this treasure behind? It's a fortune for us. It's ours. Leave it behind!'

'Take care, my friend. Is the gold-fever taking hold of you? Didn't this dead man you've just buried teach you the vanity of human things?'

'That's all right, sir,' Joe answered; 'but, after all, gold! Mr Kennedy, aren't you going to help me to pick up a few millions?'

'What could we do with them?' said the Scot, who could not suppress a smile. 'We're not here to seek our fortunes, and we ought not to take it.'

'Your millions would be a bit heavy,' the doctor continued 'and they would hardly go into your pockets.'

'But, after all,' Joe replied, driven back to his last line of defence, 'can't we take the ore as ballast instead of sand?'

'All right. I'll agree to that,' said Fergusson. 'But you mustn't grumble when we have to throw a few thousands overboard.'

'A few thousands!' Joe exclaimed. 'Can all this be gold?'

'Yes, my friend. This is a storehouse into which Nature has been pouring her treasures for centuries. There's enough to enrich whole nations, an Australia and a Canada together in the heart of a desert.'

'And all no use!'

'Perhaps. In any case, I'll tell you what I'll do to console you.'

'It won't be easy, sir,' Joe replied, crestfallen.

'Listen. I'll make a note of the exact position of this place and give it to you, and when you get back to England you can tell your neighbours, if you think so much gold will bring them happiness.'

'Well, sir, I see you're right; so as there's nothing else to be done, let's fill the car and what's left at the end of the journey will still be so much to the good.'

Joe set to work eagerly, and had soon piled into the car nearly a thousand pounds of quartz fragments in which the gold was set like a hard vein. The doctor watched him with a smile, and while the work went on he took a reckoning and found the position of the missionary's tomb to be lat. 4°55′ N., long. 22°23′ E. Then, casting a last look at the mound under which the young Frenchman's body lay, he returned to the car. He would have liked to erect a rough and modest cross over this solitary tomb in the African desert, but there was not a tree in sight.

'God will remember where it is,' he said.

Another equally serious question was at the same time passing through Fergusson's mind. He would have given much to find a little water, for he wanted to replace that he had thrown overboard in the container when the negro was hanging to the car; but in this arid region it was impossible. This continued to cause him anxiety; obliged as he was continually to feed his burner, he had begun to run short for drinking purposes. He resolved, therefore, to neglect no opportunity for replenishing his supply.

When he reached the car he found it encumbered with the stones picked up by the avaricious Joe. He got in without a word. Kennedy took up his usual position and Joe followed them, not without throwing a covetous glance at the treasure in the ravine. The doctor lit his burner and the spiral grew hot. After a few minutes the hydrogen began to flow and the gas dilated, but the balloon did not budge. Joe watched uneasily and did not utter a word.

'Joe,' said the doctor.

No answer.

'Joe, do you hear?'

Joe made a sign that he had heard but would not understand.

'You'll be good enough,' Fergusson went on, 'to throw out some of this quartz.'

'But, sir, you said I could — '

'I said you could replace the ballast, that was all.'

'But — '

'Do you want us to stay in this desert for ever?'

Joe cast a despairing glance towards Kennedy, but the Scotsman assumed the air of a man who is helpless.

'Well, Joe?'

'Won't your burner work?' asked the stubborn fellow.

'The burner is lit, as you see. But the balloon won't rise until you've lightened her a bit.'

Joe scratched his head, picked up a bit of quartz, the smallest of all, weighed it in his hand repeatedly, throwing it up and catching it. It weighed three or four pounds. He then threw it overboard. The *Victoria* did not budge.

'Hello!' he said. 'We're not rising yet?'

'Not yet,' the doctor answered. 'Carry on.'

Kennedy was laughing. Joe threw out ten pounds or so. The balloon remained motionless. Joe turned pale.

'My poor fellow,' said Fergusson. 'We three, I believe, weigh about four hundred pounds. You'll have to throw out at least an equal weight, to compensate for us.'

'Throw out four hundred pounds!' cried Joe pitiably.

'And something extra to lift us. Come, hurry up.'

The worthy servant, sighing deeply, set to work to lighten the balloon. From time to time he would stop, saying, 'We're rising!'

'We're not,' was the invariable reply.

'She's moving,' he said at last.

'Carry on,' repeated Fergusson.

'She's rising. I'm sure she is.'

'Carry on,' replied Kennedy.

Then Joe picked up a last block and threw it desperately out of the car. The *Victoria* rose about a hundred feet, and with the help of the burner soon cleared the neighbouring peaks.

'Never mind, Joe,' said the doctor, 'you'll still have a useful fortune left if we manage to keep all this to the end of the trip, and you'll be a rich man for the rest of your days.'

Joe did not reply but stretched himself limply on his stony bed.

'You see, Dick, what gold can do with the best servant in the world. What passions, what greed and crime the secret of such a mine awakens. It's very depressing.'

By evening the *Victoria* had travelled ninety miles westward. She was now four hundred miles in a direct line from Zanzibar.

24

The wind drops — The confines of the desert — Shortage of water — Equatorial nights — Fergusson's anxieties — The situation — Vehement replies from Kennedy and Joe — Another night

Moored to a solitary withered tree, the *Victoria* passed the night in perfect calm. The travellers were able to enjoy a little of the sleep they so sorely needed, for the excitement of the last few days had left sad memories. Towards morning the sky resumed its brilliant clearness and heat. The balloon rose in the air and, after several fruitless attempts, fell in with a gentle current which bore them north-west.

'We're not making much headway,' said the doctor. 'Unless I'm mistaken, we've done half our journey in about ten days, but at the rate we're going now, it will take us a month to finish it. The worst of it is, we're threatened with a failure of the water supply.'

'But we'll find some,' Dick replied. 'We're bound to come across some river, some stream or pond in this great stretch of country.'

'I wish we could.'

'Mightn't it be Joe's cargo that's keeping us back?'

Kennedy said this by way of pulling Joe's leg, which he did all the more readily as he had himself for a moment shared Joe's illusions. But as he had not betrayed his feelings he could pose as a firm spirit, of course only in jest. Joe gave him a pitiful look. But the doctor did not reply. He was thinking, not without secret misgiving, of the vast solitudes of the Sahara, where caravans go for weeks without encountering a well to quench their thirst. He therefore scanned minutely the slightest depressions in the ground.

These precautions and recent events had done a good deal to damp the spirits of the three travellers. They talked less and buried themselves more in their own thoughts. Since his eyes had first lighted on that sea of gold, the worthy Joe was no longer the same man. He was taciturn and brooded greedily over the stones heaped up in the car, valueless today, tomorrow beyond price.

Moreover, the aspect of this part of Africa was disquieting. They were gradually entering the desert. Not a village or even a collection of huts to be seen. Vegetation was being left behind. At most there were a few stunted plants like the heather on the moors of

221

Scotland, the beginning of white sands and bare stone, a few lentisks and thorny shrubs. In the middle of this sterility the rudimentary structure of the globe was revealed in sharp ridges of living rock. These symptoms of aridity gave Dr Fergusson food for thought. It looked as though no caravan had ever faced this deserted region. It would have left visible traces of camps, whitened bones of men or animals. But there was nothing. It felt as though soon an infinity of sand would overwhelm the desolate area. And yet there could be no going back, only forward, than which the doctor asked nothing better. He could have wished for a tempest to sweep him beyond this region, and there was not a cloud in the sky. By the end of the day the *Victoria* had made thirty miles.

If only the water had not failed! But there were only three gallons left. Fergusson set aside one gallon to slake their thirst, which a temperature of 90 degrees rendered intolerable. This left two gallons to feed the burner. At most, they could produce another 480 cubic feet of gas, and the burner used up about nine cubic feet an hour, so that they could only hold on for fifty-four hours. All this Fergusson carefully worked out.

'Fifty-four hours,' he said to his companions. 'Now, as I've made up my mind not to travel by night for fear of missing a stream or a well or pool, we have three and a half days' travel left during which we must find water at all costs. I thought I ought to warn you of this serious situation because I can only reserve one gallon for drinking, and we shall have to ration ourselves strictly.'

'Ration us, then,' Kennedy replied; 'but it's too soon to despair yet. You say we've three days before us?'

'Yes, old man.'

'Very well. It's no use worrying now. In three days it will be time to make up our minds what we're going to do. Meanwhile we must keep a sharper look-out than ever.'

At the evening meal the water was strictly measured out. The quantity of brandy in the grog was increased, but it was necessary to be sparing with this liquor, which is more of a thirst-producer than a thirst-quencher.

During the night the car rested on a great plateau which sank deeply towards its centre. The fact that it was not eight hundred feet above the level of the sea gave the doctor some hope, for he remembered the views of geographical experts as to the supposed existence of a vast stretch of water in the centre of Africa If this lake existed they must reach it, but, meanwhile, no signs of change appeared in the still sky.

The peaceful night, magnificently starred, was followed by a windless day with a burning sun. From early morning the temperature was torrid. At 5 a.m. the doctor gave the signal for departure, and for a considerable time the *Victoria* hung motionless in the leaden air. The doctor might have managed to escape from the intense heat by rising to a higher zone, but that would have required a lot of water, which was out of the question. He therefore contented himself with keeping the balloon a hundred feet above the ground where a faint breeze urged her westward. Lunch consisted of a little dried meat and pemmican. By noon the *Victoria* had only advanced a few miles.

'We can't go any quicker,' said the doctor. 'We can't command, only obey.'

'Yes, Samuel,' said Kennedy, 'this is one of those cases where a propeller would be useful.'

'No doubt, Dick, always supposing it didn't require water; otherwise the position would be precisely the same. Besides, so far, nothing practical has been invented. Balloons are still at the stage of development ships were in before the discovery of steam power. It took six thousand years to think of paddles and screws, so we've a long time to wait.'

'Curse this heat!' said Joe, wiping his

dripping forehead.

'If we had some water the heat would be useful, for it expands the hydrogen in the balloon and saves the flame in the spiral. It's true, if we hadn't run short of water we shouldn't have to spare it. Damn that savage we wasted that precious container on!'

'You don't regret what you did, Samuel?'

'No, Dick, since we were able to save that poor fellow from a horrible death. But the hundred pounds of water we threw out would have been very useful. It would have meant twelve or thirteen days' travel, certain, which would have been quite enough to cross this desert.'

'We've done half the journey, at least?' Joe asked.

'In distance, yes; but as far as time is concerned, no, if the wind fails us. It's showing signs of dropping altogether.'

'Come, sir,' Joe went on. 'We mustn't complain. We've got on very well so far, and whatever I do, I can't give up hope. We'll find water, I tell you, sir.'

Meanwhile the land was sinking with every mile. The undulations of the gold mountains were dying away over the plain; sparse grass, the last efforts of exhausted Nature, replaced the fine trees of the east. A few clumps with wizened foliage still struggled against the invasion of the sand. Great rocks fallen from distant summits and smashed by their fall were scattered about in the form of sharp stones, which would soon form coarse sand and later become fine dust.

'This is Africa as you imagined it, Joe. I was right in telling you to be patient.'

'Well, sir,' Joe answered, 'it's very natural, all the same. Heat and sand. It would be absurd to look for anything else in such a country. You see,' he added, laughing, 'I hadn't much faith in your forests and plains. It didn't seem right. It's not worth while coming all this way only to find England over again. This is the first time I can really believe myself in Africa, and I'm not sorry to have a taste of the real thing.'

Towards evening the doctor found that the *Victoria* had not moved twenty miles during this burning day. As soon as the sun had disappeared behind a horizon drawn with the precision of a pencil line the hot night enveloped them.

The following day was the 1st of May, a Thursday, but day succeeded day with desperate monotony. Every morning was like the one before. Noon poured down the same relentless rays of heat, and night absorbed in its shadows the scattered heat that the following day was in its turn to bequeath to the night. The wind, now scarcely perceptible, became rather a sigh than a breeze, and the moment seemed at hand when this breath, too, would die away.

The doctor reacted to the gloom of the situation, and preserved the calm and sang-froid of tempered courage. Glass in hand, he searched every quarter of the horizon. He saw the last hills gradually fade, the last vegetation die out; in front of him stretched the whole immensity of the desert. The responsibility weighing upon him affected him much, but he showed no sign. He had dragged away these two men, who were both his friends, by the very force of friendship or duty. Had he acted rightly? Was it not venturing upon forbidden paths? Was he not in this expedition trying to pass the limits of the possible? Had not God reserved knowledge of this barren continent for later centuries?

As happens in hours of discouragement, these thoughts thronged his brain, and by an irresistible train of thought Samuel was carried away beyond logic and reason. After considering what he ought not to have done he fell to wondering what was to be done next. Would it be impossible to retrace his steps? Were there not higher currents which would bear him back towards less arid country? He knew the country they had passed but not that which lay ahead. And so, his conscience becoming insistent, he decided to have a frank talk with his two companions. He explained the situation clearly, showed them what had been done and what remained to do. At a pinch they could turn back, or at least try to. What did they think?

'I will follow my master,' Joe answered. 'I'll suffer what he suffers, and can stand it better than he can. I'll go where he goes.'

'And you, Kennedy?'

'I, my dear Sam, am not given to despair. No one realised better than I did the dangers of this venture. But I wanted to forget as soon as you were faced with them. I'm with you, body and soul. As things are, my view is we should go on to the end. Besides, it seems to me that there's just as much danger in going back. Forward, then. You can rely on us.'

'Thank you. You're good fellows,' the doctor replied with feeling. 'I knew I could rely on you, but I wanted to hear you say so. I'm very grateful.'

And the three men shook hands warmly.

'Listen to me,' Fergusson continued. 'According to my calculations we're not more than three hundred miles from the Gulf of Guinea. The desert can't go on for ever, for the coast is inhabited and the country is known for some distance inland. If necessary we'll make for the coast, and we're bound to come across some oasis or well where we can renew our supplies of water. But what we want is a wind, and without it we shall stay becalmed in the air.'

'We must make up our minds to wait,' said Kennedy.

But in vain each in turn scanned the horizon during this interminable day. Nothing appeared that could rouse the slightest hope. The last undulations of the ground vanished in the setting sun, whose horizontal rays stretched like long lines of fire over this vast expanse. It was the desert. The travellers had not covered fifteen miles and had used up, as on the previous day, one hundred and thirty-five feet of gas to feed the burner, while two pints of water out of eight had had to be sacrificed to slake their burning thirst. The night was calm, too calm. The doctor did not sleep a wink.

25

*Another balloon — Traces of a
caravan — A well*

The next day brought the same clear sky, the
same still air. The *Victoria* rose to four
hundred feet but hardly made the slightest
progress westward.

'We're in the heart of the desert,' said the
doctor. 'Look at the stretch of sand. What a
strange sight. What an odd whim of Nature.
Why should there be all that luxuriant
vegetation over there, and here this parched
waste, and in the same degree of latitude,
under the same sun?'

'The reason doesn't worry me,' Kennedy
replied, 'as much as the fact. The important
thing is that it is so.'

'We may as well philosophise a bit, old
man. It can't do any harm.'

'Philosophise away, then, I'm quite agreeable. At least, we've plenty of time. We're
hardly moving. The wind's afraid to blow. It's
asleep.'

'It won't last,' said Joe. 'I think I see some
strips of cloud in the east.'

'Joe's right,' the doctor said.

'Good,' said Kennedy. 'We could put up with a good cloud with rain and a fresh wind in our faces.'

'We'll see, Dick; we'll see.'

'But it's Friday, sir, and I'm suspicious of Fridays.'

'Well, I hope today will show the error of your forebodings.'

'I hope so, sir. Phew!' he said, wiping his face. 'I like warmth, and especially in summer, but it can be overdone.'

'Have you any fear of the effect of the heat on our balloon?' Kennedy asked the doctor.

'No; the gutta-percha with which the silk is proofed can stand much higher temperatures. I've sometimes got a temperature of 158 degrees out of the coil and the envelope doesn't appear to have suffered.'

'A cloud! A real cloud!' Joe cried just at that moment, for his piercing eye scorned any kind of glass.

He was right. A thick bank of cloud was now rising slowly but distinctly above the horizon. It looked deep and swollen. It was made up of a heap of small clouds, each preserving its individual shape, from which the doctor concluded that there was no breeze affecting them. It was about eight in the morning when this compact mass appeared, and it was not until eleven that it reached the disc of the sun, which vanished completely behind the thick curtain. At the same moment the lower edge cleared the horizon, from which a brilliant light poured.

'It's a single cloud,' said the doctor. 'We mustn't count too much on it. Look, Dick! It's still the same shape as it was this morning.'

'Yes, Samuel, there's not going to be any rain or wind; not for us, at any rate.'

'I'm afraid not. It's keeping very high.'

'Well, suppose we go up to meet this cloud since it refuses to break on us?'

'I don't imagine that will help much,' replied the doctor. 'It will mean using up gas and also a good deal of water. But as things are, we must leave nothing undone. We must go up.'

The doctor turned up the flame of the burner inside the coil. A fierce heat was developed, and soon the balloon rose under the influence of the expanding hydrogen. When she reached about a hundred feet, she encountered the thick mass of the cloud and entered a dense fog, keeping the same elevation. But there was no breath of wind. The very fog seemed devoid of humidity, and objects exposed to its contact were scarcely damp. The *Victoria*, perhaps, moved forward more perceptibly in the mist, but that was all.

The doctor was disappointed at the poor result of his move, when he heard Joe exclaim in accents of keen surprise: 'Good Lord!'

'What is it, Joe?'

'Look, sir! Look, Mr Kennedy! that's strange!'

'What is it?'

'We're not alone here. It's a plot! They've pinched our idea.'

'Is the man going mad?' said Kennedy.

Joe looked like a statue of amazement. He stood transfixed

'Can the sun have affected the poor fellow's brain?' said the doctor, turning towards him.

'Are you going to tell me what's the matter?' he asked.

'But, just look, sir!' said Joe, pointing to a speck in space.

'Holy St Andrew!' cried Kennedy in his turn. 'It's impossible. Look, Sam! Look!'

'I see,' the doctor replied calmly.

'Another balloon with passengers like ourselves!'

Two hundred feet away, a balloon was floating in the air with car and passengers, following exactly the same route as the *Victoria*.

'Well, we've only to signal to it,' said the doctor. 'Get out the flag, Kennedy, and let's show our colours.'

Apparently the same idea occurred to the

passengers of the second balloon at exactly the same moment, for the same flag repeated identically the same greeting from a hand waved in the same way.

'What does that mean?' Kennedy asked.

'They're a lot of monkeys,' Joe exclaimed. 'They're making fun of us.'

'It means,' replied Fergusson, laughing, 'that it's you who are making that signal, my dear Dick. It means that we ourselves are in that other car. That balloon is simply the *Victoria*.'

'Well, sir, begging your pardon, you'll never make me believe that.'

'Get up on to the side, Joe, and wave your arms, and then you'll see.'

Joe obeyed and saw his every gesture immediately repeated.

'It's only a mirage,' said the doctor. 'That's all. Merely an optical illusion. It's due to the unequal rarefication of the air strata.'

'It's wonderful,' said Joe who, reluctant to give in, continued his experiments with a wild waving of his arms.

'A strange sight,' said Kennedy. 'It's nice to see the good old *Victoria*. She looks well and behaves with dignity, you know.'

'However you explain it,' Joe replied, 'it's uncanny, all the same.'

But the mirage was gradually dimming.

The clouds lifted to a very high level, leaving behind them the *Victoria*, who made no attempt to follow, and an hour later they had disappeared above her. The wind, which had been scarcely perceptible, now seemed to grow fainter still. The doctor, in despair, dropped towards the earth. The travellers, whom this incident had drawn out of their meditations, fell back upon their gloomy thoughts, overcome by the searing heat.

About four o'clock Joe reported an object standing out from the immense plateau of sand, and a little later saw two palm trees not far ahead.

'Palms!' said Fergusson. 'Then there must be a spring, a well!'

He took up his glass and assured himself that Joe's eyes had not deceived him.

'Water at last. Water! Water!' he repeated. 'We're saved; for though we're not moving fast, we are moving, and we'll get there in time.'

'Well, sir,' said Joe, 'what about a drink meanwhile? The air's stifling.'

'Yes, let's have a drink, Joe.'

No one waited to be asked. The whole pint vanished, reducing the supply to three pints and a half.

'Ah! that's good!' said Joe. 'That's jolly good! Beer never tasted like that!'

'That's one of the advantages of going

without,' replied the doctor.

'Taking them altogether they're not great,' said Kennedy, 'and I'd gladly renounce water on condition I was never deprived of it.'

At six o'clock the *Victoria* was floating over two miserable withered palms, leafless ghosts of trees more dead than alive. Fergusson looked at them anxiously. At their foot could be seen the half-crumbled stones of a well which seemed to have been reduced to mere dust under the fierce heat of the sun. There was no sign of humidity. Samuel's heart contracted and he was about to impart his fears to his companions when their exclamations diverted his attention.

Westward, as far as the eye could see, stretched a long line of bleached bones. Fragments of skeletons surrounded the spring. A caravan must have struggled there, leaving this long trail of bones in its wake. The weakest had fallen one by one in the sand; the stronger, having reached the longed-for well, had met a horrible death at its edge. The travellers looked at one another and blenched.

'Don't let us go down,' said Kennedy; 'let's get away from this ghastly sight. We shan't find a drop of water.'

'No, Dick, we must have a clear conscience. We may just as well spend the night here as anywhere else. We'll search this well to the bottom. There has been a spring here; perhaps we shall find some trace of it.'

The *Victoria* touched ground. Joe and Kennedy put into the car a weight of sand equivalent to their own and disembarked. They ran to the well and climbed down inside it by steps which were crumbling to dust. The spring seemed to have been dried up for many years. They dug in the dry, fine sand; dry as a bone. Not a trace of damp did they find.

The doctor saw them emerge again, sweating, beaten, covered with fine dust, downcast, depressed and despairing. He realised that their search had been fruitless as he had expected. He said nothing but felt that henceforward he would require courage and strength for three.

Joe brought back the fragments of a shrivelled water-skin, which he threw away angrily among the bones which strewed the ground. During supper the travellers did not exchange a single word and ate with effort. And yet so far they had not really experienced the torments of thirst. Their despair was for the future.

26

The distance covered by the *Victoria* the previous day was not more than ten miles, and had cost them 162 cubic feet of gas. On Saturday morning the doctor gave the signal for departure.

'The burner can only hold out six hours more,' he said. 'If in the next six hours we don't find a well or spring, God only knows what will become of us.'

'There's not much wind this morning, sir,' said Joe. 'But perhaps it will get up,' he added, noticing Fergusson's ill-concealed distress.

Vain hope! They were in a dead calm; one of those relentless calms that grip ships in tropical seas. The heat became intolerable and the thermometer under the shade of the awning showed 113 degrees. Joe and Kennedy, stretched out side by side, tried to forget their situation in sleep, or at least torpor. The forced inactivity left them hours of painful leisure. The most pitiable of men are those without work or material occupation to distract their thoughts. But here there was nothing to attend to, no further effort to be made. The situation had to be submitted to; it could not be improved.

The agonies of thirst began to make themselves cruelly felt. The brandy, far from appeasing their compelling need, only increased it, justifying the name 'tiger's milk' given to it by the natives of Africa. They had rather less than two pints of liquid left, and that was hot. The eyes of all brooded covetously over the precious water and none dared touch it with his lips. Two pints of water in the heart of the desert!

Dr Fergusson, deep in thought, was asking himself whether he had acted prudently. Would it not have been better to preserve the water he had fruitlessly decomposed to hold them in the air? Certainly he had made a little headway, but was he any nearer his goal? What difference would it have made if he had been sixty miles farther back, since there was no water to be found? And again, if the wind did rise, would it not blow as strongly there as here, stronger even if it came from the east? But hope urged Samuel forward. And yet those two wasted gallons of water would have sufficed for a halt of nine days in this desert, and what changes might not come about in nine days! Perhaps, too, he should have kept this water, and risen by throwing out ballast, even if he had had to lose gas to come down again. But gas was the balloon's blood, her life.

A thousand such reflections jostled through his head, which he held in his hands without raising it for hours at a time.

'We must make one last effort,' he told himself about ten in the morning; 'one last attempt to find a breeze that will get us away. We must stake everything on a last throw.'

And while his companions were asleep he raised the hydrogen to a high temperature. The balloon swelled under the expansion of the gas and rose straight up through the vertical rays of the sun. The doctor searched the air from a hundred to a thousand feet but found no breath of wind. The place from which he started was still directly below him. An absolute calm seemed to extend to the last limits of breathable air. At last the water gave out and the burner died for want of gas. The Bunsen battery ceased to function and the *Victoria*, contracting, dropped gently to the sand on the very spot that still bore the imprint of the car. It was noon. A reckoning showed their position as lat. 6° 51′ N., long.

19° 35′ E., nearly five hundred miles from Lake Tchad and more than four hundred from the West Coast of Africa. As they touched, Dick and Joe woke from their heavy torpor.

'We're stopping?' said the Scotsman.

'We must,' Samuel replied gravely.

His companions understood. The ground here was at sea-level; indeed, of late it had been constantly sinking, so the balloon was maintained in perfect equilibrium, completely motionless.

As they disembarked, the travellers filled the car with a weight of sand equal to their own. Each was absorbed in his own thoughts and for several hours they did not speak. Joe prepared a supper of biscuit and pemmican which they hardly touched. A sip of hot water completed this dismal meal.

During the night no watch was kept, but no one slept. The heat was stifling. Next morning only half a pint of water remained, which the doctor set aside, resolving not to touch it save in the last extremity.

'I'm suffocating,' Joe gasped a little later. 'It's hotter than ever, and I'm not surprised,' he added after consulting the thermometer: '140 degrees!'

'The sand is scorching. It might be fresh from a furnace,' said Kennedy. 'And not a cloud in this grilling sky. It's enough to drive one mad!'

'Don't let us give in,' said the doctor. 'These fierce heats are always followed by storms in this latitude, and they come with the swiftness of lightning. In spite of the dreadful serenity of the sky great changes come about in less than an hour.'

'But, surely, there would be some sign,' said Kennedy.

'Well,' said the doctor, 'I rather think the barometer shows a slight tendency to drop.'

'Pray Heaven you're right, Sam. We're nailed down here like a winged bird.'

'With the difference, however, old man, that our wings are intact, and I sincerely hope we shall be able to use them yet.'

'Oh, for a wind!' cried Joe. 'Just enough to take us to a stream, and we shall be quite all right. We've got enough grub, and if only we could get some water, we could wait for months without taking any harm. But thirst is awful.'

Thirst, added to the unceasing glare of the desert, was eating into their souls. There was not the slightest break in the ground, not a sand-hill, not a stone to distract their eyes. The flatness sickened them and produced the disorder known as desert sickness. The relentless stillness of the arid blue sky and the yellow immensity of sand eventually struck terror into them. In this burning atmosphere the heat seemed to quiver as over a red-hot furnace. Watching this calm, and seeing no reason why the situation should ever end, for immensity is a kind of eternity, filled their souls with despair. These unfortunate men, deprived of water in this fearful heat, began to experience symptoms of hallucination. Their eyes dilated, their sight became blurred.

When night had fallen the doctor resolved to fight this disquieting mood by means of a sharp walk. He intended to spend a few hours crossing this plain of sand, not with the idea of searching but simply for exercise.

'Come on,' he said to his companions. 'Believe me, it will do you good.'

'It can't be done,' replied Kennedy. 'I couldn't walk a step.'

'I'd much rather sleep,' said Joe.

'But sleep and rest are fatal. Try and rouse yourselves. Now then, come along!'

As the doctor could get no response, he set out alone through the starry clearness of the night. His first steps were painful, the steps of a man weakened and unused to walking; but he soon realised that the exercise would be beneficial. He went on several miles in a westerly direction and his mind was already feeling easier when he was suddenly seized with giddiness. It was as if he were leaning over an abyss. He felt his knees giving way. The vast solitude terrified him. He was as a mathematical point, the centre of an infinite circumference, of the void. The *Victoria* had disappeared completely in the darkness. An uncontrollable panic took possession of the doctor, the impassive, intrepid traveller. He tried to retrace his steps, but in vain. He called aloud, but not the slightest echo answered him, and his voice fell into space like a stone into a bottomless pit. He sank exhausted on the sand, alone amid the great silence of the desert.

At midnight he came round, to find himself in the arms of the faithful Joe, who, uneasy at his master's prolonged absence, had hastily followed his tracks, which were clearly printed in the sand. He had found him unconscious.

'What's happened, sir?' he asked.

'It's nothing, my dear fellow. A momentary weakness, that's all.'

'Nothing, indeed, sir! But get up; lean on me and we'll get back to the *Victoria*.'

Leaning on Joe's arm, the doctor returned the way he had come.

'It was unwise, sir. You shouldn't do these things. You might have been waylaid,' he added, laughing. 'Come, sir, let's be serious.'

'Go on. I'm listening.'

'We must really make up our minds. We can't go on like this for many days more, and if the wind doesn't come, it's all up with us.'

The doctor did not reply.

'Well, someone must sacrifice himself for the rest and it's only natural it should be me.'

'What do you mean? What's your idea?'

'It's quite simple. Take some food and walk straight ahead until I get somewhere. I'm bound to, sooner or later. Meantime, if Heaven sends you a favourable wind, you mustn't wait for me; you must start. As for me, if I come to a village I'll manage to get along with a few Arab words you can write out for me, and I'll bring back help or die in the attempt. What do you think of it, sir?

'It's mad, but does credit to your heart, Joe. It's out of the question. You're not going to leave us.'

'After all, sir, we must try something. It can't do any harm for, as I say, you won't wait for me, and at a pinch I may do some good.'

'No, no, Joe; we mustn't separate. It would only make it worse for the others. It was fated that this should be and it's probably arranged that it will be different later. So let us wait patiently.'

'All right, sir, but I'll tell you one thing. I'll

give you another day, but I won't wait longer than that. Today is Sunday, or rather Monday, for it's one o'clock in the morning. If we don't get a move on by Monday, I'll risk it. I've quite made up my mind.'

The doctor did not reply. Soon afterwards he reached the car and took his place beside Kennedy, who was lying perfectly still; but that did not mean he was asleep.

27

*Terrific heat — Hallucinations — The
last drops of water — A night of despair
— Attempted suicide — The simoon
— The oasis — A lion and lioness*

In the morning the doctor's first thought was
to consult the barometer. At most, there
was the faintest drop.

'No good! No good!' he muttered to himself.

He left the car and took a look at the
weather. The same heat, the same clear sky,
the same implacable conditions.

'Must we give up hope?' he exclaimed.

Joe said nothing. He was wrapped up in his
own thoughts, meditating his plan.

Kennedy got up feeling very ill, a prey to
an alarming attack of nerves. He was suffering
horribly from thirst. His blistered tongue and
lips could hardly articulate a sound. There were
a few drops of water left. They all knew it. The
thoughts of each were drawn towards it as to
a magnet, but no one dared go near it.

The three companions, the three friends,
looked at one another with haggard eyes and

with a feeling of brute greed which betrayed itself most in Kennedy, whose powerful frame succumbed more readily to this intolerable privation. Throughout the day he was in the grip of delirium. He walked up and down, uttering hoarse cries, gnawing his fists, on the point of opening his veins to drink the blood.

'Oh!' he muttered; 'they're right to call this the land of thirst, the land of despair!' Then he relapsed into a state of coma. Nothing was heard from him but the hissing of his breath between his parched lips.

Towards evening Joe began to show symptoms of mania. This vast sea of sand appeared to him as an immense pool of cool and limpid waters. More than once he threw himself down on the scorching sand to drink and got up again with his mouth full of dust.

'Damnation!' he cried angrily. 'It's salt-water!'

Then, while Fergusson and Kennedy lay stretched out motionless, he was seized with an overpowering temptation to drain the few drops of water that were being held in reserve. It grew too much for him. He dragged himself on his knees towards the car, fastened his eyes greedily upon the bottle containing the liquid, looked at it with a desperate glance, seized it, and raised it to his lips.

At this moment he heard the words: 'Water! Water!' in accents that tore the heart. It was Kennedy, dragging himself towards him. The poor fellow was a pitiable sight. He remained on his knees, the tears welling from his eyes. Joe, also in tears, offered him the bottle and, to the very last drop, Kennedy drained the contents. 'Thank you,' he gasped, but Joe did not hear him; he had fallen prone on the sand.

What happened during that dreadful night is known to no one, but on the Tuesday morning, under the douche of fire pouring from the sun, the wretched men felt their limbs gradually shrivelling When Joe tried to get up he found it impossible. He was unable to carry out his plan. He took a look round him. In the car the doctor lay prostrate, his arms folded over his chest, gazing at an imaginary point in space with imbecile fixity. Kennedy was a terrifying sight. His head swayed from side to side like that of a caged animal.

Suddenly the Scotsman's eye rested upon his carbine, the butt of which was projecting over the side of the car.

'Ah!' he cried, raising himself by a superhuman effort. He dashed at the weapon, desperate, insane, and placed the muzzle to his mouth.

'Sir! Mr Kennedy!' said Joe, throwing

himself upon him.

'Leave me alone! Get away!' moaned the Scotsman, and the two struggled desperately.

'Clear out or I'll kill you,' Kennedy went on. But Joe clung to him fiercely. They fought together for nearly a minute, the doctor appearing not to notice them. Then suddenly in the struggle the carbine went off. At the sound of the report the doctor got up, erect as a spectre. He looked around him. Then a sudden light came into his eye. He stretched his hand towards the horizon and, in a voice in which there was nothing human, rasped out: 'Look! Look over there!'

There was such energy in his gesture that Joe and Kennedy broke away and both looked. The plain was rising and falling like a sea lashed by a storm. Waves of sand broke one upon another, throwing up clouds of dust. From the south-east a huge, twisting column was approaching with incredible swiftness. The sun vanished behind a dense cloud whose gigantic shadow extended to the balloon. Grains of fine sand swept along with the quick flow of liquid and, little by little, the rising tide advanced.

A gleam of hope shone in Fergusson's eyes. 'The simoon!' he cried.

'The simoon!' Joe repeated, without much idea of what the word meant.

'Good!' muttered Kennedy, in the delirium of despair. 'All the better. We're going to die.'

'Yes, all the better!' replied the doctor. 'But we're going to live.' And he began rapidly to throw out the sand holding down the car. His companions, at last understanding, rejoined him and took their places at his side. 'And now, Joe,' said the doctor, 'throw out fifty pounds or so of your gold.'

Though he felt a swift pang of regret, Joe did not hesitate. The balloon rose.

'It was time,' said the doctor.

And indeed the simoon was sweeping towards them with the swiftness of lightning. A little longer and the *Victoria* would have been crushed to pieces — annihilated. The huge column was upon them. The *Victoria* was swept by a hail of sand.

'More ballast!' the doctor cried to Joe.

'Aye, aye, sir,' replied the latter, hurling out an enormous piece of quartz.

The *Victoria* rose rapidly above the column, but, caught in the great whirlpool of air, she was torn along at dizzy speed over this foaming sea of sand. Samuel, Dick and Joe did not speak but looked and hoped, refreshed by the whirlwind. By three o'clock the tumult had ceased. The sand fell again and formed a great quantity of little hills. The sky resumed its former calm. The *Victoria*, motionless again, was floating within sight of an oasis, an island of trees on the surface of the sandy ocean.

'Water! There's water there!' cried the doctor. And immediately, opening the upper valve, he let the hydrogen escape and came down gently, two hundred yards from the oasis. In four hours the travellers had covered two hundred and forty miles.

The moment the car came to a halt Kennedy jumped out, followed by Joe.

'Your gun!' cried the doctor. 'Take your guns, and look out.'

Dick seized his carbine and Joe one of the guns. They quickly approached the trees and plunged into the fresh foliage which promised abundant springs. They paid no heed to a number of large, broad footmarks freshly imprinted here and there on the humid earth. Suddenly, twenty yards away, a roar rang out.

'A lion!' said Joe.

'Good!' snapped the exasperated Kennedy. 'We'll fight him. We're strong enough when it's only a question of fighting.'

'Take care, sir. All our lives may depend on the life of one of us.'

But Kennedy was not listening. He strode forward, eyes blazing, carbine cocked, terrible in his audacity. Under a palm an enormous black-maned lion was crouching, ready to spring. Scarcely had he caught sight of Kennedy than he hurled himself through the air; but before he touched the ground a bullet struck him in the heart. He fell dead.

'Hurray!' cried Joe.

Kennedy dashed towards the well, slipping on the wet steps, and threw himself down by a fresh spring into which he greedily plunged his lips. Joe followed his example, and the silence was broken only by the lapping sound made by thirsty animals.

'Steady, sir,' said Joe, taking a long breath. 'We mustn't overdo it.' But Dick, without answering, went on drinking. He plunged his head and hands into the healing water. He was intoxicated.

'And what about Dr Fergusson?' said Joe. This brought Kennedy to his senses. Filling a bottle he had brought, he dashed up the steps. But what was his amazement when he found a huge opaque body blocking the entrance. Joe, who was following him, had to draw back too.

'We're shut in!'

'Impossible! what does this mean — ?'

Dick did not finish. A terrible roar made him realise with what new enemy he had to deal.

'Another lion!' cried Joe.

'No. A lioness. Damn the brute! Wait,' said

the hunter, hastily reloading his carbine. An instant later he fired, but the animal had disappeared. 'Come on!' he cried.

'No, sir. You didn't kill her. The body would have rolled down here. She's waiting to spring on whichever of us comes out first, and it will be all up with him.'

'But what's to be done? We must get out. Dr Fergusson's waiting.'

'Let's draw her. You take my gun and pass me the carbine.'

'What's the idea?'

'You'll see.'

Taking off his canvas jacket, Joe stuck it on the end of the gun and held it out above the opening as a bait. The animal dashed at it in fury. Kennedy was ready, and with a shot broke its shoulder. The roaring animal rolled down the steps, knocking Joe over. Joe already imagined he could feel the animal's great claws piercing his flesh, when a second shot rang out, and the doctor appeared at the opening, his gun still smoking in his hand.

Joe got up hastily, climbed over the animal's body and passed the bottle of water to his master. To raise it to his lips and half-empty it was for Fergusson the work of a moment, and from the bottom of their hearts the three travellers thanked Providence, who had so miraculously saved them.

28

*A delicious evening — Joe's cooking
— Dissertation on raw meat — The story
of James Bruce — The bivouac — Joe's
dreams — The barometer drops — The
barometer rises again — Preparations for
departure — The hurricane*

The evening was a delightful one and, after a comforting meal, it was spent under the cool shade of the mimosas. The tea and grog were not spared. Kennedy had explored the oasis in all directions, and had beaten the undergrowth. The travellers were the only inhabitants of this earthly paradise. They stretched themselves out on their blankets and spent a peaceful night, which blotted out the memory of past discomforts. The next day, the 7th of May, the sun was shining with full brilliance, but its rays failed to penetrate the thick curtain of shade. As they had plenty of provisions, the doctor decided to wait in this place for a favourable wind. Joe had brought with him his portable kitchen and indulged in a great number of culinary experiments, using water lavishly.

'What a strange alternation of troubles and enjoyment!' Kennedy exclaimed. 'Abundance after want; luxury after misery! I jolly nearly went off my head.'

'My dear Dick,' the doctor said, 'without Joe you wouldn't be here to discourse on the instability of human things.'

'He's a good fellow,' said Dick, offering Joe his hand.

'Don't mention it, sir,' Joe replied. 'You'd do the same for me; but I hope there'll be no need.'

'What poor things we are to allow ourselves to despair for so little.'

'You mean for so little water, sir? It must be a very important thing.'

'It is, Joe. People hold out much longer without food than without drink.'

'I can quite believe that. Besides, at a pinch, a man can eat whatever turns up, even his fellow-men, though that must be hard to digest.'

'The savages seem to manage it all right,' said Kennedy.

'Yes; but they're savages and they're used to eating raw meat. That's a custom I could never get used to.'

'Yes, it is repulsive,' the doctor went on; 'so much so that no one would credit the stories of the first African travellers when they reported that several tribes fed on raw meat. In this connection a curious adventure happened to James Bruce.'

'Tell us about it, sir. We've plenty of time,' said Joe, stretching himself luxuriously on the cool grass.

'Certainly. James Bruce was a Scotsman from Stirling who between 1768 and 1772 explored the whole of Abyssinia as far as Lake Tyana in search of the Nile sources and then returned to England, where he did not publish the account of his travels until 1790. His story was received with extreme scepticism, as no doubt ours will be. The customs of the Abyssinians seemed so different from what people are used to in England that no one would believe him. Among other details James Bruce had stated that the people of East Africa ate raw meat. This roused the whole public against him. He could say what he liked; no one would listen. Bruce was a very brave man and very stubborn. This scepticism exasperated him. One day, when he was in an Edinburgh drawing-room, a Scotsman took up the subject, which had become a daily joke, and with regard to the point of raw meat declared flatly that the thing was neither possible nor true. Bruce went out and in a few moments returned with a raw steak, salted and peppered in the

African manner. 'Sir,' he said to the Scotsman, 'by doubting what I've told you, you have offered me a serious insult; in believing it impossible, you are entirely in the wrong, and to prove this to everyone, you're going to eat this raw steak now or give me satisfaction for what you have said.' The Scotsman was frightened and obeyed, pulling dreadful faces. Then, with perfect coolness, James Bruce added: 'Even admitting the statement isn't true, sir, you at least can't continue to maintain that it's impossible.''

'A good answer,' said Joe. 'If the Scotsman got indigestion it served him right, and if anyone doubts our story when we get back to England — '

'Well, Joe, what will you do?'

'I'll make them eat the remains of the *Victoria*, and without pepper or salt.'

They all laughed at Joe's remark. And so the day passed in cheerful conversation. With returning strength hope revived, and with hope, courage. The past faded away before the future with miraculous rapidity. Joe would have liked to stay for ever in this enchanted refuge, the kingdom of his dreams. He felt at home there. He made his master tell him its exact position, which he solemnly entered in his notebook: lat. 8° 32′ N., long. 15° 48′ E.

Kennedy had only one regret — that there

was no shooting in this miniature forest. As he said, there weren't many wild animals.

'What about the lion and lioness, old man?' replied the doctor. 'You've soon forgotten them.'

'Oh, those creatures!' he said, with the true hunter's scorn for the killed quarry. 'But, as a matter of fact, their presence here at all gives good reason to suppose that we're not very far from more fertile country.'

'An uncertain proof, Dick. These animals often cover considerable distances when they're hard pressed by hunger and thirst. We shall do well to keep an extra keen look-out tonight, and light fires.'

'In this heat!' said Joe. 'Well, if we must, we will; but it seems a pity to burn this nice little wood which has been so useful to us.'

'We'll take special care not to set fire to it,' answered the doctor. 'Some day others may be glad to find shelter in the middle of the desert.'

'We'll see to that, sir. But do you think anyone knows about this oasis?'

'Of course. It's a halting-place for caravans crossing the centre of Africa. A visit from them might not be to your liking, Joe.'

'Are there any more of those beastly Nyam Nyams in these parts?'

'Without a doubt. It's the common name for all these people, and in the same climate the same races are bound to have similar habits.'

'Pah!' said Joe. 'Well, after all, it's only natural. If savages had the tastes of gentlemen, what difference would there be? At any rate, these good people wouldn't have needed any persuasion to swallow the Scotsman's steak, and the Scotsman into the bargain.'

After this very sensible remark Joe went off to prepare the fires for the night, making them as small as possible. Fortunately these precautions were unnecessary and, one after the other, all fell into a deep sleep.

The next day there was still no change in the weather, which remained obstinately fine. The balloon hung motionless, not the slightest oscillation indicating a breath of wind. The doctor began to grow anxious. If the expedition was going to drag out in this way they would run short of provisions. After almost dying for want of water were they to be reduced to death by starvation? But he was reassured at seeing the mercury of the barometer drop quite appreciably. There were obvious signs of an approaching change. He therefore resolved to get ready to leave so that he could take advantage of the first opportunity. The food and water containers were all filled to their full capacity.

Fergusson had then to re-establish the

equilibrium of the balloon, and Joe was compelled to sacrifice a considerable part of his precious ore. With restored health, his ambitious ideas had returned, and he pulled several grimaces before obeying his master, but the latter convinced him that he could not lift such a weight. When he was offered his choice between water and gold Joe hesitated no longer, but threw a large quantity of his precious ore on to the sand.

'There's something for the next people who come along after us,' he said. 'They'll be very surprised to find a fortune in a place like this.'

'Suppose some scientific traveller should come across these samples — ?' said Kennedy.

'You needn't have any doubts about that, old man; you may be sure he'd be very surprised, and would publish his surprise in many volumes. Some day we shall hear of a wonderful vein of auriferous quartz in the middle of the African desert.'

'And Joe will be responsible for it.'

The chance of hoaxing a scientist cheered the worthy Joe and made him smile. During the rest of the day the doctor waited vainly for a change in the weather. The temperature rose, and without the shade of the oasis the heat would have been intolerable. The thermometer showed 149 degrees in the sun. A veritable rain of fire poured down through the air. It was the hottest weather they had yet encountered. In the evening Joe again prepared the bivouac for the night, and during Fergusson's and Kennedy's watches no incident occurred. About 3 a.m., however, during Joe's watch, the temperature suddenly dropped, the sky clouded over and the darkness increased.

'Wake up!' cried Joe, rousing his two companions. 'Wake up! Here's the wind!'

'At last,' said the doctor, scanning the sky. 'It's a storm. Back to the car.'

It was quite time. The *Victoria* was stooping under the force of the hurricane and dragging the car, which left a furrow in the sand. If any part of the ballast had happened to fall overboard the balloon would have gone and all hope of finding it again would have been lost for ever. But the fleet-footed Joe ran as fast as he could and held the car down, the balloon sinking to the sand, where it seemed likely to be torn. The doctor went to his usual post, lit his burner, and threw out the extra ballast. The travellers took a last look at the trees of the oasis, which were bending to the storm and, picking up the east wind two hundred feet from the ground, they soon vanished into the night.

29

*A French author's fantastic notion
— Speke and Burton's exploration
linked up with Barth's*

From the very moment of their departure the travellers were dashed along at great speed. They were anxious to get away from this desert which had nearly proved so disastrous to them. About a quarter-past nine in the morning they caught sight of some signs of vegetation, grasses floating on the sea of sand and revealing to them, as to Christopher Columbus, the proximity of soil. Green blades pushed their way timidly between rocks which were themselves to become the shoals of this ocean. Hills, as yet of low elevation, undulated on the horizon, their outline, blurred by mist, being indistinctly defined. The country was growing less monotonous. The doctor greeted this change of scene with delight and, like a sailor keeping his watch, he felt inclined to shout: 'Land! Land!'

An hour later the continent stretched below their eyes, still wild, but less flat, less bare. A few trees stood out against the grey sky.

'We're in civilisation again!' said Kennedy.

'Civilisation, sir? That's one way of putting it. There's not a soul to be seen yet.'

'That won't last long at the rate we're travelling,' Fergusson answered.

'Are we still in negro country, sir?'

'Yes, Joe, until we get to that of the Arabs.'

'Arabs, sir, real Arabs, with camels?'

'No, without camels. Camels are rare, not to say unknown, in this region. They're not to be found until you come a few degrees farther north.'

'What a pity!'

'Why, Joe?'

'Because if the wind turned against us they might be useful.'

'How?'

'I've got an idea, sir. We could harness them to the car and make them tow us. What do you think, sir?'

'The idea has occurred to others before you, Joe, and it has been exploited in a novel by a witty French writer, M. Méry. Some travellers have their balloons towed by camels. A lion eats the camels, swallows the tow-line and tows them in its turn, and so on. You see, it's all mere fancy and in no way connected with our method of locomotion.'

Joe, a little humiliated to find that his idea had already occurred to someone else, tried to think what animal could have eaten the lion, but as he could not think of one he returned to his contemplation of the scenery. A fair-sized lake stretched below him in an amphitheatre of high hills which could as yet hardly be called mountains. Among these wound fertile valleys with tangled thickets of many kinds of trees. These were dominated by the elæis, with leaves fifteen feet long and its stem covered with sharp thorns. The bombax threw the fine down of its seed to the passing wind. The strong perfume of the pendanus, the *kenda* of the Arabs, made the air fragrant even at the height at which the *Victoria* was travelling. The papaw, with its palmate leaves, the sterculier, which produces the Sudanese nut, the baobab and the banana-tree completed the luxuriant flora of these tropical regions.

'It's a splendid country,' said the doctor.

'There are some animals,' said Joe; 'the people won't be far off.'

'Oh, what fine elephants!' exclaimed Kennedy. 'Couldn't we manage a little hunting?'

'How are we to stop in this wind, Dick? No, you'll have to suffer a taste of the torture of Tantalus. You'll make up for it later on.'

There was indeed plenty to stir the

imagination of a sportsman. Dick's heart beat hard and his fingers tightened on the butt of his Purdey. The fauna of the country was worthy of its flora. The wild ox wallowed in the thick grass which buried it completely. Grey, black and tawny elephants of enormous size passed like a tornado through the forests, smashing, tearing and wrecking, and leaving behind them a trail of ruin. Cascades and watercourses poured to the northward down the wooded slopes, and here hippopotamus splashed noisily, and manatees twelve feet long displayed their fish-like bodies on the banks, exposing their round udders, swollen with milk. There was a whole menagerie of rare animals in a wonderful setting where countless multi-coloured birds flitted among the trees and shrubs. This prodigality of Nature made it clear to the doctor that this was the splendid kingdom of Adamawa.

'We're getting into touch with modern discovery,' he said. 'I've picked up the broken trail of the explorers. We're in luck, my friends! We're going to connect the work of Burton and Speke with the explorations of Dr Barth. We've left the English to find a German, and we shall soon come to the farthest point reached by that brave discoverer.'

'Judging by the distance we've come, there seems to be a good stretch of country between the two,' said Kennedy.

'It's easy enough to calculate. Have a look at the map and see what is the longitude of the southern point of Lake Victoria reached by Speke.'

'About the 37th meridian.'

'And the town of Yola, where we ought to arrive tonight? Barth got there.'

'The 12th, about.'

'That makes 25 degrees, then; or, at sixty miles to the degree — fifteen hundred miles.'

'A nice little jaunt,' said Joe.

'It will be done, however. Livingstone and Moffat are still travelling towards the interior. Nyasa, which they discovered, is not very far from Lake Tanganyika, found by Burton. Before the end of the century all these great stretches of country will be explored without a doubt. But,' added the doctor, looking at the compass, 'it's a pity the wind is taking us due east. I wanted to go north.'

After twelve hours' travelling the *Victoria* found herself on the confines of Nigeria. The first inhabitants of this country, Choua Arabs, were nomads driving their flocks from one pasture to another. The huge crests of the Alantika Mountains projected over the horizon; mountains which no European foot had yet trodden and whose height is estimated at about eight thousand feet. Their western slope forms the watershed of all the rivers of this part of Africa; they are the Moon Mountains of this region.

At last the three men sighted a real river and from the huge ant-hills on its banks the doctor recognised the Benue, one of the chief tributaries of the Niger, which the natives call the 'Cradle of the Waters.'

'This river,' the doctor informed his companions, 'will one day become the natural line of communication with the interior of Nigeria. The steamboat *Pleiades* has already explored it as far as Yola. You see, we are now in known country.'

Numbers of slaves were at work in the fields, tending the sorghum, a kind of maize, which is their staple food. The appearance of the *Victoria*, flying like a meteor through the air, caused wide-eyed amazement. In the evening she hove to, forty miles from Yola. Ahead of her in the distance rose the two sharp peaks of Mount Mendif. The doctor had the anchors thrown out and moored to the crest of a high tree. But a sharp wind beat the *Victoria* down so that she lay almost horizontal, which at times made the position of the car extremely dangerous. Fergusson did not close his eyes once during the night. He was often on the point of cutting the cable to run before the wind. At last the storm died down and the oscillation of the balloon ceased to give cause for anxiety. The following day the wind moderated, but it carried the travellers away from Yola which, as it had recently been rebuilt by the Fellanis, had aroused Fergusson's curiosity. However, as there was no alternative, they had to resign themselves to travelling northwards, and even slightly east.

Kennedy suggested making a halt in this district where the hunting seemed good. Joe claimed that the need of fresh meat was beginning to make itself felt, but the wild nature of the country and the hostile attitude of the population, which was shown by the firing of guns at the *Victoria*, decided the doctor to hold his course. They were crossing country which is constantly the scene of massacre, fire, and war, where the sultans stake their kingdoms in bloody fighting. Many populous villages of elongated huts stretched between the wide pastures, where the thick grass was speckled with violet flowers. The huts, looking like huge hives, were protected by bristling palisades. The wild slopes of the hills, as Kennedy several times remarked, were reminiscent of the glens in the Scottish Highlands.

In spite of his efforts, the doctor was being carried due north-east, towards Mount

Mendif, the summit of which was buried in the clouds. The high peaks of this range separate the Niger from the Lake Tchad basin.

Soon Bagele hove in sight with eighteen villages clinging to its sides, like a litter of young animals at their mother's breasts. Seen from above, where the whole effect was commanded, it was a magnificent spectacle. The ravines were covered with fields of rice and pea-nut.

At 3 p.m. the *Victoria* was face to face with Mount Mendif. As it had been impossible to avoid it, it would have to be cleared. By raising the temperature another 180 degrees, the doctor gave the balloon an additional lift of 1600 lbs and rose over eight thousand feet. This was the greatest elevation attained during the voyage and the temperature became so low that the doctor and his companions were obliged to resort to their rugs. Fergusson was anxious to come down again as soon as possible as the envelope of the balloon showed a tendency to crack. However, he had time to observe the volcanic origin of the mountain, the extinct craters of which were now merely deep abysses. Large accumulations of bird-droppings gave to the sides of the mountain the appearance of limestone. There was enough to fertilise the whole of the United Kingdom.

At five o'clock the *Victoria*, sheltered from the southern winds, was gently following the slopes of the mountain when she came to a stop in a large clearing far from any habitation. As soon as she touched land, precautions were taken to moor her firmly, and Kennedy, gun in hand, dashed down the slope. It was not long before he returned with half a dozen wild duck and a sort of snipe, which Joe dealt with in his best manner. After they had enjoyed a pleasant meal the night was spent in deep sleep.

30

*Mosfeia — The sheik — Denham,
Clapperton and Oudney — Vogel —
The capital of Loggum — Toole
— Becalmed over Kernak — The
governor and his court — The attack
— Incendiary pigeons*

On the following day, the 11th of May, the
Victoria resumed her adventurous journey.
The travellers had the confidence in her that
a sailor has in his ship. In spite of the terrible
hurricanes, tropical heat, hazardous risings,
and even more dangerous descents, she had
always and everywhere come out of her
difficulties successfully. It might be said that
Fergusson guided her with a wave of his
hand. So, though ignorant of where he would
eventually land, the doctor had no further
fears as to the ultimate issue of the voyage. In
this land of savages and fanatics, however,
prudence forced him to take the strictest
precautions; he therefore recommended his
companions to keep their eyes open for
anything that might happen at any moment.

The wind bore them on a slightly more

northerly course, and about nine o'clock they caught sight of the large town of Mosfeia, built upon an eminence, itself shut in between two mountains. The situation was impregnable, a narrow way between a swamp and a wood providing the sole means of access.

Just at this moment a brilliantly-robed sheik was entering the town, escorted by men on horseback, and preceded by trumpeters and runners who pushed back the branches to make way for him. The doctor came down lower to examine these natives more closely, but as the balloon grew bigger, signs of utter panic showed upon their faces, and they at once made off at full speed. The sheik alone stood his ground. Picking up his long musket he cocked it and waited proudly. The doctor approached to within fifty yards of him and in his best manner greeted him in Arabic. At these words out of the sky the sheik alighted from his horse and prostrated himself in the dust of the road. The doctor was unable to distract him from his worship.

'These people can't help but take us for supernatural beings,' the doctor said. 'The first Europeans they saw they took for a super-human race. When this sheik tells his story he is sure to embroider it with all the resources of an Arab's imagination. You can guess the sort of legend that will be woven around us.'

'That might be a nuisance,' replied Kennedy. 'In the interests of civilisation it would be better to be taken for ordinary men. It would give these niggers a different idea of European power.'

'I agree, Dick. But what can we do? At whatever length you explained to the local wise men the mechanism of a balloon, they would never understand you. They would cling to the idea of supernatural intervention.'

'You were talking about the first Europeans to explore this country, sir,' said Joe. 'Who were they, if I may ask?'

'My dear fellow, we are on the very road followed by Major Denham. It was at Mosfeia that he was received by the Sultan of Mandara. He had come from Bornu and was accompanying the sheik on an expedition against the Fellahs. He witnessed the attack on the town, which put up a brave resistance with their arrows against the muskets of the Arabs, and routed the sheik's troops. It was all merely a pretext for murder, pillage and raids. The major was robbed of all he had, even his clothing; and if he hadn't managed to slip under his horse's belly and escape from his conquerors at a desperate gallop, he would never have got back to Kuka, the capital of Bornu.'

'But who was this Major Denham?'

'A brave Englishman who between 1822 and 1824 commanded an expedition into Bornu, accompanied by Captain Clapperton and Dr Oudney. They left Tripoli in March, reached Murzuk, the capital of Fezzan, followed the road later taken by Dr Barth to return to Europe, and arrived in Kuka, near Lake Tchad, on the 16th of February, 1823. Denham explored Bornu, Mandara, and the east shore of the lake, while, on the 15th of December, 1823, Captain Clapperton and Dr Oudney penetrated the Sudan as far as Sakatu, Oudney dying of exhaustion in Murmur.'

'So this part of Africa has contributed a large number of victims to science?' observed Kennedy.

'Yes, it's a deadly district. We're making straight for the kingdom of Baghirmi that Vogel crossed in 1836 on his way to Wadai, where he disappeared. The young fellow — he was only twenty-three — was sent to join Dr Barth. They met on the 1st of December, 1854, and Vogel then began his exploration of the country. In his last letters, about 1856, he announced his intention of surveying the kingdom of Wadai, where no European had then set foot. He appears to have got as far as Wara, the capital, where, according to some, he was taken prisoner, others saying he was put to death for attempting to climb a sacred mountain in the neighbourhood. But it doesn't do to be in a hurry to assume the death of an explorer, for that prevents a search being made. Dr Barth's death, for instance, was officially announced times without number, which often caused him justifiable irritation. So it is very possible that Vogel is still in the hands of the Sultan of Wadai, who would have hopes of getting a ransom for him. Baron Neimans was starting for Wadai when he died at Cairo, in 1855. We now know that von Heuglin, with the Leipzig expedition, is on Vogel's track, so we ought soon to have definite news about the fate of this interesting young traveller.'[1]

Mosfeia had long since vanished beyond the horizon. Mandara was displaying its amazing fertility, with its forests of acacia, red-blossomed locust and plantations of cotton and indigo. The Shari, which empties itself into Lake Tchad eighty miles away, swept on its impetuous course. The doctor traced it for his companions on Barth's maps.

'You see,' he said, 'the work of this able

---

[1] Letters addressed from El Obeid written by Munzinger, the new chief of the expedition, after the doctor's departure, unfortunately leave no doubt about Vogel's death.

man is extremely accurate. We are heading straight for the Loggum district, and perhaps even for Kernak, the capital. That's where poor Toole died, hardly twenty-two. He was a young Englishman, a subaltern of the 80th Regiment who, a few weeks before, had joined Major Denham in Africa, where he so soon met his death. This great country may well be called the white man's grave.'

Canoes, about fifty feet long, were making their way down the Shari. At a height of a thousand feet the *Victoria* attracted little attention from the natives, but the wind, which hitherto had been blowing pretty strongly, showed a tendency to drop.

'Are we going to be becalmed again?' said the doctor.

'Never mind, sir. At any rate, we needn't be afraid of the desert, and we shan't run short of water.'

'No, but the people here are more formidable still.'

'Look,' said Joe. 'There's something that looks like a town.'

'It's Kernak. The wind will just manage to get us there and, if we like, we shall be able to make an exact plan of it.'

'Can't we get down nearer?' asked Kennedy.

'Nothing easier, Dick. We're right over the town. Let me lower the burner a little and we'll soon be down.'

Half an hour later the *Victoria* was hanging motionless two hundred feet from the ground.

'We are now nearer to Kernak than a man on the dome of St Paul's would be to London,' said the doctor, 'so we can view it at our ease.'

'What's that hammering noise all over the place?'

Joe looked carefully and saw that the noise was made by large numbers of weavers in the open air beating their cloth, which was stretched out on enormous tree trunks.

The capital of Loggum could now be seen in its entirety, as on an unfolded map. It was a real town, with rows of houses and fairly broad streets. In the middle of a large square a slave-market was in progress. Buyers were numerous, for the Mandarans, who have very small hands and feet, are much sought after and fetch high prices. When the *Victoria* was sighted, there was a recurrence of the effect she had already so often produced. It began with shouting, which gave place to dumbfounded amazement. Business was abandoned, work interrupted, and the place relapsed into silence. The travellers remained perfectly still and observed every detail of this populous city. They even came down within sixty feet of the ground, whereupon the ruler of Loggum emerged from his residence, accompanied by musicians blowing into harsh buffalo horns in a way that seemed certain to burst everything except their own lungs. He unfurled his green standard. The crowd gathered round him. Dr Fergusson tried to make himself heard, but in vain. These people, with their high foreheads, closely curling hair and almost aquiline noses, looked proud and intelligent, but the presence of the *Victoria* seemed to have a strangely disturbing effect upon them. Horsemen could be seen galloping in all directions, and it soon became evident that the chief's troops were being mustered to deal with this extraordinary enemy. It was no use for Joe to wave handkerchiefs of every conceivable colour; he produced no effect.

Meanwhile the sheik, surrounded by his court, called for silence and declaimed a speech of which the doctor could not understand a word. It was a mixture of Arabic and Baghirmi. From the universal language of gesture, however, he realised that it was a definite invitation to go away. He would have asked nothing better, but the absence of wind made it impossible. His standing still exasperated the sheik, and the courtiers began to scream to try and frighten the monster away.

These courtiers were odd-looking fellows,

in their vividly-striped robes. They had enormous stomachs, some being quite pot-bellied. The doctor surprised his companions by telling them that this was a way of doing honour to the sultan. The rotundity of the stomach indicated the degree of ambition of its owner. These corpulent fellows gesticulated and shouted; especially one, who, if his dimensions had met with their just reward, must have been the prime minister. The negro crowd mingled their shrieks with those of the court and mimicked their gesticulations like monkeys, ten thousand arms waving as one.

These efforts at intimidation being apparently found inadequate, more drastic methods were adopted. Soldiers armed with bows and arrows ranged themselves in battle order. But the *Victoria* had already been dilated and quietly rose out of range. The governor seized a musket and levelled it at the balloon, but Kennedy was watching him, and a bullet from his carbine smashed the weapon in the sheik's hand. This unexpected coup produced a general rout. Every man bolted into his hut, and for the rest of the day the town remained completely deserted.

Night fell, but the wind still refused to blow. They had to reconcile themselves to hanging suspended three hundred feet above the ground. Not a light relieved the darkness. A silence reigned like that of death. The doctor redoubled his alertness; this calm might conceal a trap. He was right to keep on the lookout, for about midnight the whole town burst into a blaze of light. Hundreds of fiery lines intersected one another like rockets, forming a network of flame.

'That's odd!' said the doctor.

'But, God forgive me, it looks as though the fire was rising towards us,' said Kennedy.

It was true. Amid the din of dreadful shrieks and the crash of muskets this mass of fire was rising towards the *Victoria*. Joe got ready to throw out ballast, but Fergusson soon found the explanation of the phenomenon. Thousands of pigeons with some inflammable material fixed to their tails had been launched against the *Victoria*. In terror they flew upward, striping the air with zigzags of fire, Kennedy got ready to fire his whole armament into the middle of the mass, but what could he do against such a countless army? Already the pigeons were round the car and the balloon, whose envelope, reflecting the light, seemed to be caught in a mesh of fire.

Without hesitation the doctor threw out a lump of quartz and was soon out of reach of this dangerous attack. Two hours later the birds could be still seen flashing through the night, then gradually their numbers diminished, and finally they could be seen no more.

'Now we can sleep in peace,' said the doctor.

'Not a bad idea for savages,' Joe remarked.

'Yes; pigeons are often used to set fire to the thatch of villages, but this time the village flew higher even than those fiery messengers.'

'There's no doubt about it: a balloon has no enemies to fear,' said Kennedy.

'Oh, hasn't it!' the doctor answered.

'What, then?'

'The carelessness of its crew; so keep a good look-out, my friends, everywhere and always.'

31

They set off in the dark — Still three
— Kennedy's instincts — Precautions
— The course of the Shari — Lake Tchad
— The water — The hippopotamus
— A wasted bullet

About three in the morning Joe, whose watch it was, at last saw the town moving away from below their feet. The *Victoria* was off again. Kennedy and the doctor woke up, and the latter, consulting his compass, was glad to see that the wind was bearing them north-northeast.

'We're in luck,' he said. 'Everything's going in our favour. We shall sight Lake Tchad before the day's out.'

'Is it a big lake?' Kennedy asked.

'It's a good size, Dick. At its longest and broadest it must measure a hundred and twenty miles.'

'It'll be a bit of a change to travel over water.'

'But I don't think we've anything to grumble at. We've had a good deal of change and the best possible conditions.'

'No doubt, Samuel; except for the trying time in the desert, we haven't met with any serious danger.'

'There's no doubt the good old *Victoria* has behaved wonderfully. Today is the 12th of May, and we left on the 18th of April. That makes twenty-five days. Another ten and we'll be there.'

'Where?'

'I've no idea. But what does it matter?'

'You're right, Sam. We can rely on Providence to guide us and keep us fit, as has been the case so far. We don't look as though we had crossed the most pestilent country in the world.'

'We could always rise, and that's what we've done.'

'Give me a balloon, every time!' cried Joe. 'Here we are after twenty-five days, healthy, well-fed and rested; perhaps over-rested, for my legs are beginning to get rusty, and I shouldn't be sorry to stretch them with a thirty-mile walk.'

'You'll be able to do that through the streets of London, Joe. But after all, we started out as three, like Denham, Clapperton and Overweg, and like Barth, Richardson and Vogel; but we've been luckier than they were, and there are still three of us. But it's very important we shouldn't separate. If the

284

Victoria had to rise to escape some sudden danger while one of us was on the ground, it's quite likely we should never see each other again. I must tell you frankly, Kennedy, that I don't like you going off shooting.'

'But surely you don't want me to give it up, Samuel. There's no harm in replenishing our supplies and, besides, before we left you made me imagine a whole lot of splendid hunting and up to now I've done very little in that line.'

'You're forgetting your successes, Dick; or perhaps it's your modesty. If I remember right, not to mention small game, you already have an antelope, an elephant and two lions on your conscience.'

'Oh, yes. But what's that to an African sportsman who has to watch all the animals of creation wandering in front of his gun? Hello! Just look at that herd of giraffe!'

'Those, giraffes?' said Joe. 'They're no bigger than your fist.'

'That's because we're a thousand feet above them, but from close to, you'd see they are three times your height.'

'And what about that herd of gazelle?' Kennedy went on, 'and those ostriches legging it like the wind?'

'Ostriches!' said Joe. 'They're hens, just ordinary hens!'

'Come, Samuel, can't we get a bit closer?'

'We can, Dick, but we're not going to land. After all, what's the good of shooting them when they're no use to you? I could understand wanting to kill a lion, or a tiger-cat, or a hyena; that would always make one dangerous animal the less. But to shoot an antelope or a gazelle simply for the empty satisfaction of your hunting instincts really isn't worth while. After all, old man, we're going to keep at a hundred feet, and if you spot a fierce animal we shall be glad to watch you put a bullet in its heart.'

The *Victoria* was gradually dropping but still kept at a comfortable height. In this wild and thickly-populated country it was necessary to be on the look-out for unexpected dangers.

The travellers were now directly following the Shari, whose delightful banks were buried beneath leafy trees of many shades. Lianas and climbing plants wound in all directions, producing strange combinations of colour. Crocodiles disported themselves in the sunshine or dived under the water with the agility of lizards, landing again on the numerous green islands that broke the course of the river. Covered with this rich, luxuriant nature the surroundings of Mafate passed below them. About nine o'clock in the morning Dr Fergusson and his friends at last reached the southern shore of Lake Tchad. Here at last was this Caspian Sea of Africa whose existence had so long been relegated to the realms of fable; this inland sea touched only by the expeditions of Denham and Barth. The doctor attempted to establish its present configuration, which differed widely from that of 1847. In fact, it is impossible to make a chart of this lake. It is surrounded by spongy, almost impassable swamps in which Barth almost perished. From year to year these marshes, which are covered with reeds and papyrus fifteen feet high, merge into the lake itself. Often, even the very towns spread along its shores are submerged, as happened in 1856 to Ngornu. Where hippopotami and alligators now dive was once the site of Bornu dwellings.

The sun shone brilliantly on the tranquil water, which to northward stretched as far as the eye could see. The doctor was anxious to sample the water, which has long been thought to be salt. There was no danger in coming down to the surface of the lake, so the car skimmed over it like a bird at a height of five feet. Joe dipped a bottle in and brought it up again half full. It was tasted and found hardly drinkable, with a slight flavour of natron.

While the doctor was noting down the

result of his experiment a shot rang out beside him. Kennedy had been unable to resist a desire to fire at an enormous hippopotamus. The animal, which was breathing peacefully on the surface, vanished at the noise of the report, and the sportsman's conical bullet did not seem to have had any other effect.

'We ought to have harpooned him, sir,' said Joe.

'And how?'

'With one of the anchors. It would have made the right sort of hook for an animal like that.'

'That's really rather a good idea of Joe's — ' said Kennedy.

'Which I'll ask you not to put into practice,' replied the doctor. 'The beast would soon have us away where we didn't want to go.'

'Especially now we've settled the quality of the Tchad water. Is that kind of fish eatable, Dr Fergusson?'

'That fish, as you call it, Joe, is a pachydermatous mammal. Its flesh is said to be excellent, and a good deal of trade is carried on in it between the tribes on the shores of the lake.'

'Well, in that case, I'm sorry Mr Kennedy didn't have better luck.'

'These animals are only vulnerable in the

belly and between the thighs. Mr Kennedy's bullet won't have made the least impression. But if the landing looks good we'll halt at the northern end of the lake. You'll find a regular menagerie, Kennedy, and can blaze away as you like.'

'Good!' said Joe. 'I hope you'll have a try at the hippopotamus. I'd like to taste the meat. It certainly doesn't seem natural to cross the centre of Africa and live on woodcock and partridges, just as if you were in England.'

32

The capital of Bornu — The Biddiomah Islands — Vultures — The doctor's anxiety — His precautions — An attack in mid-air — The envelope torn — The drop — Splendid devotion — The northern shore of the lake

Since reaching Lake Tchad the *Victoria* had fallen in with a breeze veering more to the west and a few clouds then tempered the heat of the day. Over the water the air had been fresh, but about one o'clock the balloon, having crossed this part of the lake diagonally, travelled for another seven or eight miles over land. The doctor was at first disappointed at this change of direction but forgot his grievance when he saw Kuka, the famous capital of Bornu. He had a momentary glimpse of the town girdled with its walls of white clay. A few crude mosques rose clumsily above the group of Arab houses which looked like a collection of dice. In the courtyards of the houses and in the public squares, palms and rubber-trees grew, crowned by a dome of foliage over a hundred feet wide. Joe pointed out that these

290

huge parasols were appropriate to the intensity of the sun and drew conclusions flattering to Providence.

Kuka really consisted of two distinct towns separated by the 'Dendal,' a broad boulevard six hundred yards long, now thronged with pedestrians and horsemen. On one side the rich part of the town flaunts its lofty well-ventilated dwellings, while on the other is huddled the poor quarter, a dismal collection of low, conical huts, where a needy population vegetates, for Kuka is neither a commercial nor an industrial centre.

Kennedy thought it looked like Edinburgh situated in a plain, with its two perfectly defined towns. But the travellers were hardly able to obtain more than a fleeting glimpse, for, with the suddenness which is characteristic of the air-currents of this district, a contrary wind seized hold of them and brought them back some forty miles over Lake Tchad.

The view was now completely changed. They could count the many islands of the lake, which are inhabited by the Biddiomahs, blood-thirsty pirates who are as much feared in the district as the Tuaregs in the Sahara. These savages were getting ready to give the *Victoria* a formidable reception with arrows and stones, but she soon left the islands

291

behind, flitting over them like a gigantic insect. Joe, who was watching the horizon, turned to Kennedy and said: 'My word, Mr Kennedy; you're always dreaming about shooting, there's something in your line.'

'What is it, Joe?'

'And this time my master won't interfere.'

'But what is it?'

'Don't you see that flock of big birds flying towards us?'

'Birds?' said the doctor, seizing his glass.

'I see them,' Kennedy replied. 'There's at least a dozen of them.'

'Fourteen, sir, begging your pardon,' Joe remarked.

'It's only to be hoped they're of a kind dangerous enough to prevent the humane Fergusson from interfering.'

'I shall have no objection,' replied Fergusson, 'but I'd rather they were not there.'

'You're not afraid of them, sir?' said Joe.

'They're bearded vultures, unusually big ones, and if they attack us — '

'Well, we'll put up a good fight, Samuel. We've a useful arsenal for their reception. I don't think they can be very formidable.'

'We'll see,' the doctor replied.

Ten minutes later the flock had come within range and the fourteen birds were making the air re-echo with their raucous cries. They swept towards the *Victoria*, more angry than frightened.

'What a din!' said Joe. 'I don't suppose they like us trespassing on their country and making bold to fly like they do.'

'They certainly look pretty fierce,' said Kennedy. 'They'd be nasty if they were armed with Purdey Moores!'

'They don't need them,' replied Fergusson, who had become very grave.

The vultures were circling through wide arcs which gradually narrowed round the *Victoria*. They drove through the sky at incredible speed, every now and again dashing straight at the balloon with the swiftness of a bullet. The doctor, filled with anxiety, decided to rise to escape from their dangerous proximity. He expanded the hydrogen and the balloon soon began to climb. But the vultures climbed with her, showing little inclination to leave her.

'They don't seem to like the look of us,' said Kennedy, cocking his carbine. The birds were indeed coming closer, and several, less than fifty feet away, seemed to be defying Kennedy's gun.

'I'm itching terribly to have a shot at them,' he said.

'No, no, Dick. Don't infuriate them if you can help it. You'd only make them attack us.'

'But I can easily deal with them.'

'You're wrong, Dick.'

'We've a bullet for each of them.'

'And suppose they made a dash at the upper part of the balloon, how should we get at them? Imagine yourself faced with a lot of lions on land or sharks in mid-ocean. The present position is just as dangerous for us.'

'Do you really mean that, Samuel?'

'I do, Dick.'

'In that case, let's wait.'

'Yes, wait. Get ready for an attack but don't fire unless I tell you.'

The birds were now massing quite a short distance away. Their naked throats, distended by the effort of their screams could be clearly seen, as well as their gristly crests, covered with purple spots and erect with anger. They were of the largest size, their bodies more than three feet long, and the inner side of their white wings shone in the sunlight. They looked alarmingly like a shoal of winged sharks.

'They're coming after us,' said the doctor, seeing them rise with the balloon. 'It's no good going up; they can fly higher than we can.'

'Well, what are we going to do?' Kennedy asked.

The doctor made no reply.

'Look here, Samuel,' the Scotsman went on, 'there are fourteen of these birds. We can put in seventeen shots if we fire all our guns. Shan't we manage to wipe them out or, at any rate, scatter them? I'll undertake to settle a certain number.'

'I'm not questioning your skill, Dick. I'm quite ready to regard all you aim at as dead; but I repeat, they've only to attack the upper half of the balloon and they'll be out of your sight. They'll tear the envelope which holds us up, and we've three thousand feet to fall.'

Just then one of the most savage of the birds darted straight at the *Victoria*, beak and claws open, ready to bite and tear.

'Shoot!' cried the doctor.

The word was hardly out of his mouth when the bird, struck dead, was hurtling downwards through space. Kennedy had seized one of the double-barrelled guns. Joe had the other at his shoulder. Frightened by the report, the vultures drew away for a moment, but almost at once returned to the charge with terrific fury. With his first shot Kennedy broke the neck of the nearest. Joe smashed the wing of the next.

'Only eleven more,' he said. But the birds now changed their tactics and with one accord rose above the *Victoria*. Kennedy looked at Fergusson. In spite of his courage and coolness the latter turned pale. There was a moment of awful silence. Then they heard the hiss of tearing silk and the car began to drop from below their feet.

'We're done!' cried Fergusson, casting a glance at the barometer, which was shooting up rapidly. Then he added: 'Ballast, throw out ballast!'

In a few seconds every lump of quartz had gone overboard. 'We're still dropping! . . . Empty the water cans! . . . Joe, do you hear? . . . We're dropping into the lake!'

Joe obeyed. The doctor leaned over. The lake seemed to be rushing towards him like a rising tide. Objects on the ground were growing perceptibly bigger. The car was only two hundred feet from the surface of Lake Tchad.

'The stores! The stores!' cried the doctor, and the box containing them was hurled into space. The fall became less rapid but they were still falling.

'Go on, throw out something else!' the doctor cried once more.

'There is nothing,' said Kennedy.

'Yes, there is,' Joe replied laconically, and with a rapid wave of his hand, he vanished over the side of the car.

'Joe! Joe!' yelled the doctor. But Joe was out of earshot. The *Victoria*, relieved of his weight, started upwards again and reached a height of a thousand feet, while the wind blowing into the deflated envelope bore her towards the northern shores of the lake.

'He's done for,' said Kennedy, with a gesture of despair.

'To save us,' Fergusson replied. And these strong men felt the tears running down their cheeks. They leaned over in an effort to see some sign of poor Joe, but they were already far away.

'What's to be done now?' asked Kennedy.

'Drop to the ground as soon as possible, Dick, and then wait.'

After travelling sixty miles the *Victoria* came down on a deserted shore at the north end of the lake. The anchors caught a low tree and Kennedy made them fast. Night came on, but neither Fergusson nor Kennedy could sleep for a moment.

33

*Conjectures — Re-establishing the
equilibrium of the Victoria — Fergusson's
fresh calculations — Kennedy goes shooting — Complete exploration of Lake
Tchad — Tangalia — The return — Lari*

The next day, the 13th of May, the travellers
at once recognised the part of the shore in
which they were. It was a sort of island of
firm ground in the middle of a huge swamp.
Around this patch of solid earth stood reeds
as big as trees in Europe, stretching as far as
the eye could see. These impassable swamps
established the position of the *Victoria*
beyond all doubt. It was only necessary to
observe the shores of the lake; the great
stretch of water broadened out continuously,
especially in the east, and nothing appeared
on the horizon, neither shore nor island. The
two friends had not yet ventured to speak of
their unfortunate companion. Kennedy was
the first to give expression to his conjectures.

'Joe may not be lost,' he said. 'He's a clever
fellow and can swim like a fish. He used to
have no difficulty in swimming across the

Firth of Forth at Edinburgh. He'll turn up again, though I don't know when or how. But we must leave no stone unturned to give him a chance to rejoin us.'

'Heaven grant you're right!' the doctor replied, much moved. 'We'll go round the world to find him. First let's see how we stand. The first thing is to rid the *Victoria* of this outer envelope, which is now useless. We shall be getting rid of a considerable weight, six hundred and fifty pounds, so it's worth the trouble.'

They got to work, but found themselves faced with serious difficulties. The tough silk had to be torn away strip by strip, and the strips had to be cut very small to get them through the meshes of the net. The rent made by the birds was several feet long.

This operation took quite four hours, but at last the inner balloon was completely freed and it appeared to have suffered no damage. The size of the *Victoria* was now reduced by a fifth, the difference being marked enough to surprise Kennedy

'Will it be big enough?' he asked Fergusson.

'You need have no anxiety on that score, Dick. I'll put the equilibrium right again and, if poor Joe returns, we'll manage to continue our route with him on board as well.'

'If I remember right, when we fell we

weren't very far off an island.'

'Yes, I remember. But that island, like all the islands of Lake Tchad, is sure to be inhabited by a gang of pirates and cut-throats. They're sure to have seen our disaster, and if Joe falls into their hands, unless superstition comes to his rescue, what will happen to him?'

'As I said before, you can trust him to find a way out. I'll back his skill and brains.'

'I hope you're right. Now, Dick, you go and do a little shooting round about, but don't go far away. It has become very necessary for us to replenish our stores, for we've thrown away the greater part of them.'

'All right, Samuel. I'll not be long.'

Kennedy took a double-barrelled gun and plunged into the tall grass, making for a copse not far away. Frequent reports soon told the doctor that the sport was good. Meanwhile he was busy taking stock of the things still left in the car and establishing the equilibrium of the second balloon. There remained about thirty pounds of pemmican, a supply of tea and coffee, about a gallon and a half of brandy and an empty water container. All the dried meat had gone.

The doctor knew that, owing to the loss of the hydrogen in the other balloon, his lifting force was reduced by about 900 lbs. He had therefore to work on this difference in re-establishing his equilibrium. The new *Victoria* had a capacity of 67,000 cubic feet and contained 33,480 cubic feet of gas. The expanding gear seemed in good order. Neither the battery nor the spiral seemed to have been damaged. The lift of the new balloon was therefore about 3000 lbs. Adding together the weight of the apparatus, the passengers, the water, the car and its accessories, and allowing for a further addition of fifty gallons of water and a hundred pounds of fresh meat, the doctor arrived at a total of 2830 lbs. He could therefore carry seventy pounds of ballast for emergencies and the balloon would be in equilibrium with the surrounding air.

He made his plans accordingly, replacing Joe's weight by extra ballast. These various preparations occupied the whole day and were brought to an end as Kennedy returned. The sportsman had had a good day and brought back a regular load of geese, wild duck, woodcock, snipe, teal and plover. He set about dressing the game and smoking it. Each bird, spitted on a thin stick, was hung over a fire of green wood, and when they seemed ready to Kennedy, who incidentally knew what he was about, they were all stowed in the car. The following morning he finished off the provisioning.

Night found the pair still at work. Their supper consisted of pemmican, biscuits and tea. Fatigue, which had first given them appetite, now gave them sleep. During his watch, each searched the darkness and at times thought he heard Joe's voice. Unfortunately that voice they longed to hear was far away. At the first glimmer of daylight Fergusson woke Kennedy.

'I've been trying for a long time to think what is the best thing to do to find Joe,' he said.

'I'll fall in with whatever you've decided, Samuel. Tell me.'

'First and foremost, it's important that Joe should have news of us.'

'Of course. It would be awful if the good fellow thought we were deserting him!'

'Not he, he knows us too well. Such an idea would never cross his mind, but he must know where we are.'

'But how?'

'We'll get back into the car and go up.'

'What if the wind carries us away?'

'Luckily it won't. Look, Dick. The breeze will take us back over the lake, and if that was a nuisance yesterday it's in our favour today. All we shall have to try to do, then, is to keep over this big stretch of water all day. Joe can't fail to see us. He'll be looking out all the time. We may even manage to find out where he is.'

'Provided he's alone and free, he certainly will look out.'

'And if he's a prisoner,' the doctor replied, 'as these natives don't as a rule shut their prisoners up, he'll see us and realise what we're trying to do.'

'But after all,' Kennedy resumed, — 'for we must take everything into account, — what are we to do if we find no sign, if he's left no trace?'

'We shall have to try to get back to the north end of the lake, keeping in sight as far as possible. We'll wait there and explore the banks on that side, which Joe will certainly make for, and we won't leave before we've done all we can to find him.'

'Let's get away, then,' said Kennedy.

The doctor took the exact position of this strip of firm ground that they were leaving. From his map he estimated that it was north of Lake Tchad, between the town of Lari and the village of Ingemini, both of which had been visited by Major Denham. Meanwhile Kennedy completed his supplies of fresh meat. Although the surrounding marshes showed traces of rhinoceros, manatee and hippopotamus, he did not fall in with a single one of these huge animals.

At 7 a.m., and not without great difficulties, which Joe had managed to overcome so successfully in the past, the anchors were freed from the tree. The gas expanded and the new *Victoria* rose two hundred feet into the air. She hesitated at first, twisting on her own axis; but in the end, caught in a brisk current, she headed over the lake and was soon travelling at a speed of twenty miles an hour. The doctor continued to keep her at a level varying between two hundred and five hundred feet. Kennedy frequently fired his carbine. Above the islands they dropped perhaps incautiously close, their eyes searching the woods, thickets and undergrowth; everywhere where any shade or rocky cleft might have offered Joe a refuge. They came down also near some long canoes that were crossing the lake. On seeing them, the fishermen threw themselves into the water and swam back to their island in unconcealed terror.

'Two hours gone,' said Kennedy. 'Nothing so far.'

'We must wait, Dick, and keep our hearts up. We can't be far from where the accident took place.'

By one o'clock the *Victoria* had travelled ninety miles, when she encountered a fresh current almost at right angles, and this took

304

her sixty miles to eastward. She was now over a very large and thickly populated island which the doctor took to be Farram, where the capital of the Biddiomahs was situated. They expected to see Joe emerge from every bush, running for his life and shouting to them. Had he been free, they could have got him away without difficulty, and even if he had been a prisoner, they could have repeated the manœuvre employed in the case of the missionary. But nothing appeared, nothing stirred. It seemed hopeless.

At 2.30 the *Victoria* came in sight of Tangalia, a village on the eastern shore of the lake which marked the extreme point reached by Denham's expedition. This persistent direction of the wind made the doctor anxious. He felt himself being driven back eastward, towards the centre of Africa, towards the boundless deserts.

'We must certainly halt,' he said, 'and even land. For Joe's sake especially, we must get back over the lake. But first of all, let's try to find a current in the opposite direction.'

For over an hour he tried various zones. The *Victoria* still drifted over terra firma. But at a thousand feet, fortunately, a very strong breeze took them back north-west.

It was impossible that Joe should be kept a prisoner on one of the islands of the lake. He would certainly have found some way of making his presence known. He might have been carried off overland. This was what the doctor thought when once more he came within sight of the northern shore. The idea of Joe's being drowned was inadmissible, but a horrible idea occurred to the two men: alligators abound in these parts! Neither of them, however, had the courage to voice this fear, which was obviously in the minds of both. At last the doctor said bluntly:

'Crocodiles are only to be met with on the shores of the islands or of the lake itself. Joe will be sharp enough to keep out of their way. In any case, they're not very dangerous. The Africans bathe as they like without fear of being attacked.'

Kennedy offered no reply. He preferred to remain silent rather than discuss this terrible possibility. About five o'clock in the evening the doctor pointed out the town of Lari. The inhabitants were working at the cotton harvest outside cabins built of plaited reed in the middle of clean and carefully kept enclosures. This collection of about fifty huts occupied a slight depression in a valley between low mountains. The strength of the wind carried them farther than the doctor wanted, but it shifted a second time and took them back to the exact point of their departure, the island of firm ground where they had spent the preceding night. The anchor, instead of finding the branches of a tree, took hold in some clumps of reed mixed with the thick mud of the marsh and of considerable resistance. The doctor had a good deal of difficulty in checking the balloon, but finally, with nightfall, the wind dropped and the two friends, reduced almost to despair, kept watch together.

34

At three in the morning a gale sprang up, so violent that the *Victoria* could not remain near the ground without danger. The reeds rubbed against her envelope, threatening to tear it.

'We must get off, Dick,' said the doctor. 'We can't stay here.'

'But what about Joe?'

'I'm not going to desert him. I should think not. Even if the gale carries us a hundred miles north we'll come back. But by staying here we shall be risking the safety of all three.'

'I don't like the idea of starting without him,' said the Scotsman in accents of deep regret.

'Do you think it's less hard for me than for you?' Fergusson continued. 'But we can't help ourselves.'

'I'm with you,' Kennedy replied. 'Let's start.'

But starting presented great difficulties. The anchor, which was deeply buried, resisted all their efforts and the balloon, dragging in the opposite direction, made its hold firmer. Kennedy could not get it away. Further, in the existing circumstances, his position grew very dangerous for there was risk of the *Victoria*'s rising before he could rejoin her. The doctor, not wishing to run such a risk, told him to get back into the car and resigned himself to cutting the anchor rope. The *Victoria* leapt three hundred feet and headed due north. Fergusson had to let the storm have its way. He folded his arms and gave himself up to his sad reflections.

After a few moments of complete silence he turned to Kennedy, who was equally silent.

'We may have been tempting Providence,' he said. 'It's not for men to attempt such a voyage.' And he sighed deeply.

'It's only a few days since we were congratulating ourselves on having come through many dangers,' Kennedy replied. 'We all shook hands.'

'Poor Joe; he was a kind-hearted fellow, plucky and straightforward. After his wealth had dazzled him a moment he willingly sacrificed it. Now he's far away and the wind is rapidly taking us farther away still.'

'Come, Samuel, suppose he has found

refuge among the lake tribes. Couldn't he do as the other travellers did, who have been there before us, like Denham and Barth? They got back.'

'But, my dear Dick, Joe doesn't know a word of the language. He's alone and helpless. The travellers you mention only got along by sending the chief lots of presents; besides, they were surrounded by an escort armed and equipped for such expeditions. And even then they couldn't avoid terrible suffering. What do you expect would happen to poor old Joe? It's awful to think of. I'm sorrier about it than I've ever been about anything.'

'But we'll come back, Samuel.'

'Yes, we'll come back, Dick; even if it means abandoning the *Victoria*, coming back to Lake Tchad on foot, and getting into communication with the Sultan of Bornu. The Arabs can't have unpleasant memories of their first European.'

'I'll go with you, Samuel,' Kennedy replied resolutely. 'You can rely on me. We'll give up the rest of the trip if necessary. Joe has sacrificed himself for us. We'll do as much for him.'

This resolve revived their courage somewhat. They felt themselves fortified by the same idea. Fergusson did all he could to find a contrary current that might take him back to the lake, but as yet without success, and besides it was impracticable to land in this denuded country in such a gale.

In this way the *Victoria* passed over the country of the Tibbus. She left behind her Belad el Djerid, a thorny wilderness forming the fringe of the Sudan, and penetrated the sandy desert scored by the long trails of caravans. The last line of vegetation was soon lost on the southern horizon, not far from the chief oasis of that part of Africa, whose fifty wells are shaded by magnificent trees. But it was impossible to stop. An Arab encampment, gaily-striped tents and a few camels stretching their snake-like heads over the sand, broke the solitude, but the *Victoria* passed over it like a shooting star, covering a distance of sixty miles in three hours, with Fergusson helpless to control her course.

'We can't stop,' he said. 'We can't go down. Not a tree. Not a break in the ground! Are we going to cross the whole Sahara like this? Heaven is obviously against us.'

As he uttered these words in impotent exasperation he saw the sands of the desert in the north rising in a dense cloud of dust and twisting under the force of the opposing winds. In the middle of the whirlwind a whole caravan, bruised, broken, and overthrown, was being buried under the avalanche of sand. The horses, thrown into panic, were uttering muffled but heart-rending moans. Shouts and shrieks came from the suffocating mist. From time to time a brightly-coloured garment would flash across the chaos, while the roaring of the wind dominated the whole scene of destruction.

Soon the sand gathered into compact masses and, where shortly before had stretched a smooth plain, there rose a still moving mound, the enormous tomb of the engulfed caravan. The doctor and Kennedy, with pale faces, watched this terrible drama. They had lost all control over their balloon, which was whirled about by the contrary currents and no longer responded to the expansion or contraction of the gas. Caught in the surging air, she twirled with dizzy speed, the car heaving about in all directions. The instruments hanging under the awning were dashed together and threatened to break. The pipes of the spiral bent and seemed ready to snap at any moment. The water containers were hurled crashing from their places. Though only two feet apart, the men could not make themselves heard, while with one hand clutching the rigging they strove to keep on their feet under the fury of the hurricane.

Kennedy, his hair blowing in the wind, looked on without a word. The doctor's courage had revived in the face of danger, and no trace appeared on his face of the tumult of his feelings; not even when, after a final spin, the *Victoria* suddenly came to a standstill in an unexpected lull. The north wind had gained the upper hand and was driving her swiftly but smoothly back over the route travelled during the morning.

'Where are we off to now?' Kennedy shouted.

'Leave that to Providence, Dick. I was wrong to doubt; Providence knows better than we what is best for us, and here we are heading back again towards the places we had given up hope of seeing again.'

The surface of the ground, which had been so smooth as they came, was now broken as by waves after a storm. A succession of ridges, hardly yet settled into stillness, ruffled the surface of the desert. The wind was blowing strongly and the *Victoria* flew through space. The direction followed was somewhat different from that of the morning, so that about nine o'clock, instead of coming back to the shores of Lake Tchad, they saw the desert still stretching before them. Kennedy pointed this out.

'It doesn't matter much,' the doctor

replied. 'The important thing is to be going south. We shall come across the towns of Bornu, Wuddie or Kuka, and I shall not hesitate to stop there.'

'So long as you're satisfied, I am,' Kennedy answered; 'but God grant we shan't be reduced to crossing the desert like those unfortunate Arabs! It was a horrible sight.'

'And it's quite a frequent one, Dick. Crossing the desert is more dangerous than crossing the ocean, for the desert has all the perils of the sea, including that of being swallowed up, and, in addition, intolerable fatigue and privation.'

'It seems to me,' said Kennedy, 'that the wind is showing a tendency to drop. The sand-dust is less dense, the waves of sand are smaller and the horizon is clearing.'

'All the better. We shall have to search it carefully with a glass and let no point escape us.'

'I'll see to that, Samuel, and as soon as the first tree appears I'll let you know.'

And Kennedy, glass in hand, took up a position in the forward part of the car.

35

*Joe's story — The island of the
Biddiomahs — Worship — The engulfed
island — The shores of the lake — Snakes
in a tree — The Victoria passes — The
Victoria disappears — Despair — The
swamp — A last despairing cry*

What had happened to Joe while his master
was making this fruitless search?

When he threw himself into the lake, Joe's
first movement on coming to the surface was
to raise his eyes upwards. He saw the
Victoria, already high above the lake and
mounting rapidly, gradually dwindling. Soon
she was caught in a swift air-current and
disappeared northwards. His master, his
friends, were saved.

'It's lucky I thought of throwing myself
out,' he told himself. 'Mr Kennedy would
have been sure to think of the same thing,
and would certainly have done what I did; for
it's only natural for a man to sacrifice himself
to save two others. It's a matter of arithmetic.'
Reassured on this point, Joe began to think of
himself. He was in the middle of a huge lake,

surrounded by unknown and probably fierce tribes; an additional reason for summoning all his self-reliance to get out of this nasty situation. He did not, however, feel any signs of fear. Before the attack by the vultures, which he had found very natural, he had noticed an island on the horizon. He now decided to make for this and brought to bear all his skill in swimming, after first getting rid of his heavier clothing. A swim of five or six miles was little to him, so while he was in the middle of the lake his one thought was to swim strong and straight. After an hour and a half the distance separating him from the island was considerably diminished. But, as he approached land, a thought which had already passed fleetingly across his mind began to take a firm hold. He knew that the banks of the lake were haunted by enormous alligators of whose voracity he was fully aware. Eager as he always was to find everything in this world natural, the worthy fellow could not shake off a feeling of dismay. He was afraid that white flesh might be particularly to the crocodiles' taste, and therefore went forward with extreme caution, keeping a keen look-out. Hardly was he within a hundred yards of a shady bank, covered with green trees, when a puff of air heavy with the sickly smell of musk reached his nostrils.

'There we are,' he said to himself. 'Just what I was afraid of. There's an alligator somewhere about.'

He dived swiftly, but not sufficiently so to avoid contact with a huge body whose scaly skin scraped against him as it passed. He gave himself up for lost and began to swim with desperate vigour. Reaching the surface, he took a long breath and dived again. Then followed a quarter of an hour of inexpressible anguish which all his philosophy failed to overcome, when he thought he heard behind him the sound of the great jaw ready to snap. He was swimming just below the surface, as quietly as possible, when he felt himself seized, first by the arm and then by the middle of his body.

Poor Joe! His last thought was for his master as he began a struggle of despair. Then he realised that he was being dragged, not towards the bottom of the lake, as is the habit of crocodiles before devouring their prey, but to the surface. Scarcely had he had time to take breath and open his eyes than he found himself between two niggers, black as ebony, who were holding him tightly and uttering strange cries.

'Hello!' Joe could not help exclaiming. 'They're niggers, not crocodiles! That's a jolly sight better! But how can these chaps dare to bathe in these places?'

Joe was unaware that the inhabitants of the islands of Lake Tchad, like many other negroes, dive with impunity into water infested with alligators, paying no heed to their presence. The amphibia of this lake especially have a justified reputation for being harmless.

But had he only fallen out of the frying-pan into the fire? This question he left the event to decide and, as there was no alternative, he allowed himself to be led to the bank without betraying any fear.

'These people must have seen the *Victoria* skimming over the lake like a flying monster,' he said to himself. 'They would see me fall, and they're bound to have some respect for a man who has fallen from Heaven. Let's see what they are going to do.'

He had just reached this point in his reflections when he arrived on land and found himself in the middle of a shrieking mob; men and women of every age but all of the same colour. They belonged to a tribe of Biddiomahs, who are as black as jet. Nor was there any need for him to blush at the scantiness of his costume. He found himself in the height of fashion. But before he had time to take stock of the situation, he saw that he was undoubtedly regarded as an object of worship. This naturally reassured him, in spite of his memory of what had happened at Kazeh.

'I see I'm going to be made a god again, a son of the moon or something! Well, it's as good a job as any when there's no other. The thing is to gain time. If the *Victoria* happens to come back this way I'll make the most of my new position to let my worshippers see a miracle.'

While these thoughts were passing through Joe's mind the crowd closed in on him, prostrated themselves, shouted, touched him and began to grow familiar. At least, however, they were thoughtful enough to offer him a splendid feast of sour milk and rice crushed in honey. The good fellow, making the best of the situation, then had one of the best meals of his life and gave his people an impressive idea of the way the gods eat on great occasions.

When evening came on, the sorcerers of the island took him respectfully by the hand and led him towards a hut surrounded with talismans. Before entering, Joe cast an uneasy glance at the bones that were heaped up round this sanctuary. Moreover, he had plenty of time to reflect on his situation when he was shut up in his cabin.

During the evening and part of the night he

heard festive singing, the throbbing of a sort of drum, and the clang of metal, so sweet to African ears. Yelling in chorus, the natives were performing one of their interminable dances round the sacred cabin, with contortions and grimaces of every conceivable kind. Joe could hear the deafening din through the walls of his hut which were built of mud and reeds. No doubt under any other circumstances these strange ceremonies would have afforded him considerable interest, but his mind soon became racked by a very unpleasant idea. Though trying to look on the bright side of things, he found it dull and even depressing to be lost in this savage country in the middle of such people. Of the men who had ventured into these parts few had come home again. Moreover, could he rely on this worship of which he found himself the object? He had good reason to believe in the vanity of human greatness. He wondered whether in this country adoration might not be pushed to the point of eating the adored one. In spite of the outlook, after some hours of reflection fatigue got the better of his black thoughts and Joe fell into a fairly deep sleep, which no doubt would have lasted until daybreak had not an unexpected sensation of damp awakened the sleeper. The damp soon became water, and this water rose until he was immersed as far as the waist. 'What on earth's this?' he wondered. 'A flood; a cloud-burst; or a new torture invented by these niggers? I'm hanged if I'll wait till it gets up to my neck!' So saying, he burst through the wall with a blow from his shoulder and found himself in the middle of the lake. Of the island there was not a trace; it had been submerged during the night. In its place was the immensity of Lake Tchad. 'A nice country for land-owners!' Joe said to himself, beginning to swim vigorously.

The good fellow had been delivered by a phenomenon not infrequent on Lake Tchad. More than one island, apparently as solid as rock, had vanished in this way, the unfortunate survivors of these terrible catastrophes being frequently rescued by the dwellers on the shore. Joe did not know this custom, but he did not fail to take advantage of it. Catching sight of a stray canoe, he quickly swam to it. It was a trunk of a tree crudely hollowed out. Fortunately it contained a pair of paddles and Joe, making use of a fairly rapid current, let himself drift.

'Let's see where we are,' he mused. 'The North Star will help me. It's always ready to show the way north to anybody.'

He noted with satisfaction that the current was carrying him toward the north shore of the lake, and he let himself go. About two in the morning he set foot on a promontory covered with thorny reeds, which seemed unduly searching even to a philosopher. But he found a tree specially designed to offer him a bed in its branches. For greater safety Joe climbed it and, without sleeping much, awaited the dawn.

When morning broke, with the swiftness characteristic of equatorial regions, Joe cast a glance over the tree which had sheltered him during the night. A somewhat astonishing spectacle struck terror into his heart. The branches of this tree were literally swarming with snakes and chameleons. They completely hid the foliage. It was like some new species of tree bringing forth reptiles. The whole mass crawled and twisted in the first rays of the sun. Joe experienced a feeling of terror mingled with loathing and threw himself to the ground amidst the hissing of the creatures.

'Well, who'd have believed that!' he said.

He did not know that Dr Vogel's last letters had reported this peculiarity of the shores of the Tchad, where reptiles are more numerous than in any other country in the world. After what he had seen, Joe decided to be more circumspect in future and, taking his direction by the sun, set out north-east. He was very careful to avoid cabins and huts, or in fact anything that could serve as a receptacle for human beings.

His eyes were constantly fixed on the sky. He hoped to catch sight of the *Victoria*, and though he searched in vain during that day's march, his confidence in his master did not flag. He must have had great force of character to accept his situation so philosophically. Hunger began to join forces with fatigue, for a man cannot renew his strength on a diet of roots or the sap of such shrubs as the *mele* or the fruit of the doum palm, and meanwhile, according to his reckoning, he had travelled about thirty miles westward. Many parts of his body were scored by the thousands of thorns which bristle on the reeds of the lake, the acacia and mimosa, and his bleeding feet made walking extremely painful. But he managed to hold out against his sufferings, and when night came on he decided to spend it on the shores of the lake. There he had to suffer the maddening stings of myriads of insects, for flies, mosquitoes and ants half an inch long literally covered the ground. After two hours there was not a shred left of Joe's scanty clothing; the insects had devoured it completely. It was a terrible night which brought not an hour's sleep to the weary traveller. Meanwhile wild boars, buffaloes and ajoubs, a rather dangerous kind of sea-cow, plunged about in the bushes and beneath the waters of the lake, their fierce cries making the night hideous. Joe did not dare to stir, though his resignation and patience were hard put to it to cope with such a situation.

At last it was day again and Joe got up hurriedly. His disgust can be imagined when he saw what a loathsome creature had shared his bed — a toad five inches long, a monstrous, repulsive beast, was staring at him with its great round eyes. Joe felt sick and, his horror reviving some of his strength, he dashed off and plunged into the waters of the lake. This bath calmed somewhat the hunger that tortured him and, after chewing a few leaves, he set out again with a dogged stubbornness for which he found it difficult to account. He was no longer acting consciously, and yet he felt within himself a power that raised him above despair.

Meanwhile he was tortured by terrible hunger. His stomach, less resigned than himself, began to complain. He was forced to tie a creeper tightly round his body. Fortunately he could quench his thirst at any moment, and when he remembered his sufferings in the desert, he found comparative comfort in being spared the torture of this imperative need.

'Where can the *Victoria* be?' he asked himself. 'The wind's from the north. It should bring her back over the lake. Dr Fergusson is sure to have overhauled the balloon, but yesterday ought to have been enough for that. It's quite possible that today — but I'd better go on as though I was never going to see them again. After all, if I managed to get to one of the big towns of the lake, I'd be in the same position as the travellers my master told us about. Why shouldn't I get out of it all like they did? Hang it all, some of them got back! . . . Come on. We must buck up.'

Musing thus and going ahead all the time through the forest, brave Joe suddenly found himself in the middle of a group of savages. He stopped in time and was not seen. The negroes were busy poisoning their arrows with the juice of the euphorbia as the people of this region do; they make a kind of solemn ceremony of it.

Standing perfectly motionless and holding his breath, Joe lay hidden in the midst of a copse where, raising his eyes, he saw through a gap in the foliage the *Victoria* — the *Victoria* herself — making for the lake hardly a hundred feet above him. It was impossible to attract her attention. A tear came into his eye, not of despair, but of gratitude. His master was looking for him, was not deserting him! He had only to wait for the departure of the blacks and then he would be able to leave his retreat and run to the lake side.

But the *Victoria* was now lost in the distance. Joe resolved to wait for her. She would be sure to come back. She did so, in fact, farther westward. Joe ran, waved his arms and shouted — but all in vain. A violent wind was driving the balloon along at tremendous speed. For the first time, courage and hope failed the poor fellow. He gave himself up for lost. He thought his master was now gone for ever. He dared not think; he tried to keep the subject away from his mind.

Like a madman, feet bleeding, body bruised, he walked the whole day and part of the night, dragging himself along, at times on his hands and knees. He saw the time coming when his strength would fail him, and then it would be the end. Labouring along like this, he at last found himself facing a swamp, or rather what he knew to be a swamp, for it had been dark for several hours. Without warning he found himself involved in clinging mud. In spite of his efforts, in spite of his despairing struggles, he felt himself being dragged down little by little into the sticky ooze. A few minutes later it was up to his waist.

'This is death,' he thought; 'and what a death! . . . '

He struggled frenziedly, but his efforts only served to bury the poor fellow deeper in the grave he was making for himself. There was not the smallest bit of wood to stop himself with, not a reed to take hold of! . . . He realised that the end had come . . . His eyes closed.

'Master! Sir! Help! . . . ' he cried. And this lonely cry of despair, already stifled, died away into the night.

36

Since taking up his post of observation in the front of the car, Kennedy had not ceased to scan the horizon with close attention. After some time he turned to the doctor and said: 'Unless I'm mistaken, there's a band of men or animals moving over there. It's impossible to make them out yet. But in any case they're moving quickly for they're raising a cloud of dust.'

'Might it not be a contrary wind?' said Fergusson. 'A sand storm coming to drive us back north?' And he got up to look.

'I don't think so, Samuel,' Kennedy replied. 'It's a herd of gazelle or buffalo.'

'Perhaps, Dick; but they're at least nine or ten miles from us and I can make nothing of them even with the glasses.'

'In any case I shan't lose sight of them.

There's something curious going on that puzzles me. At times it looks like cavalry manœuvring. Ah! I was right; they're horsemen. Look!'

The doctor looked closely.

'I believe you're right,' he said. 'It's a detachment of Arabs or Tibbus. They're travelling in the same direction as ourselves, but we are travelling faster and gaining easily. In half an hour we shall be able to see and decide what we ought to do.'

Kennedy had picked up his glass again and was watching attentively. The mass of horsemen grew clearer. Some broke away from the rest.

'It must be a manœuvre or a hunt,' Kennedy continued. 'It looks as though those fellows were chasing something. I'd very much like to know what it's all about.'

'Patience, Dick. We'll soon catch them up and even pass them if they keep to the same route. We're doing twenty miles an hour, and there are no horses that can keep up that speed.'

Kennedy continued to watch and a few minutes later said: 'They're Arabs, galloping hell for leather. I can see them distinctly. There's about fifty of them. I can see their burnouses blowing in the wind. It's a cavalry exercise. Their chief is a hundred yards ahead and they're galloping after him.'

'Whatever they are, Dick, we've nothing to be afraid of; and if necessary I'll rise.'

'Wait a bit, Samuel. Wait!'

'That's strange,' added Dick after another look. 'There's something I don't understand. Judging by their efforts and the irregularity of their line, they look more as though they were chasing something than following.'

'Are you sure, Dick?'

'Quite. There's no doubt about it. It's a hunt, but a manhunt. That's not the chief ahead, it's the quarry.'

'Quarry!' said Samuel with feeling.

'Yes.'

'Don't let's lose sight of him, and let's wait.'

They quickly gained three or four miles on the horsemen, who were sweeping forward at headlong speed.

'Samuel! Samuel!' cried Kennedy in a trembling voice.

'What is it, Dick?'

'Are my eyes deceiving me? Can it be possible?'

'What do you mean?'

'Wait.' And Kennedy quickly wiped the glass of his binoculars and began to watch again.

'Well?' said the doctor.

'It's he, Samuel!'

'He?' cried the doctor.

The word 'He' explained everything. There was no need to mention names.

'He's on horseback. Less than a hundred yards ahead. He's flying for his life!'

'Yes, it's Joe,' said the doctor, turning pale.

'He can't see us the way he's going.'

'He will,' Fergusson replied, lowering the flame of his burner.

'But how?'

'In five minutes we'll be fifty feet from the ground; in a quarter of an hour we'll be over him.'

'We must shout and let him know.'

'No, he can't turn; he's cut off.'

'What can we do, then?'

'Wait.'

'Wait! And the Arabs?'

'We'll catch them up and pass them. We're only two miles behind. If only Joe's horse holds out.'

'Good God!' exclaimed Kennedy.

'What's the matter?'

Kennedy had uttered a cry of despair on seeing Joe thrown to the ground. His horse, evidently played out, had collapsed.

'He's seen us,' cried the doctor. 'He's getting up and waving to us. But the Arabs will get him! What's he want? Ah! Good lad!'

'Hurray!' shouted the Scotsman, who could

no longer control himself.

The instant he rose from his fall, and while one of the first horsemen was bearing down upon him, Joe leaped like a panther, swerved aside, threw himself on to the horse's croup, seized the Arab by the throat with his strong nervous fingers, strangled him, hurled him on to the sand and continued his terrific race. A great cry from the Arabs rose into the air, but, absorbed as they were in their pursuit, they had not seen the *Victoria*, five hundred yards behind them and less than thirty feet above the ground. They themselves were not twenty lengths behind Joe's horse.

One of them was perceptibly gaining and was about to stab Joe with his lance, when Kennedy, with steady eye and firm hand, stopped him short with a bullet and brought him to the ground. Joe did not even turn his head at the report. At the sight of the *Victoria* part of the troop pulled up and fell prostrate in the dust. The rest continued the chase.

'But what's Joe doing?' cried Kennedy. 'Why doesn't he stop?'

'He's doing better than that, Dick. I see! He's keeping our course, relying on our intelligence. Ah! Good lad! We'll snatch him from under their noses. Only two hundred yards more.'

'What are we going to do?'

'Put down your gun.'

'Right,' said Kennedy, obeying.

'Can you hold one hundred and fifty pounds of ballast in your arms?'

'Yes; more if you like.'

'No, that'll do.' And the doctor piled sacks of sand into Kennedy's arms.

'Keep at the back of the car and be ready to drop this out at one throw. But on your life don't do it till I tell you!'

'Don't worry.'

'If you do, we'll miss him; he'll be lost.'

'Leave it to me.'

The *Victoria* was now almost over the troop of horsemen who were riding neck or nothing behind Joe. The doctor, in the fore part of the car, held the ladder uncoiled, ready to throw it out when the moment came. Joe had kept his lead of about fifty feet. The *Victoria* overhauled them.

'Ready!' said Fergusson to Kennedy.

'Aye, aye!'

'Joe! Look out! — ' the doctor shouted with all his strength and dropped the ladder, the bottom rungs of which raised a cloud of dust.

At the doctor's shout Joe, without pulling in his horse, looked round. As the ladder swept past him he caught hold of it.

'Now!' the doctor cried to Kennedy.

'It's gone'; and the *Victoria*, relieved of a

weight greater than Joe's, rose a hundred and fifty feet.

Joe clung stoutly to the ladder as it swung to and fro. Then with an indescribable gesture to the Arabs and climbing with the agility of a clown, he reached his companions, who received him in their arms. The Arabs uttered a cry of surprise and rage. The fugitive had been snatched from them at full speed and the *Victoria* was rapidly drawing away from them.

'Doctor! Mr Kennedy!' gasped Joe; and succumbing to emotion and fatigue, he fainted, while Kennedy, almost delirious with excitement, kept repeating: 'Saved! Saved!'

'Thank God!' said the doctor, who had resumed his usual impassivity.

Joe was almost naked. His bleeding arms and bruised body all testified to his sufferings. The doctor dressed his wounds and laid him under the tent. He soon recovered consciousness and asked for a glass of brandy, which the doctor had not the heart to refuse, as Joe was not to be treated as an ordinary man. After drinking, he shook hands with them both and declared himself ready to relate his story. This, however, he was not allowed to do, and the excellent fellow fell back into a deep sleep, of which he was obviously in great need.

The *Victoria* then headed diagonally towards the west. Driven by a strong wind they found themselves again over the fringe of the thorny wilderness, where the palms were bent and torn by the storm. That evening, after travelling two hundred miles since Joe's rescue, they passed the tenth meridian.

37

*Westward — Joe's awakening — His
obstinacy — The end of Joe's story
— Tagelel — Kennedy's anxiety
— Northward — A night near Agades*

During the night the wind rested from its
efforts of the day before and the *Victoria* hung
peacefully over the crest of a great sycamore.
The doctor and Kennedy took turns to watch,
and Joe spent the time in a profound sleep
which lasted twenty-four hours.

'That's the remedy he needs,' said Fergusson.
'Nature will put him right.'

During the day the wind freshened again,
but its direction was capricious. It veered
suddenly from north to south, but finally the
Victoria was carried westward. The doctor,
map in hand, recognised the kingdom of
Damerghu, an undulating country of great
fertility, its villages formed of huts built with
long reeds twisted with branches of asclepia.
The corn-stacks in the cultivated fields were
raised on low scaffolding to protect them
from mice and white ants. Soon they reached
the town of Zinder, which could be

336

recognised by its wide square for executions. In the centre stands the tree of death with the executioner watching at its foot, and whoever passes beneath its shade is hanged on the spot. Consulting his compass, Kennedy could not refrain from remarking: 'We're going north again.'

'What does it matter? Even if it leads us to Timbuktu we shan't complain. It will be the finest expedition ever made — '

'And the healthiest,' Joe broke in, sticking his good-natured, beaming face through the curtains of the tent.

'Here's good old Joe,' cried Kennedy, 'the man who saved our lives. How are you?'

'I'm all right, sir. It's only natural. I never felt better. Nothing could make a man feel fitter than a little pleasure-trip after a bath in Lake Tchad. What do you think, sir?'

'You're a fine fellow,' replied Fergusson, wringing his hand. 'You've given us a very painful and anxious time.'

'But what about you, sir? Do you think I wasn't anxious about you? You can be sure you gave me an awful fright.'

'We shall never agree, Joe, if you take things like that.'

'I see his fall hasn't changed him,' Kennedy added.

'Your sacrifice was wonderful, Joe, and

saved our lives. The *Victoria* was falling into the lake, and once there nothing could have got her out.'

'But if my sacrifice, as you are good enough to call my somersault, saved you, it must have saved me too, for we're all three safe and sound now. So on that score you've nothing to blame yourselves for.'

'We'll never convince a fellow like Joe,' said Kennedy.

'The best way is to say no more about it,' Joe answered. 'What's done is done. Good or bad, it's over and finished with.'

'You're a pig-headed fellow,' said the doctor, laughing. 'At least, you'll be kind enough to tell us your story?'

'If you really want me to. But first I want to dress and cook this fat goose; for I see Mr Kennedy hasn't been wasting his time.'

'You're right, Joe.'

'Well, we must see how this African game suits a European stomach.'

The goose was soon cooked over the flame of the burner, and gradually vanished. Joe did his share like a man who has not eaten for several days. After some tea and grog he told his companions the story of his adventures. He spoke with a certain feeling, though regarding his adventures with his usual philosophy. The doctor could not refrain from gripping his hand several times when he saw his good servant more concerned with his master's safety than his own. When he came to tell of the submersion of the island of the Biddiomahs, the doctor explained to him the frequency of this phenomenon on Lake Tchad.

At last Joe came to the moment when, engulfed in the swamp, he uttered his last despairing cry.

'I thought it was all over with me, sir,' he said, 'and I thought of you. I began to struggle. I won't tell you how. I'd made up my mind I wouldn't let myself be swallowed up without arguing the point, when, two yards away, I saw — what do you think? A rope end, freshly cut. I made a last effort and somehow or other I got up to it. I caught hold and pulled and the rope held. I hauled away and in the end found myself on firm land. At the end of the rope I found an anchor . . . Oh, sir! It was a real anchor of refuge, if you'll let me say so. I knew it. It belonged to the *Victoria*. You'd landed in this very place. I followed the direction of the rope, which told me the way you'd gone, and after a bit of a struggle I got clear of the bog. I felt cheered up a lot, and stronger, as I walked on, part of the night, away from the lake. At last I came to the edge of a big forest. There, in an enclosure, I found some horses quietly feeding. Any man can ride a horse when it comes to a pinch, can't he? I didn't stop to think but jumped on to the back of one and off we dashed north at full gallop. I won't tell you about the towns I didn't see or the villages I kept away from. I dashed across sown fields, passed huts, climbed over palisades, rode my horse on, shouting and urging. I came to the end of the cultivated land. A desert was what I wanted. I could see better in front of me and farther. I was still hoping to see the *Victoria* waiting for me as I dashed along. But there was nothing. After three hours I came like an idiot into an Arab encampment. Then there was a chase! . . . You see, Mr Kennedy, a man who hunts doesn't know what hunting is unless he's been hunted himself; and I shouldn't advise him to try, if he can help it. My horse was done up and fell. They were pressing me hard. I jumped up behind one of the Arabs. I had no special grudge against him and I hope he won't bear me any ill-will for strangling him. But I'd seen you . . . You know the rest. The *Victoria* was following my tracks and you picked me up like a rider picking up a ring. I was right in counting on you, wasn't I? Well, sir, you see how easy it all was. Nothing more natural in the world. I'm quite ready to have it all over again, if it's any good to you.

Besides, as I told you, sir, it isn't worth talking about.'

'Good old Joe!' the doctor said warmly. 'We were quite right in relying on your intelligence and skill.'

'Not at all, sir. A man has only to deal with things as they come and he'll get out of anything. The best way is to take things as they come.'

While Joe was telling his story, the balloon had rapidly crossed a broad stretch of country. Soon afterwards Kennedy pointed out on the horizon a collection of huts which looked like a town. The doctor consulted his map and found it to be Tagelel in Damerghu.

'Here we pick up Barth's route,' he said. 'This was where he separated from Richardson and Overweg. Richardson was to follow the Zinder route, and the other make for Maradi; and you'll remember that of these three Barth was the only one who got back to Europe.'

'So we're going due north,' said Kennedy, following the *Victoria*'s course on the map.

'Due north, Dick.'

'And you don't mind?'

'Why should I?'

'Well, this route takes us to Tripoli and over the great desert.'

'Oh we shan't go as far as that, old man; at least I hope not.'

'Well, where are you expecting to stop?'

'Wouldn't you like to see Timbuktu?'

'Timbuktu?'

'Of course,' said Joe. 'No one ought to come to Africa without seeing Timbuktu.'

'You'll be the fifth or sixth European to set foot in that mysterious town.'

'I'm for Timbuktu!'

'We will get between the 17th and 18th parallels and then we'll look for a favourable wind to take us west.'

'Right!' Kennedy replied. 'But have we to go much farther north?'

'A hundred and fifty miles at least.'

'Get some sleep, sir,' said Joe; 'and you too, Mr Kennedy. You'll need it, for I must have made you lose a lot.'

Kennedy lay down under the tent, but Fergusson, upon whom fatigue had little effect, remained at his post of observation. Three hours later the *Victoria* was flying at great speed over some stony country with ranges of high bare mountains with granite bases. Isolated peaks were as much as four thousand feet high. Giraffes, antelopes and ostriches were springing about with wonderful agility in the forests of acacia, mimosa and date-palms; for vegetation was establishing a hold again after the aridity of the desert. It was the country of the Kailuas, a tribe who veil their faces with strips of cotton like their dangerous neighbours, the Tuaregs.

At 10 p.m., after a splendid trip of two hundred and fifty miles, the *Victoria* came to a standstill over an important town. The moon lit up one part which was largely in ruins, and the domes of several mosques rising here and there caught the white light. The doctor took a reckoning from the stars and found that they were at Agades, once the centre of a far-reaching commerce, and already in ruins at the time of Dr Barth's visit.

The *Victoria*, unseen in the darkness, touched ground two miles above Agades in a large field of millet. The night was comparatively calm and day broke about five in the morning, when a light wind veered the balloon towards the west, with a slight tendency to south. Fergusson, at once seizing this opportunity, rose rapidly and made off away from the rising sun.

38

*Rapid travelling — Prudent resolutions
— Caravans — Continual rain — Gao
— The Niger — Golberry, Geoffrey and
Gray — Mungo Park — Laing — René
Caillié — Clapperton — John and
Richard Lander*

The 17th of May passed calmly and without incident. They were on the confines of the desert, with a moderate wind bringing the *Victoria* back south-west. She veered neither to right nor left, her shadow drawing a perfectly straight line over the sand.

Before leaving, the doctor had prudently replenished his supplies of water, as he was afraid of being unable to land in this country infested by Awelimmidian Tuaregs. The plateau, which was eighteen hundred feet above sea-level, fell away towards the south. Having cut across the Agades-Murzuk road, much used by camels, the travellers reached lat. 16° N., long. 4° 55′ E., in the evening, after one hundred and eighty miles of monotonous travel.

During the day Joe completed the preparation of the last of the game, which had only been partially dressed before. At supper he served a very appetising dish of snipe. The wind was good and the doctor resolved to hold his course during the night, which was made bright by an almost full moon. The *Victoria* rose to a height of five hundred feet and during the night journey of about sixty miles her motion would not have disturbed the light sleep of a child.

On Sunday morning there came a fresh change in the wind, which veered to the south-east. A few crows were flying through the air, and towards the horizon could be seen a flock of vultures, which fortunately kept at a distance. The sight of these birds led Joe to congratulate his master on his idea of a double balloon.

'Where should we be now if we'd only had one envelope?' he said. 'The second balloon is like a ship's pinnace; if you get shipwrecked you always have it to fall back on.'

'You're right, my friend. But my pinnace is causing me some anxiety. It doesn't come up to the ship herself.'

'What do you mean?' asked Kennedy.

'I mean that the new *Victoria* is not as good as the old. Whether the silk has been too severely tried, or the gutta-percha has melted through the heat of the coil, I don't know, but I notice a certain wastage of gas. So far it hasn't been much, but it is noticeable. We have a tendency to drop, and to keep up I'm forced to expand the hydrogen more than I used to.'

'Great Scott!' said Kennedy. 'I don't see any remedy for that.'

'There isn't one, Dick. That's why we shall do well to press on and avoid even halting at night.'

'Are we still a long way from the coast?' asked Joe.

'What coast, Joe? We don't know where fate will take us. All I can tell you is that Timbuktu is still four hundred miles to westward.'

'And how long will it take us to get there?'

'If the wind doesn't shift much I think we ought to strike it about Tuesday evening.'

'In that case,' said Joe, pointing to a long file of men and animals winding across the desert, 'we shall get there quicker than that caravan.'

Fergusson and Kennedy leaned out and saw a long string of creatures of every kind. There were over one hundred and fifty camels, of the kind which for twelve mutkals of gold (about five pounds) go from Timbuktu to Tafilet with a load of five hundred pounds. Each carried under its tail a small bag to receive its excrement, the only fuel that can be relied on in the desert. These Tuareg camels are among the finest that exist. They can remain from three to seven days without drinking and two without food. They are faster than horses and obey intelligently the voice of the khabir, the guide of the caravan. They are known in the country as *meharis*.

These details were given by the doctor while his companions watched the multitude of men, women and children labouring through the shifting sand, which was only held by a few thistles, clumps of dry grass and shrivelled bushes. The wind wiped out all trace of their footprints almost instantly. Joe asked how the Arabs managed to guide themselves in the desert and reach the wells that are thinly scattered over this vast solitude.

'The Arabs,' Fergusson replied, 'have been endowed by Nature with a wonderful instinct for finding their way. Where a European would be completely at sea, they never even hesitate. An insignificant stone, a pebble, a tuft of grass, the different shades of the sand, are sufficient to enable them to march with confidence. During the night they guide themselves by the Pole Star. Their average speed is not more than two miles an hour, and they rest during the midday heat; so you can imagine the time they take to cross the Sahara, a distance of more than nine hundred miles.'

But the *Victoria* had already vanished from the astonished eyes of the Arabs, who must have envied her her speed. In the evening they crossed long. 2° 20′ E., and during the night they had travelled more than another degree. On Monday the weather changed completely. Rain began to fall with great violence and they had to force their way through this deluge, further handicapped by the increase of weight due to the water on the balloon and in the car. This continuous downpour explained the marshy swamps of which the surface of the country was entirely composed. Vegetation again made its appearance with mimosas, baobabs and tamarisks.

Such was Songhay with its villages capped by roofs turned down like Armenian bonnets. There were few mountains, and only just enough hills to produce ravines and reservoirs over which guinea-fowl and snipe skimmed. Occasionally an impetuous torrent broke the path. These the natives crossed by clinging to a creeper stretched from tree to tree. The forests then gave place to jungle alive with alligator, hippopotamus and rhinoceros.

'It won't be long before we sight the Niger,' said the doctor. 'Near great rivers the country changes. These moving roads originally brought vegetation with them, just as later they will bring civilisation. So in its course of two hundred and fifty miles the Niger has sown upon its banks the most important cities of Africa.'

'Oh,' said Joe, 'that reminds me of the fellow who thought it very wise of Providence to arrange that rivers should always run through big towns.'

At noon the *Victoria* passed over a small town, a collection of rather wretched huts. This was Gao, once a great capital.

'That's where Barth crossed the Niger on his way back from Timbuktu,' said the doctor. 'And here's the river. It was very famous in antiquity; the rival of the Nile to which superstition attributed a celestial origin. Like the Nile it has always been an object of interest to students of geography. And its exploration has claimed even more victims than the other river.'

The Niger flowed between widely-separated banks, its waters rolling strongly southwards; but the balloon was travelling so quickly that the three men only just had time to observe its curious windings.

'I wanted to tell you about this river,' Fergusson said, 'and it's far behind us already. It has had many names; the Dhiouleba, the Mayo, the Egghirrew, the Quorra, and others. It passes through a huge stretch of country and must almost rival the Nile in length. Its names simply mean 'black river,' according to the dialects of the different districts it flows through.'

'Did Dr Barth come this way?' asked Kennedy.

'No, Dick. After leaving Lake Tchad he passed through the chief towns of Bornu and crossed the Niger at Say, four degrees below Gao. He then plunged into the unexplored country contained within the bend of the Niger, and after eight months of continuous effort reached Timbuktu. With this wind we shall be there in less than three days.'

'Has anyone discovered the sources of the Niger?' asked Joe.

'A long time ago,' the doctor replied. 'The discovery of the Niger was the object of many expeditions. I can tell you the chief of these. Between 1749 and 1758 Adamson explored the river and visited Goree. Between 1785 and 1788 Golberry and Geoffrey crossed the deserts of Senegambia and got as far as the country of the Moors who murdered Saugnier, Brisson, Adam, Riley, Cochelet, and lots of others. Then came the famous Mungo Park, the friend of Walter Scott, and himself a Scotsman. He was sent out in 1795 by the London African Society, reached Bambarra, saw the Niger, travelled five hundred miles with a slave-dealer, found the river Gambia, and returned to England in 1797. On the

30th of January, 1805, he set out again with his brother-in-law Anderson, Scott the cartographer, and a band of workmen. He got to Goree, where he was reinforced by a detachment of thirty-five soldiers, and sighted the Niger again on the 19th of August. But by then, as the result of fatigue, privations, ill-treatment, bad weather and the unhealthiness of the country, there were only eleven left out of forty Europeans. Mungo Park's last letters reached his wife on the 16th of November, and a little later it was learned through a trader of the country that when he arrived at Bussa on the Niger on the 23rd of December, his boat was overturned by the cataracts and the poor fellow was murdered by the natives.'

'And that awful death didn't stop the explorations?'

'Quite the other way, Dick; for after that it was necessary not only to explore the river, but also to find Park's papers. In 1816 an expedition was fitted out in London with Major Gray in charge. It went to Senegal, entered Futa-Djallon, studied the Fullah and Mandingo populations, and returned to England without obtaining any other results. In 1822 Major Laing explored all the parts of Western Africa which border on English possessions, and it was he who first reached the sources of the Niger. According to his writings the source of this huge river was only two feet wide.'

'Easy to jump,' commented Joe.

'Easy enough,' replied the doctor, 'but according to tradition anyone trying to jump this spring is immediately engulfed. Anyone trying to draw water from it feels himself pushed back by an invisible hand.'

'And are we allowed to refuse to believe a word of it, sir?' asked Joe.

'If you like. Five years later Major Laing crossed the Sahara, reached Timbuktu, and was strangled a few miles above by the Oulad Shimans, who wanted to compel him to become a Mussulman.'

'Another victim,' said Kennedy.

'Then a brave young fellow with slender resources undertook and carried through the most astonishing expedition of modern times. I mean the Frenchman, René Caillié. After several attempts in 1819 and 1824, he started off again on the 19th of April, 1827, from Rio Nuñez. On the 3rd of August he arrived at Time, so exhausted that he couldn't go on again until January 1828, six months later. He then joined a caravan, protected by his oriental dress, reached the Niger on the 10th of March, entered the town of Jenné, embarked on the river and went down it as far as Timbuktu, where he arrived on the 30th of April. In 1670 another Frenchman, Imbert, and in 1810 Robert Adams, an Englishman, were supposed to have seen this curious town; but René Caillié must have been the first European to bring back any exact information about it. On the 4th of May he left this queen of the desert and on the 9th found the very spot where Major Laing was murdered. On the 19th he came to El-Arauan, a commercial town, and braving a thousand dangers, crossed the vast solitudes that divide the Sudan from the northern regions of Africa. At length he reached Tangier, where he took ship on the 28th of September for Toulon. In nineteen months, including six spent in illness, he had crossed Africa from west to north. If only he'd been born in England, Caillié would have been acclaimed the boldest explorer of modern times, the equal of Mungo Park; but in France he is not appreciated at his real worth.'

'He must have been a brave fellow,' said Kennedy. 'What became of him?'

'He died at the age of thirty-nine, from overstrain. They thought they had recognised his services adequately by giving him the prize of the *Société de Géographie* in 1828. In England the greatest honours would have been showered upon him. As for the rest, while he was carrying out this wonderful expedition, the same idea occurred to an Englishman, who attempted it with equal courage, if with less luck. This was Captain Clapperton, Denham's partner. In 1829 he returned to Africa, landing in the Bight of Benin on the West Coast. He picked up the trail of Mungo Park and Laing, found in Bussa documents revealing the death of Mungo Park, reached Sakatu on the 29th of August, where he was kept a prisoner and died in the arms of his faithful servant, Richard Lander.'

'And what happened to Lander, sir?' Joe asked with great interest.

'He managed to get back to the coast and went back to London with the captain's papers and an exact account of his own journey. He then offered his services to the Government to complete the exploration of the Niger. His younger brother John — they were the sons of poor parents in Cornwall — joined him, and between 1829 and 1831 they travelled down the river from Bussa to its estuary, describing every village and every mile of the way.'

'So they escaped the usual fate?' Kennedy asked.

'Yes, at any rate as far as that expedition was concerned. But in 1833 Richard set out a third time for the Niger and was shot, it is not known by whom, near the river's mouth. So you see, my friends, this country we are passing over now has been the scene of splendid sacrifices, only too often rewarded by death.'

39

The country within the bend of the Niger — A fantastic view of the Hombori Kabra Mountains — Timbuktu — Dr Barth's plan

During this tedious Monday, Dr Fergusson devoted himself to recounting to his companions many details of the country they were crossing. The flat land presented no obstacle to their progress. The doctor's only anxiety was caused by the exasperating north-east wind, which blew furiously and carried them away from the latitude of Timbuktu. The Niger, after bending northwards as far as this town, curves back like a great jet of water to fall into the Atlantic Ocean in a wide spray. The country contained within this bend is very varied, sometimes of luxuriant fertility and sometimes of extreme aridity. Uncultivated plains follow upon fields of maize, which in turn give place to vast open spaces covered with broom. All kinds of aquatic birds, pelican, teal and kingfishers, live in great flocks on the banks of the torrents and marigots.

From time to time there would appear a camp of leather tents in which Tuaregs sheltered themselves, while the women sat in the open, milking their camels or smoking their pipes by the great fires. About eight in the evening, the *Victoria* had travelled over two hundred miles towards the west and the travellers witnessed a magnificent spectacle. Some rays of moonlight had cut a path through a cleft in the clouds and filtering their way through the streaming rain, fell on the Hombori mountain chain. Nothing could have been stranger than the appearance presented by these basalt crests. Their fantastic outline was silhouetted against the blackness of the sky like the legendary ruins of some great mediæval town or ice floes as they are seen on a dark night in Arctic seas.

'That would be a good setting for *The Mysteries of Udolpho*,' said the doctor. 'Ann Radcliffe couldn't have cut those mountains into more fearsome shapes.'

'I'm blowed if I'd like to walk about alone in the dark in those weird parts,' said Joe. 'You know, sir, if it wasn't so heavy I'd like to cart that country to Scotland. It would look well on the banks of Loch Lomond, and the tourists would flock to see it.'

'I'm afraid the balloon would hardly hold it. But surely we are altering our course.

Good! The local spirits are kind to us. They're sending us a little wind from the south-east, which is just what we want.'

Indeed the *Victoria* was returning to a more northerly course, and during the morning of the 20th she passed over a tangled network of channels, torrents, and rivers, the whole intricate system of the Niger tributaries. Several of these canals were covered with thick grass and looked like fat meadows. Here the doctor found Barth's route when he took to the river to make for Timbuktu. With a breadth of nearly five thousand feet the Niger here flowed between banks rich in cruciferæ and tamarisks. Herds of gazelle disported themselves there, their ringed horns blending with the tall grass in which alligators watched for them in silence. Long files of donkeys and camels carrying merchandise from Jenné plunged through the splendid forests, and soon an amphitheatre of low houses appeared at a bend of the river. On the terraces and roofs was heaped the forage gathered from the surrounding country.

'It's Kabra,' cried the doctor in delight. 'That's the port of Timbuktu. The town is only five miles away.'

'You're pleased, sir?' asked Joe.

'Delighted, Joe.'

At two o'clock the queen of the desert, mysterious Timbuktu, which, like Athens and Rome, once had her scholars and chairs of philosophy, was revealed to the explorers' eyes. Fergusson followed the slightest details on the plan made by Barth himself and confirmed the explorer's extreme accuracy. The town forms a huge triangle on a wide plain of white sand. Its apex lies to the north like a wedge driven into the desert, its surroundings are completely bare; at most a little grass, some dwarf mimosas and stunted bushes.

As for Timbuktu itself, the reader can imagine a heap of dice and marbles. That's what it looked like from the air. The somewhat narrow streets are fringed with houses of only one storey, built of sun-baked bricks and huts of reed and straw; some conical, some square. On the terraces a few inhabitants lounged carelessly, draped in brilliant robes, lance or musket in hand. Not a woman was to be seen at this hour of the day.

'But they are said to be beautiful,' the doctor added. 'You see the three towers of the three mosques which are all that are left of a large number. What a fall from the town's ancient splendour! At the apex of the triangle over there is the Mosque of Sankore with its rows of galleries supported by beautifully-designed arcades. That over there, farther on, near the Sane-Gungu, is the Sidi Yahia Mosque. Some of the houses near it have two storeys. It's no use looking for palaces or monuments. The sheik is simply a trader and his royal residence a shop.'

'I think I can see some broken-down ramparts,' said Kennedy.

'They were destroyed by the Fellanis in 1826. At that time the town was larger by a third, for since the eleventh century Timbuktu has been generally coveted and has belonged in turn to the Tuaregs, the Songhays, the Moors and the Fellanis, and this great centre of civilisation, where in the sixteenth century a scholar like Ahmed Bala possessed a library of sixteen hundred manuscripts, is now merely a warehouse for the commerce of Central Africa.'

The town certainly appeared to have been abandoned to a state of neglect and showed clear signs of the universal indifference of cities whose day is over. Great heaps of ruins stood in the outlying parts of the town and, with the hill on which the market stood, formed the sole break in the flatness of the site. When the *Victoria* passed, there was some movement and the drum was beaten; but it is doubtful whether the last remaining scholar of the place had time to observe this new phenomenon. Driven back by the desert wind, the travellers again followed the sinuous course of the river, and soon Timbuktu was no more than a fleeting memory of their journey.

'And now,' said the doctor, 'Heaven may take us where it will.'

'So long as it's west,' Kennedy replied.

'What does it matter?' said Joe. 'It wouldn't worry me if we had to go back to Zanzibar by the same way and across the ocean to America.'

'We should have to be capable of doing so first.'

'And what are we short of, sir?'

'Gas, Joe. The lift of the balloon is getting appreciably less, and it will take it all its time to get us to the coast. I shall have to throw out ballast. We're too heavy.'

'That's what comes of having nothing to do, sir. Loafing all day in a hammock makes a man soft. He's bound to put on weight. It's a lazy way of travelling, ours, and when we get back we shall find ourselves dreadfully fat.'

'Just the sort of thing Joe *would* think,' Kennedy replied. 'But wait till we get there. Who knows what fate has in store for us? We're a long way off the end yet. Where do you expect to strike the coast of Africa, Samuel?'

'I should find it very difficult to say. We are

at the mercy of very variable winds. However, I should think myself lucky if we landed somewhere on the strip of country between Sierra Leone and Portendick. There we should find ourselves among friends.'

'And it would be good to shake their hands. But are we actually going the right way?'

'None too directly, Dick. Look at the compass needle. We are heading south, towards the sources of the river.'

'A fine chance to discover them,' said Joe, 'if someone else hadn't got there first. At a pinch, couldn't we find fresh ones?'

'No, Joe; but don't worry, I hope we shan't get as far as that.'

At nightfall the doctor threw out his last sacks of ballast and the *Victoria* rose. The burner, though working to its utmost capacity, could hardly keep her in the air. She was now sixty miles south of Timbuktu and the following morning found them on the banks of the Niger not far from Lake Debo.

40

*Dr Fergusson's uneasiness — Still south
— A cloud of locusts — View of Jenné
— View of Sego — The wind changes
— Joe's disappointment*

The river bed was now broken by large islands into narrow channels where the current was very rapid. On one stood some shepherds' huts, but it was impossible to take an exact bearing as the *Victoria*'s speed was continually increasing. Unfortunately she headed still more to southward and crossed Lake Debo in a few minutes. Fergusson, by forcing his expansion to the utmost, tried different elevations to find other atmospheric currents, but in vain. He soon gave up these attempts which increased the waste of gas by pressing it against the weakening walls of the balloon.

He said nothing, but grew very uneasy. This persistent course towards Southern Africa was upsetting his calculations. He no longer knew on what he could reckon. If he did not strike British or French territory, what would happen to them among the barbarians that infest the Guinea coast? The present direction of the wind was taking them towards the kingdom of Dahomey, which is among the most barbarous and at the mercy of a king who at public festivities was in the habit of sacrificing thousands of human victims. To fall into his hands would be fatal.

Besides, the balloon was visibly flagging and the doctor felt she was failing him. However, the weather clearing a little, he hoped that the end of the rain would bring a change in the atmospheric currents. He was soon brought back to an appreciation of the real situation by these words from Joe: 'Hello! Here's more rain; a regular deluge this time, judging from that cloud!'

'Another cloud!' said Fergusson.

'And a whopper!' Kennedy added.

'I've never seen one like that before,' Joe went on.

'It's nothing after all,' said the doctor, putting down his glass. 'It's not a rain-cloud.'

'Well, what is it, sir?' asked Joe.

'A cloud of locusts.'

'Those! Locusts?'

'Yes, thousands of them. They'll sweep over the country like a sandstorm and it will be a bad look-out, for if they come down the land will be devastated.'

'I'd like to see that.'

'Wait a bit, Joe. In ten minutes the cloud

will have reached us and you'll be able to see with your own eyes.'

Fergusson was right. This dense opaque cloud, several miles in extent, advanced with a deafening roar, its shadow darkening the country as it passed. It was a countless legion of migrating locusts. A hundred yards from the *Victoria* they swept down on a verdant countryside. Quarter of an hour later the mass rose again into the air and the travellers could then see from afar the trees and hushes completely stripped and the meadows looking as though they had been mown. It was as if a winter had suddenly plunged the country into a state of complete sterility.

'Well, Joe?'

'Well, sir, that's very odd, but quite natural. What one locust would do on a small scale thousands do on a big one.'

'Like some appalling hailstorm,' said Kennedy, 'but much more destructive.'

'And there's no way of guarding against it,' said Fergusson. 'Sometimes the people have tried burning forests and even harvests to stop the flight of these insects. But those ahead dash into the flames and stifle them with their dense mass, and the rest pass over unchecked. Fortunately there is some sort of compensation for the havoc caused. The natives collect the insects in large numbers and eat them with relish.'

'Sort of air-shrimps,' said Joe, adding that he was sorry not to have been able to try them, 'by way of education.'

The country they passed over towards evening became more marshy, the forests giving place to isolated clumps of trees. On the banks of the river could be seen tobacco plantations and marshy land on which rich grass grew. On a large island they found the town of Jenné with the two towers of its mosque, which is built of earth, the air being laden with the noxious smell of the millions of swallows' nests which had accumulated on its walls. Tops of baobab trees, mimosas and date-palms projected between the houses. Even at night the town seemed very busy. It is, in fact, a considerable commercial centre and supplies all the needs of Timbuktu, to which place boats on the river and caravans on the shady road carry the various products of its industry.

'If it were not that it would prolong our trip,' said the doctor, 'I should be tempted to land in this town. There must be many Arabs here who have travelled in France or England and who will be acquainted with our method of travel; but it would be unwise.'

'Let's put off our visit until the next time,' laughed Joe.

'Besides, unless I'm mistaken, my friends, the wind shows a slight tendency to blow from the east, and it wouldn't do to miss such a chance.'

The doctor threw out a few articles which were now useless: empty bottles and a case of meat which had gone bad, and in this way managed to keep the *Victoria* in the favourable zone. At four in the morning the first rays of the sun shone on Sego, the capital of Bambarra, which was easily recognisable by the four distinct towns of which it is composed, its Moorish mosques and the incessant crossing backwards and forwards of the ferries carrying the inhabitants from one quarter to another. But the travellers passed over too quickly to see or be seen very much. The *Victoria* was speeding due north-west and the doctor's anxiety gradually vanished.

'Two days more in this direction and at this speed and we'll be at the Senegal River.'

'In a friendly country?' asked Kennedy.

'Not altogether. If the *Victoria* should happen to fail us, we could at a pinch find French settlements. But let's hope she'll hold out a few hundred miles more and we'll reach the West Coast without fatigue, alarm or danger.'

'And then it'll be all over,' said Joe. 'Well, it can't be helped. If it wasn't for the fun of telling the yarn I shouldn't mind if I never set foot on land again. Do you think they'll believe our story, sir?'

'Who knows, Joe? At any rate there will always be one indisputable fact. We must have had a thousand witnesses of our departure from one coast of Africa, and another thousand will see us arriving at the other.'

'In that case,' replied Kennedy, 'it would seem difficult to dispute the fact that we crossed.'

'I shan't find it easy to forget the loss of my gold!' said Joe with a deep sigh. 'That would have given a bit of weight to our story and made it more convincing. At the rate of one gramme of gold for everyone who listened, I'd collect a nice little crowd, and they might even think me a fine fellow.'

41

*Nearing the Senegal — The Victoria
dropping lower and lower — Al Hadji,
the marabout — Joe's feat*

About nine in the morning of the 27th of
May a change came over the country. The
long ridges changed to hills which appeared
to be the forerunners of mountains. The balloon would have to clear the chain separating
the Niger basin from that of the Senegal,
which divides the streams running into the
Gulf of Guinea and Cape Verde Bay respectively. According to the stories of Fergusson's
predecessors this part of Africa as far as the
Senegal is dangerous. They had undergone
many privations and run many dangers among
the barbarous blacks who dwell there, and the
deadly climate had accounted for the greater
part of Mungo Park's companions. Fergusson
was therefore more determined than ever not
to set foot in this inhospitable country.

But he had not a moment's rest. The *Victoria*
was drooping markedly. It became necessary
to jettison further more or less superfluous
objects, especially when it came to clearing a

peak. And so it went on for more than a hundred and twenty miles, during which constant effort was required to keep the balloon in the air. This new stone of Sisyphus was constantly falling back. The outline of the inadequately inflated balloon already showed signs of leanness. It became elongated and the wind dug great hollows in its loose envelope. Kennedy could not refrain from pointing this out.

'Can she be leaking?' he asked.

'No,' the doctor replied; 'but the gutta-percha has evidently softened in the heat and the hydrogen is percolating through the silk.'

'How can we prevent it?'

'We can't. We must lighten her. It's the only way. Throw out everything we can spare.'

'But what?' asked Kennedy, looking round the already seriously dismantled car.

'Let's get rid of the tent; it's quite heavy.'

Joe, to whom this order was addressed, climbed outside the belt which held the net ropes together, and from there managed without difficulty to loose the thick curtains of the tent and throw them out.

'That will make a whole tribe of niggers happy,' he said; 'there's enough of it to dress a thousand natives, for they're pretty sparing with their material.'

The balloon rose a little, but it soon

became clear that she was again beginning to drop.

'Let's get out,' said Kennedy, 'and see if we can't do something with the envelope.'

'I tell you, Dick, we've no means of repairing it.'

'Then what are we going to do?'

'We'll sacrifice everything that is not absolutely indispensable. At all costs I want to avoid a halt in this district. Those forests just below us are by no means safe.'

'Why not, sir; lions; hyenas?' said Joe scornfully.

'Worse than that, my good fellow; men, and the most bloodthirsty in all Africa.'

'How do you know, sir?'

'From the explorers who have been here before us, and then the French who occupy the colony of Senegal have, of course, had relations with the surrounding tribes. Under the governorship of Colonel Faidherbe, reconnaissances were made far into the country. Officers like Pascal, Vincent and Lambert have brought back valuable information from their expeditions. They explored these countries contained in the elbow of the Senegal and found that war and pillage have left them mere heaps of ruin.'

'How did that come about?'

'In 1854 a marabout called Al Hadji gave

himself out as inspired by Mahomet and drove the tribes into war against the infidels; meaning, of course, the Europeans. He destroyed and laid waste all the country between the Senegal and its tributary the Falémé. Three hordes of savages led by him harried the country, sparing not a single village or even hut; pillaging and massacring. They even pushed into the Niger valley as far as the town of Sego, which they long threatened. In 1857 he headed north, and laid siege to the fort of Medina, which was built by the French on the river bank. This settlement was defended by a hero called Paul Holl, who held out for several months with no food, little ammunition and few guns, until he was relieved by Colonel Faidherbe. Al Hadji and his band then recrossed the Senegal and returned to Kaarta to continue their rapine and massacre. So this is the district to which he escaped with his hordes of bandits, and I assure you it wouldn't be pleasant to fall into their hands.'

'We'll see we don't, sir,' said Joe; 'even if we have to throw out our boots to lighten the balloon.'

'We aren't far from the river,' said the doctor; 'but I'm afraid our balloon won't get us to the other side.'

'Well, at any rate, let's get to the bank,'

Kennedy replied; 'that will be so much to the good.'

'That's what we are trying to do,' said the doctor. 'But there's one thing I'm anxious about.'

'What?'

'We have some mountains to get over and it won't be easy, for I can't increase the lift even with the burner in full blast.'

'Let's wait and see,' said Kennedy.

'Poor old *Victoria*!' said Joe. 'I've got as fond of her as a sailor is of his ship. It'll be hard to part with her. She's not quite what she was when we started out, but it won't do to slight her. She's served us well and it would be heartbreaking to desert her.'

'Don't worry, Joe. We won't desert her if we can help it. She'll go on serving us as long as she can. I'm only asking her for another twenty-four hours.'

'She's nearly done,' said Joe, contemplating the balloon. 'Look how thin she's getting. She can't stick it much longer. Poor old *Victoria*!'

'Unless I'm mistaken,' said Kennedy, 'there are the mountains you were talking about, Samuel, on the horizon.'

'Yes, those are the ones,' said the doctor, after examining them through his glass. 'They look to me very high and we shall have our work cut out to get over them.'

'Couldn't we go round them?'

'I don't think so, Dick. Look what a long way they stretch. They cover half the horizon.'

'They even seem to be closing round us on both sides,' said Joe.

'There's nothing for it but to go over.'

These dangerous obstacles seemed to be advancing towards them with great rapidity, or rather a very strong wind was rushing the balloon towards some sharp peaks. At all costs they would have to rise to avoid being dashed against them.

'Empty the water container,' said Fergusson. 'Keep only enough for one day.'

'There you are, sir,' said Joe.

'Is she rising?' asked Kennedy.

'A little; fifty feet perhaps,' replied the doctor, never taking his eyes off the barometer. 'But that's not enough.'

Indeed the lofty crests seemed to be dashing straight at the balloon, which was not nearly high enough to pass over them. She wanted over five hundred feet more. The supply of water for the furnace was also poured overboard, only a few pints being kept; but that again proved insufficient.

'But we've got to get over,' said the doctor.

'Let's throw out the containers as they're empty,' said Kennedy.

'Out with them.'

'Done, sir,' said Joe. 'It's hard to go overboard, bit by bit.'

'Now, Joe, no more of your sacrifices. Whatever happens, swear you won't leave us.'

'Don't worry, sir; we're not going to part.'

The *Victoria* had lifted about a hundred and twenty feet, but the mountain crest was still above her, a sheer ridge ending in a perpendicular wall of rock, still more than two hundred feet above the car.

'Another ten minutes,' the doctor mused, 'and the car will be smashed against the rocks, unless we manage to get over somehow.'

'What next, sir?' asked Joe.

'Keep only the pemmican; throw out all the rest of the meat.'

The balloon was relieved of another fifty pounds and rose distinctly, but it was of little use unless they could get above the level of the mountains. The situation was appalling. The *Victoria* was dashing forward and it seemed inevitable that she would be shattered in pieces. The shock would be terrific. The doctor looked round the car and found it almost empty.

'If necessary, Dick, you'll be ready to sacrifice your guns.'

'My guns!' exclaimed the Scotsman in agitation.

'I wouldn't ask you, old man, if it wasn't

absolutely necessary.'

'Oh, look here, Samuel — '

'Your guns and powder and shot might cost us our lives.'

'We're on it!' cried Joe. 'Look out!'

They only required another sixty feet to clear the mountain. Joe seized the blankets and hurled them overboard, while Kennedy, without a word, did the same with several bags of powder and shot. As the balloon lifted above the dangerous crest, her upper part caught the sunlight; but the car was still slightly below some loose rocks, against which they were on the point of crashing.

'Kennedy!' shouted the doctor. 'Throw out your guns or we're lost!'

'Half a minute, Mr Kennedy,' Joe called. 'Wait!' And Kennedy, turning his head, saw him disappear over the side.

'Joe! Joe!' he yelled.

'He's gone!' said the doctor.

The crest of the mountain at this point was about twenty feet broad and the other side was less sheer. The car just reached the level of this fairly flat area. With a loud grinding noise it scraped over the sharp loose stones.

'She's going! She's going! She's over!' cried a voice which made Fergusson's heart bound.

The brave Joe was hanging by his hands to the lower edge of the car, running over the crest, and so relieving the balloon of his entire weight. He had even to hold her back vigorously to prevent her running away from him. When he reached the reverse slope and the abyss yawned before him, Joe heaved himself up and, clinging to the ropes, climbed back beside his companions.

'Quite easy, after all,' he said.

'That was splendid, Joe! You've saved us again,' cried the doctor enthusiastically.

'Oh, I didn't do it for you, sir,' Joe replied. 'It was to save Mr Kennedy's carbine. I certainly owed it that much after the business with the Arabs. I like paying my debts. And now we're quits,' he added, handing Kennedy his favourite weapon. 'I couldn't bear to see you parted from it.'

Kennedy wrung his hand, but was unable to utter a word. Now all that was required of the *Victoria* was to descend, which she found easy. She was soon back at two hundred feet above ground, where she was in equilibrium. The ground looked as though it had been the scene of some great upheaval and presented many projections which would be difficult to negotiate with the balloon out of hand. As night was rapidly coming on, the doctor, with great reluctance, had to make up his mind to halt until morning.

'We must look out for a likely spot,' he said.

'Oh, so you've made up your mind to it at last,' Kennedy remarked.

'Yes, for some time I've been thinking over a plan we'll try. It's only six o'clock, so we shall have time. Throw out the anchors, Joe.'

Joe obeyed, and the two anchors hung below the car.

'I can see some big forests,' said the doctor. 'We'll run over them and anchor to a tree. Nothing would persuade me to spend the night on the ground.'

'Shan't we be able to get out?' asked Kennedy.

'What would be the good? I repeat, it would be dangerous to separate. Besides, I want you to help me in a difficult job.'

The *Victoria*, which was skimming over an extensive forest, soon came to a sudden stop; her anchors had taken hold. The wind dropped as night came on, and she rested almost motionless over the vast area of green formed by the crests of the sycamores.

42

*A battle of generosity — The final sacri-
fice — The expanding apparatus — Joe's
skill — Midnight — Kennedy's watch
— He falls asleep — The fire — The
shouting — Out of range*

The first thing Dr Fergusson did was to take
a reckoning on the stars. He found he was
hardly twenty-five miles from the Senegal.

'The most we can do is to cross the river,'
he said, pointing to his map; 'but as there are
no boats and no bridge, we must at all costs
cross in the balloon, and to do this we must
lighten her still more.'

'But I don't see how we're going to manage
it,' Kennedy replied, fearing for his guns,
'unless one of us makes up his mind to
sacrifice himself and remain behind. It's my
turn and I claim the honour.'

'Certainly not, sir,' exclaimed Joe. 'I've got
used to it — '

'It's not a question of jumping, Joe, but of
getting to the coast on foot. I'm a good
walker and a good shot — '

'I'll never agree to it,' Joe replied.

'Your battle of generosity is unnecessary, my friends,' said Fergusson. 'I hope we shan't be driven to anything of that kind. Besides, if necessary, rather than separate we'll tramp across the country together.'

'There's some sense in that, sir,' said Joe. 'A little walk won't do us any harm.'

'But first,' the doctor went on, 'we'll have a last try to lighten the *Victoria*.'

'How?' asked Kennedy. 'I'm very curious to know how you're going to do it.'

'We must get rid of the burner, the battery and the spiral. They give us a good nine hundred pounds to carry.'

'But how are you going to expand the gas, in that case, Samuel?'

'I shan't. We shall have to do without.'

'But after all — '

'Listen to me, my friends. I've calculated very exactly the lifting force we are left with. It's sufficient to carry the three of us with the few things we still have. We shan't weigh five hundred pounds, including the two anchors, which I intend to keep.'

'My dear Samuel,' Kennedy replied, 'you understand these things better than we do, and you're the only one in a position to judge the situation. Tell us what we've to do and we'll do it.'

'Hear, hear!'

'Well, as I said, however serious the step may be, we must sacrifice our apparatus.'

'Let's do it, then!' replied Kennedy.

'To work!' said Joe.

It was no small job, as it involved taking down the apparatus piece by piece. They began by taking out the mixing chamber, then that containing the burner, and finally, the chamber in which the water was decomposed. It required the united strength of the three men to wrench them from the bottom of the car, to which they had been stoutly fixed; but Kennedy was so strong, Joe so skilful, and the doctor so resourceful, that they succeeded in the end. The various sections were thrown over one by one, making great gaps in the foliage of the sycamores as they disappeared.

'The niggers will get a bit of a shock when they find these in the wood,' said Joe. 'They're quite capable of making idols of them.'

They next turned their attention to the tubes connecting the balloon with the coil. Joe managed to cut through the rubber joints, a few feet above the car, but the tubes were more difficult to deal with as they were held by their upper ends and fixed by brass wire to the safety-valve.

At this juncture Joe displayed wonderful skill. His feet bare to avoid tearing the envelope, he managed, in spite of the swaying of the balloon, to climb up the net to the top where, with great difficulty and hanging by one hand to the slippery surface, he removed the outer nuts holding the pipes. These then came away easily and were drawn out through the lower appendix, which was hermetically closed again by means of a strong ligature. The *Victoria*, relieved of this considerable weight, rose and pulled strongly on the anchor ropes.

This work was successfully finished by midnight after much labour. A hurried meal was taken of pemmican and cold grog, for the doctor had no more heat for Joe's use. Joe and Kennedy were dropping with fatigue.

'Lie down and sleep, my friends,' said Fergusson. 'I'll take the first watch. I'll wake Kennedy at two, and at four Kennedy will wake Joe. We'll start at six, and may Heaven continue to be kind to us during the last day!'

Without waiting for further persuasion the two men lay down in the bottom of the car and were soon in a deep sleep. The night was peaceful. A few clouds were crushing themselves against the last quarter of the moon, whose faint rays hardly relieved the darkness. Fergusson, his elbows on the side of the car, looked around him, scrutinising closely the dark curtain of foliage which stretched below his feet and hid the ground. He was suspicious of the slightest sound and tried to find an explanation even of the light rustle of the leaves.

He was in that state of mind, exaggerated by solitude, when vague terrors invade the mind. At the close of such a voyage, when so many obstacles have been surmounted and the end is in sight, anxiety increases, excitement grows stronger, and a successful termination seems to elude the imagination.

Moreover there was nothing reassuring about their present situation in the middle of a barbarous country and relying on means of transport which, after all, might fail them at any moment. The doctor could no longer place complete reliance on his balloon. The time was past when he could take risks in handling her because he was sure of her powers.

While these thoughts were passing through his mind the doctor from time to time thought he could hear vague noises in the great forest. He even imagined he could see flames flickering between the trees. After looking closely, he brought his night glass to bear upon the place, but nothing appeared and the silence seemed to have grown deeper still. Fergusson thought it must have been an hallucination, for he listened without hearing the slightest sound. As his watch was now over, he woke Kennedy, urged him to keep a very careful look-out, and then took his place beside Joe, who was sleeping like a log.

Kennedy quietly lit his pipe, rubbed his eyes, which he found it hard to keep open and, leaning his head on his elbow in a corner, began to smoke vigorously to keep sleep at bay. Absolute silence reigned around him, a light breeze stirred the crests of the trees, and the balloon swayed gently, lulling the Scotsman to sleep in spite of himself. He tried to fight against it; several times he opened his eyes and looked into the night without seeing and finally, succumbing to weariness, he fell asleep.

How long he had been unconscious he did not know, when suddenly he was awakened by a strange crackling noise. He rubbed his eyes and rose to his feet. He could feel an intense heat on his face. The forest was in flames.

'Fire! Fire!' he shouted, without too clear an idea of what had happened. His two companions woke up.

'What's the matter?' asked Fergusson.

'Fire!' cried Joe . . . 'But who can — '

At this moment a roar of yells broke from under the trees, which were brilliantly illuminated.

'Oh, it's the savages!' Joe cried. 'They've set

fire to the forest to make sure of burning us.'

'It must be the Talibas, Al Hadji's marabouts!' said the doctor.

A circle of flames surrounded the *Victoria*. The cracking of the dead wood mingled with the hissing of the green branches. Creepers, leaves, the whole living tangle of vegetation, writhed in the destroying flames. The eye could see nothing but an ocean of fire, from which the great trees stood out black, their branches covered with glowing embers. The glow of the burning mass was reflected in the clouds and the travellers seemed to be imprisoned within a sphere of fire.

'Let's get away!' cried Kennedy. 'We must land. It's our only chance.'

But Fergusson laid a firm hand on his arm and, dashing to the anchor rope, severed it with one blow of the axe. The towering flames were already licking the envelope of the balloon, but, loosed from her bonds, the *Victoria* rose over a thousand feet at one bound. A terrible clamour, punctuated by the report of firearms, rose from the forest. The balloon, caught in a breeze which came with the dawn, headed away towards the west. It was 4 a.m.

43

The Talibas — The pursuit — A country laid waste — The wind moderates — The Victoria droops — The last provisions — The Victoria's bounds — Armed defence — The wind freshens — The Senegal River — The Guina Falls — Hot air — Crossing the river

'If we hadn't taken the precaution of lightening the balloon last night,' said the doctor, 'we should have been lost.'

'That's the advantage of taking things in time,' Joe replied. 'You then get a chance to escape. Nothing more natural.'

'We're not out of the wood yet,' replied Fergusson.

'What are you afraid of?' asked Kennedy. 'The *Victoria* can't come down without your permission, and what if she did?'

'What if she did, Dick? Look!'

They had just crossed the edge of the forest and could see thirty horsemen, wearing broad trousers and floating burnouses. They were armed, some with lances, the rest with long muskets, and on their swift fiery steeds were following the *Victoria,* which was not travelling fast, at a short gallop.

When they saw the travellers, they uttered savage cries and brandished their weapons, their ugly fury showing plainly on their bronzed faces, the ferocity of which was increased by their scanty but bristling beards. They rode easily over the low plateau and gentle slopes which dropped towards the Senegal.

'Yes, those are the fellows,' said the doctor. 'The cruel Talibas, the fierce bandits of Al Hadji. I'd rather be surrounded by wild animals in the heart of the forest than fall into those bandits' hands.'

'They certainly don't look very friendly,' said Kennedy; 'and they're lusty-looking fellows!'

'Luckily those animals they're riding can't fly; that's always something,' Joe replied.

'Look at those ruined villages, those burnt huts,' said Fergusson. 'That's some of their work. They've devastated what used to be a broad stretch of cultivated land.'

'At any rate, they can't get at us,' Kennedy replied; 'and if we manage to get the river between ourselves and them, we'll be all right.'

'Yes, Dick; but we can't afford to drop,' the doctor replied, with a glance at the barometer.

'In any case, Joe,' Kennedy went on, 'it won't do any harm to have our guns ready.'

387

'No; we might as well do that, sir. It's lucky we didn't drop them out after all.'

'My carbine!' sighed Kennedy. 'I hope I shan't ever be parted from it.' And Kennedy loaded it with the greatest care. He had a fair quantity of powder and shot left.

'What's our height now?' he asked Fergusson.

'About a hundred and fifty feet. But we can't rise and fall, looking for favourable currents. We're in the *Victoria*'s hands.'

'That's awkward,' said Kennedy. 'It's not much of a wind, but if we had a gale like that of the last few days we should have left those fellows out of sight long ago.'

'They're keeping up with us easily,' said Joe. 'They're having a nice little ride.'

'If only we were within range it would be rather fun to knock them off their horses one by one,' said Kennedy.

'It would,' Fergusson replied. 'But we should be within range ourselves and the *Victoria* would offer too easy a target for those long muskets of theirs; and if they tore her, you can imagine the position we should be in.'

The Talibas continued to pursue them all through the morning. By eleven o'clock they had only covered fifteen miles to the westward. The doctor scanned the slightest cloud that appeared on the horizon, as his constant fear was a change in the weather.

What would happen to them if they were to be driven back towards the Niger? Besides, he found that the balloon was showing a distinct tendency to droop. She had already dropped three hundred feet since they started and the Senegal was still a dozen miles away. At their present speed they must expect another three hours of travel.

Just at this moment his attention was attracted by a fresh outburst of shouting. The Talibas were urging forward their horses in great excitement. The doctor consulted the barometer and realised what was happening.

'We're dropping?' asked Kennedy.

'Yes,' Fergusson replied.

'The devil!' thought Joe.

Quarter of an hour later the car was less than a hundred and fifty feet from the ground, but the wind had freshened. The Talibas reined in their horses, and a volley rang out.

'Too far, you fools!' cried Joe. 'It's just as well to keep fellows like you at a distance.' And, taking aim at one of the foremost horsemen, he fired. The Taliba rolled to the ground. His companions halted and the *Victoria* drew away from them.

'They're a cautious lot,' said Kennedy.

'Because they think they're sure to get us,' the doctor replied; 'and they'll succeed if we drop any more. We must rise at all costs.'

'What is there to throw out?' asked Joe.

'All the rest of the pemmican. That will be thirty pounds less.'

'There you are, sir,' said Joe, obeying his master's orders; and the car, which was almost touching the ground, rose again amid fresh shouts from the Talibas. But a quarter of an hour later the *Victoria* was again dropping rapidly. The gas was escaping through the pores of the envelope. Shortly afterwards the car was just skimming the ground. Al Hadji's negroes dashed towards her; but, as happens in such cases, hardly had she touched ground than the *Victoria* leapt upwards, again to fall a mile farther on.

'So we're not going to get away,' said Kennedy in exasperation.

'Throw out our reserve of brandy, Joe,' cried the doctor; 'and the instruments, and anything that weighs anything at all; our last anchor too, since we must!'

Joe tore down barometers and thermometers, but all these weighed little and, after rising for a moment, the balloon fell back again at once towards the ground. The Talibas were in hot pursuit only two hundred yards behind.

'Throw out the two guns!' shouted the doctor.

'I'll fire them first at any rate,' Kennedy replied; and four shots struck the mass of horsemen. Four Talihas fell amid the frenzied cries of the troop. The *Victoria* rose again and leaped over the ground with huge bounds like a great rubber ball. These three men, escaping for their lives in these gigantic leaps and, like Antaeus, seeming to gather fresh force each time they touched the ground, must have presented a strange sight. But there had to be an end to this state of affairs. It was nearly midday. The *Victoria* was becoming exhausted and empty, her shape lengthening, her envelope flabby and flapping in the breeze, the folds of distended silk rasping one against the other.

'Heaven is deserting us,' said Kennedy. 'We'll have to come down.'

Joe did not reply. He was watching his master.

'No,' the latter said. 'We've still a hundred and fifty pounds we can drop.'

'How?' exclaimed Kennedy, thinking his friend had gone mad.

'The car!' he answered. 'Hang on to the net. We can hold on there and get to the river. Hurry up!'

The brave men did not hesitate. They clung to the meshes of the net as the doctor had said, and Joe, hanging by one hand, cut the ropes of the car, which fell just as the balloon was finally collapsing.

'Hurrah! Hurrah!' he cried as the balloon rose three hundred feet. The Talibas, urging on their horses, were sweeping on at a desperate gallop, but the *Victoria*, finding a fresher breeze, gained on them and made rapidly towards a hill which hid the western horizon. This was lucky for the travellers, for they were able to clear it, whereas the pursuing horde were forced to turn north-ward to go round this final obstacle. The three friends hung on to the net, which they had to tie below them so that it formed a sort of floating pocket. Suddenly, as they cleared the hill, the doctor cried: 'The river! The river! The Senegal!'

Two miles away the river was rolling its broad mass of water. The opposite bank, low and fertile, offered them a safe refuge and a favourable landing.

'Quarter of an hour more and we're saved,' said Fergusson.

But this was not to be. The empty balloon was gradually dropping towards a stretch of completely bare country, consisting of long slopes and stony plains where a few bushes and some thick sun-dried grass were the only signs of vegetation. Several times the *Victoria* touched ground and rose again, but her bounds were weakening in height and length. At last the upper part of the net caught the high branches of a baobab, the only tree to be seen in the wilderness.

'This is the end,' said Kennedy.

'And only a hundred feet from the river,' said Joe.

The three unhappy men set foot to the ground and the doctor dragged his companions off towards the Senegal. At this place a prolonged roar could be heard rising from the stream, and when they reached the bank Fergusson recognised the Falls of Guina. Not a boat on the bank; not a living creature.

Over a breadth of two thousand feet the Senegal was plunging with a deafening roar from a height of five hundred feet. The stream flowed from east to west and the line of rocks that barred its course ran north and south. Half-way down the fall some rocks projected in strange shapes like huge antediluvian animals petrified in the middle of the water. The impossibility of crossing this gulf was obvious. Kennedy could not repress a gesture of despair, but Dr Fergusson, in accents of dauntless courage, exclaimed:

'We're not done yet!'

'I knew it,' said Joe, with a confidence in his master that nothing could shake.

The sight of the dried grass had inspired the doctor with a bold idea It was their one chance. Quickly he brought his companions back towards the envelope of the balloon.

'We've at least a quarter of an hour's start on those ruffians,' he said. 'There's no time to waste, my friends. Pick a lot of that dry grass; I shall want at least a hundredweight.'

'What for?' asked Kennedy.

'I've no gas left. Well, I'm going to cross the river on hot air!'

'Really, Samuel!' cried Kennedy. 'You're a great man!'

Joe and Kennedy set to work, and soon a great stack of grass was piled up near the baobab. Meanwhile the doctor had widened the orifice of the balloon by cutting away its lower part, taking care to get rid of any hydrogen that might be left through the valve. He then piled a quantity of dried grass under the envelope and set fire to it. It does not take long to fill a balloon with hot air. A heat of 180 degrees is sufficient to halve the weight of the enclosed air by expanding it. The *Victoria* therefore soon began to resume her rounded form. There was plenty of grass. The fire blazed brightly under the doctor's care, and the envelope swelled visibly. It was then a quarter to one.

At this moment the troop of Talibas came into sight two miles to the north; their shouts and the thunder of their galloping horses could be heard.

'They'll be on us in twenty minutes,' said Kennedy.

'Grass, Joe! Grass! We'll be up in ten minutes.'

'Here you are, sir.'

The *Victoria* was two-thirds filled.

'Catch hold of the net again.'

'Right away,' Kennedy answered.

Ten minutes later the jerking of the balloon showed that she was about to rise. The Talibas were coming on rapidly and were now hardly five hundred yards away.

'Hold tight!' cried Fergusson.

'All right, sir; all right.'

The doctor kicked a fresh heap of grass into the fire and the balloon, fully dilated by the increase of temperature, flew off, rustling the branches of the baobab.

'We're off!' cried Joe.

A volley answered him and a bullet ploughed through his shoulder; but Kennedy, leaning down and firing his carbine with one hand, brought one more of the enemy to the ground. Indescribable yells of rage hailed the escape of the *Victoria*, which rose to nearly eight hundred feet. A swift wind took hold of her and she swayed about alarmingly, while the brave doctor and his companions looked down into the depths of the falls that yawned below them. Ten minutes later, without having exchanged a single word, the three men were gradually dropping towards the other bank of the river.

Here stood a group of ten men wearing French uniform, amazed and terrified. Their astonishment when they saw the balloon rise from the right bank of the river can be imagined. They half thought it was some supernatural phenomenon. But their officers, a naval lieutenant and a midshipman, had heard through the European papers of Dr Fergusson's audacious adventure, and at once understood what was happening.

Gradually deflating, the balloon with the aeronauts clinging to her net was dropping, and it was doubtful whether she would reach land, so the Frenchmen dashed into the river and caught the three Englishmen in their arms just as the *Victoria* was finally collapsing, a few feet from the left bank.

'Dr Fergusson?' exclaimed the lieutenant.

'Yes,' the doctor replied quietly, 'and his two friends.'

The Frenchmen led the travellers away from the river while the half-deflated balloon, caught in the rapid current, plunged like a great bubble over the Guina Falls.

'Poor old *Victoria*!' said Joe.

The doctor could not hold back a tear.

44

CONCLUSION

*The inquiry — The French stations
— The Basilic — Saint Louis — The
French frigate — The return to London*

The expedition then on the banks of the river
had been sent by the Governor of Senegal
and consisted of two officers, Lieutenant
Dufraisse of the Marine Infantry and Midshipman Rodamel, a sergeant, and seven men.

The last two days had been spent seeking
the most suitable site upon which to establish
a station at Guina, and they were still engaged
in their search when they witnessed the arrival
of Dr Fergusson. It is easy to imagine the
congratulations with which the three travellers were received. The Frenchmen, who had
themselves assisted at the conclusion of the
audacious venture, naturally became Dr Fergusson's witnesses. The doctor therefore asked
them at once to report officially his arrival at
the Guina Falls.

'You won't mind signing the report?' he
asked Lieutenant Dufraisse.

'I'm at your service,' the latter replied.

The Englishmen were taken to a temporary station on the banks of the river, where every attention and abundant food were lavished upon them, and here the report which today figures in the archives of the London Geographical Society was drawn up in the following terms:

GUINA FALLS *24th May, 1862*. We, the undersigned, declare that today we witnessed the arrival of Dr Fergusson and his companions, Richard Kennedy and Joseph Wilson, clinging to the net of a balloon, which balloon fell a few yards from us into the river and, dragged away by the current, was swept over the Guina Falls. In confirmation of which, we sign the present report drawn up by the aforementioned gentlemen.
SAMUEL FERGUSSON, RICHARD KENNEDY, JOSEPH WILSON.
DUFRAISSE, *Lieutenant d'Infanterie de marine*.
RODAMEL, *enseigne de vaisseau*.
DUFAYS, *sergent*.
FLIPPEAU MAYOR, PELISSIER, LORIS, RASCAGNET, GUILLON, LEBEL, *soldats*.

Thus was concluded the amazing voyage of Dr Fergusson and his brave companions, as confirmed by indisputable evidence. They were now among friends in the middle of tribes who were on friendly terms with the French establishments. They had reached the Senegal on Saturday, the 24th of May, and on the 27th they proceeded to the station of Medina, on the bank of the river a little farther to the north. Here the French officers received them with open arms and drew upon all the resources of their hospitality. The doctor and his companions were able to embark almost immediately on the small steamboat *Basilic*, which took them down the Senegal as far as its estuary.

A fortnight later, the 10th June, they arrived at Saint Louis, where they met with a magnificent reception from the Governor. They were now completely recovered from their excitement and fatigue. As Joe repeated to anyone who would listen to him: 'It was quite an ordinary trip, ours, after all, and I don't advise anyone to go and do the same thing who wants excitement. It was very dull at times towards the end, and if it hadn't been for the adventures at Lake Tchad and the Senegal I really think we should have been bored to death.'

An English frigate was about to sail and the three travellers boarded her. On the 25th June they reached Portsmouth, and were in

London on the following day.

We will not describe the welcome they received from the Royal Geographical Society, nor the cordiality with which they were entertained. Kennedy at once set out for Edinburgh with his famous carbine, being in a hurry to reassure his old nurse. Fergusson and the faithful Joe remained as we have known them, but, unknown to themselves, a change had come about; they had become friends.

The whole European press could not say enough in praise of the audacious explorers, and the *Daily Telegraph* issued an edition of 977,000 copies the day it published its account of the journey.

At a public meeting of the Royal Geographical Society, Dr Fergusson gave a lecture on his aeronautical expedition, and he and his two companions received the gold medal awarded to the most noteworthy exploration work of the year 1862.

★   ★   ★

The chief result of Dr Fergusson's expedition was to confirm in the most precise manner the geographical facts and surveys reported by Barth, Burton, Speke and others. Thanks to the expeditions at present being undertaken by Speke and Grant, Heuglin and

Munzinger, who are making for the sources of the Nile and Central Africa, we may before long be able to check in their turn the discoveries made by Dr Fergusson in that vast area lying between the 14th and 33rd meridians.

We do hope that you have enjoyed reading this large print book.

Did you know that all of our titles are available for purchase?

We publish a wide range of high quality large print books including:
Romances, Mysteries, Classics
General Fiction
Non Fiction and Westerns

Special interest titles available in large print are:
The Little Oxford Dictionary
Music Book
Song Book
Hymn Book
Service Book

Also available from us courtesy of Oxford University Press:
Young Readers' Dictionary
(large print edition)
Young Readers' Thesaurus
(large print edition)

For further information or a free brochure, please contact us at:
Ulverscroft Large Print Books Ltd.,
The Green, Bradgate Road, Anstey,
Leicester, LE7 7FU, England.
Tel: (00 44) 0116 236 4325
Fax: (00 44) 0116 234 0205